# Death Conquers

## Mortis Series: Book Eight

# J.C. DIEM

# Titles by J.C. Diem:

## Mortis Series
Death Beckons
Death Embraces
Death Deceives
Death Devours
Death Betrays
Death Banishes
Death Returns
Death Conquers
Death Reigns

## Shifter Squad Series
Seven Psychics
Zombie King
Dark Coven
Rogue Wolf
Corpse Thieves
Snake Charmer
Vampire Matriarch
Web Master
Hell Spawn

## Hellscourge Series
Road To Hell
To Hell And Back
Hell Bound
Hell Bent
Hell To Pay
Hell Freezes Over
Hell Raiser
Hell Hath No Fury
All Hell Breaks Loose

## Fate's Warriors Trilogy
God Of Mischief
God Of Mayhem
God Of Malice

## Loki's Exile Series
Exiled
Outcast
Forsaken
Destined

## Hunter Elite Series
Hunting The Past
Hunting The Truth
Hunting A Master
Hunting For Death
Hunting A Thief
Hunting A Necromancer
Hunting A Relic
Hunting The Dark
Hunting A Dragon

## Half Fae Hunter Series
Dark Moon Rising
Deadly Seduction
Dungeon Trials
Dragon Pledge

Unseelie Queen

# Chapter One

Lying on the dirty concrete floor of the murky and unwelcoming mausoleum, misery and guilt warred for supremacy. My willingness to live had come to an end the instant Luc had died, yet I continued to exist.

Luc had survived for seven centuries before I'd come along and had turned his life upside down. As a justice bringer for the vampire Court, my one true love had been sent to Australia to hunt down my maker and to end his life. Unfortunately, he'd been too late to stop Silvius from turning me and creating the creature that would ultimately bring about the doom of our kind.

*You can't blame yourself for the near extinction of your species,* my inner voice said almost timidly. *This was all fated to happen and you couldn't have done anything to change any of it.* If that was true, then fate had a lot to answer for. It had put my kin through untold horrors and it had all but wiped out our kind. Worldwide, there were less than forty vampires now, or there had been before I'd retreated into solitude. I

4

couldn't dredge up the energy, or the interest to check whether the numbers had changed.

I wasn't sure how long it had been since I'd returned to the tomb where I'd first been created. After Luc's remains had disappeared, I'd left France in a fog of despair and loneliness. Breaking down into particle form, I'd allowed myself to drift aimlessly on the winds. Subconsciously, I'd been heading back to my former home city of Brisbane all along.

With Luc gone, there was no reason for me to continue with my quasi-life, so I'd set out to will myself to die. So far, it wasn't going as well as I'd hoped. Sometimes, my body was whole. The rest of the time, I degenerated into an inert clump of microscopic particles. My misery and guilt were the only things that remained constant.

At the moment, my body was solid. I'd left my bloodstained clothes behind in France and hadn't bothered to find anything else to wear. My nakedness was covered by an old blanket that I'd stolen from a dog a long time ago. Any normal vampire would have been shivering while lying on the floor of a dingy mausoleum. Far from normal, I was no longer affected by the cold. It was one of the perks my friends and I had received after spending a few weeks on an alien planet.

Thinking about my friends triggered a new talent that I'd acquired during the time I'd spent in my self-imposed solitary confinement. While my body was determined to remain imprisoned, my mind had plans of its own. Some part of me craved contact with my friends and stubbornly continued to seek them out. My senses returned to France time and again, locating the five remaining vampires who were like a family to me.

Little by little, I'd learned to distinguish them from each other. I always seemed to be drawn to Geordie first, perhaps because he cared about me the most. The first time I'd brushed his thoughts with mine had come as a shock. His sorrow was deep and his loneliness was even greater than mine. While he was shattered by Luc's death, he was even more devastated by my disappearance. I was his best friend, the only person he thought truly understood him and I'd walked away without even saying goodbye.

That first instant of contact with the teen's mind had opened up a new world for me. I'd spent almost every waking moment since then flitting from mind to mind. I read the thoughts of random humans all around the planet. It was distressing to find so many people contemplating suicide, murder, robbery, rape, or causing other types of harm to others. There were many base desires that humans secretly harboured. Maybe I was just drawn to negative thoughts because of my own deep and abiding misery.

After realizing just how much Geordie missed me, I'd tried to avoid spying on my friends. I already felt guilty enough for getting Luc killed and now I'd added their sorrow to my burden. Yet, I often found myself hovering near them, close enough to touch if I'd been corporeal.

Having them at the forefront of my thoughts triggered my telepathy again and I felt a prickling sensation at the back of my head. For a time, I fought off the urge to investigate, but I eventually succumbed to temptation and phased into particle form. It was far easier to concentrate when my body had broken down into a substance that was finer than ash.

With my consciousness free to wander, it sought out

Geordie and was instantly transported halfway around the world. When my disembodied mind came to a stop, I was among my friends once more. I always seemed to sense it when I was the main topic of their conversation. The nanobots that I'd been infused with on Viltar were probably to blame for my new mental powers. They'd changed something in my physiology. I could now teleport my body, or send my consciousness anywhere in the world in the blink of an eye.

The trick that I was about to use was one that I'd already had some practice with. I'd learned how to possess my own body parts long ago. Possessing another body was almost as easy. It was impossible to read all five of my friends' minds at once, so I'd resorted to hijacking the eyes and ears of Geordie. It enabled me to listen in on their conversation without anyone knowing I was there.

Geordie twitched as if he'd been bitten by a horsefly when I entered his mind, but he gave no other indication that he now had someone else watching through his eyes.

"I wish there was some way we could contact Natalie," Gregor was saying. Around forty in mortal years, his blond hair was longish and his face was classically handsome. Clad in one of his usual tweed suits, he was back to being sophisticated and elegant. He was a far cry from the warrior he'd been forced to become during our stay on Viltar.

"Natalie will return to us when she is ready," Kokoro said and placed a hand on Gregor's back. He gave her a sorrowful smile and slid his arm around her waist. A former prophetess, Kokoro's once white eyes were now the usual black that any vampire over the age of three hundred possessed. She'd regained her eyesight and had lost her visions after feeding from one of our ancient ancestors. The second Viltaran she and my close friends had fed from had given them immortality.

*If they were truly immortal, then Luc wouldn't be dead,* I reminded myself. While the others could now heal what would normally be a mortal wound for our kind, it seemed that only I was able to piece myself back together after being blown apart.

"Do you think she would return if she knew about the missing ships?" Igor asked. Kokoro was the oldest of the group at forty thousand years. Igor was next oldest at fifteen thousand. He'd been born in Russia long before it had had a name or any real form of organized civilization. Stoic and gruff, Igor had been the first friend that Luc had made after he'd been thrust into Court life. He probably missed Luc as much as I did.

"I am certain that Natalie would come back to us if she was aware of what has been happening around the globe," Ishida said. "Surely, she would be concerned about the disappearances of aquatic life, as well as the humans that have gone missing."

Ishida had only been twelve years old when he'd been turned. Kokoro had been sent a vision that this child would lead their nation through the dark times, namely when I came into being. He'd been the emperor of the Japanese vampire nation for ten thousand years. Then I'd come along and his people had been wiped out, along with most of the European vampires. He'd abdicated his throne while we'd still been on Viltar and it had seemed that we'd never be able to return to Earth. Now that we were back, he no longer had an empire to rule over.

"Don't bet on it," Geordie said and instantly drew the

attention of everyone. If I'd been in full possession of his body, rather than just a portion of his mind, I would have clapped his hands over his mouth. I hadn't meant to speak, but I couldn't take the words back now.

"What do you mean?" Gregor asked. Smarter than anyone that I'd ever met, he was instantly suspicious of the teen.

Normally, Geordie was my staunchest supporter. It was a surprise to everyone that he wasn't automatically backing me this time. Of course, it wasn't really Geordie talking, but they didn't know that, yet. "Maybe she's tired of coming to the rescue all the time," I forced Geordie to say. "Maybe she doesn't give a crap about missing fish and wishes every last human on the planet would just die." I released his vocal cords and the adolescent echoed my earlier thought and clapped a hand over his mouth.

Gregor stared at Geordie in astonishment for a second then his gaze sharpened. "Natalie? Is that you?" He didn't wait for an answer, having jumped to the correct conclusion that I was indeed amongst them. "This is more than the mere disappearance of a few fish and humans. Something has been sucking all life out of the oceans, seemingly all around the globe. Whatever it is, it's getting closer to civilization. Only a few ships are missing at the moment, but I fear the number will increase soon."

His tone was urgent but, again, I couldn't dredge up the energy to care. I borrowed Geordie's vocal cords once more. "So? After what they did to Luc, all humans can burn in hell for all I care."

The teen spoke of his own volition when I was finished. "General Sanderson was the one who killed Luc," he reminded me. "You had your revenge on him." And what a revenge it had been. I'd warned the soldier what would happen if he harmed any of my people. He'd deserved to have his intestines yanked out through his mouth and I didn't feel one iota of guilt about that. "You cannot blame all humans for taking Luc from us, Nat," Geordie said gently.

Reminded again that I wasn't the only one who was missing Luc, I could sense that their grief hadn't lessened much while I'd been gone.

"Can you at least send out your senses and tell us what this new threat is?" Ishida asked. His disappointment in my decision to abandon them was obvious. I didn't need to delve into his thoughts to know that I'd let him down.

"No," I said through Geordie's mouth. I could, but I wouldn't.

"Why not?" Kokoro asked.

"Because I just don't care."

Gregor opened his mouth to say something then changed his mind. "Go ahead and say it," I told him.

Dark eyes sorrowful, he stared through Geordie and into me. "I do not think that you will have a choice. Fate has been in control of you from the moment you were born. It engineered your transformation into Mortis and it will continue to control you until it is finished with you."

I lifted Geordie's upper lip at the mention of the unknown entity that we referred to as fate. "Fate made a grave mistake when it killed Luc. It took the person I love the most away from me and I won't be jumping through any more hoops for it now."

"Are you absolutely sure that Lucentio is dead?" Kokoro queried.

I nodded Geordie's head. "After you all left, I eventually

fell asleep. When I woke up, Luc's bits and pieces were gone and I couldn't sense him anywhere in the area."

Igor and Gregor shared a glance. "How hard did you try to find him?" the Russian asked.

I realized this was just another ploy to try to get me to discover what was behind the mysterious fish disappearances. "Luc is gone, Igor." He flinched at Geordie's uncharacteristically steely tone. "Even if he'd managed to move himself while in that condition, he couldn't have gotten far. He wasn't anywhere in France when I tried to sense him and there's no point searching the globe for him now." I'd come to terms with the fact that my one true love was gone and I wished the others would as well.

"But, if Lucentio is truly dead, then his remains wouldn't have simply disappeared. They would have broken down into slush," Ishida pointed out.

"Maybe that won't happen to us seven. The Viltaran blood might have changed more about us than we realize," I responded. We had no way of knowing just how much my six friends had changed. Even Gregor had to concede that I might be right about this and he gave me a grudging nod.

Wresting control of his voice back, Geordie sent me a plea that lanced its way across the planet and directly through my disembodied heart. "Come home to us, *chérie*. We need you."

Again, I shook his head. "You're safer without me around. I'll just end up getting you all turned into minced meat."

Before anyone could protest, I detached myself from Geordie's brain and returned to the mausoleum. I'd listened in on many of their meetings, but that had been the first time that I'd given my presence away. I missed my friends, but it had been a mistake to visit them. It was one that I wouldn't make again.

My self-imposed penance for causing Luc's death was to spend the rest of eternity alone. I'd forfeited my right for happiness the moment General Sanderson's bullets had thumped home into my beloved's flesh. My remaining friends were safe, now that I was no longer with them. Hopefully, they would remain safe with me gone.

Apart from my few undead friends, I had no other ties to the world that I was turning my back on. The next time I felt the prickling sensation in the back of my mind, I ignored it and worked harder to will myself into nothingness.

# Chapter Two

Early on in my lonely exile, I'd learned that it was possible to dream even while my body was the consistency of dust motes. I dreamed about everything that had happened to me since I'd been transformed into a member of the exclusive undead club. Most of the memories were unpleasant and some events I'd have been happy to forget altogether. The only bright memories in the endless barrage of death, dismemberment and treachery were of Luc and my other close friends.

Drifting aimlessly, my restless mind settled on the time that I'd accidentally bitten Luc. Usually, drinking another vampire's blood meant instant death for us. Being Mortis, the rules didn't apply to me. Instead of dying, I'd been infused with Luc's memories. Like me, his life as a blood sucker hadn't been all sweetness and light.

Luc had been turned by the Comtesse, one of the nine

rulers of the European vampire Council. I'd nicknamed her 'the praying mantis' due to her wide-set, soulless eyes and general unpleasantness. Luc had become her newest toy and she'd used him as sexual entertainment for the female members of the Court. It was a role that he'd been forced to endure for four long centuries. He'd hidden his distaste at being used from everyone, including his own master. If they'd known just how much he'd despised consorting with them, they'd have tormented him more often.

Crafty as well as evil, the Comtesse had created over a thousand servants. It was against the rules for a Councillor to have more than twenty lackeys, but she'd pulled it off by ordering her other servants to pose as each new fledgling's true masters. Lady Monique, Luc's pretend master, was killed for committing treason. Upon her death, he'd been elevated to the position of a Lord of the Court. With the title had come the power to choose who he would bed. For three centuries, he'd chosen to bed no one.

"Then I met you," a familiar voice said with a hint of amusement.

Being disembodied, I heard the words in my mind rather than with my ears. It should have worried me that I hallucinated Luc from time to time. Instead, I just felt devastated that he was gone. I conjured a mental smile for my dead beloved, who now existed only in my imagination. "Remember the time you tied the sacks to my hands with my shoelaces while I was asleep?" My flesh hunger had been new and difficult to control back then. Luc had sacrificed his body more than once to satiate my needs.

He gave a husky, sheepish laugh. "I was afraid that I

would burn to death from your holy marks."

"I was so new back then that I didn't even know how to use them."

"You learned how to use your gifts quickly enough, Ladybug."

Wrinkling my non-existent nose at the nickname, I tried not to give into the despair and sense of aloneness that were threatening to overwhelm me. "Being Mortis is a curse, not a gift," I argued. "I've inflicted death on our whole species."

"Yet, you saved the human race three times. You are a heroine."

I would have rolled my eyes if they'd actually been solid. "Like I told the others, the humans could all die tomorrow and I wouldn't give a crap." I'd been one of them before I'd become the undead. I knew firsthand that a lot of them weren't worth saving.

"Why not?" I couldn't see him, since he was just a figment of my imagination, but I pictured him to be wearing a quizzical expression as he asked me that question.

"We might have saved them, but they'll never see us as heroes. They can only see us as monsters. They thanked us for saving them the first two times by killing most of our kind and locking the rest up to be tortured and experimented on. Even that wasn't enough, so they booted us off the planet. They'll never be grateful to us no matter how many times we save them. They'll always try to exterminate us once we've finished coming to the rescue."

"That is not the real reason why you hate them," he said astutely.

We both knew why I despised the race that we'd all

originated from, but he wouldn't let me be until I voiced it. "One of them murdered the person I love the most in the world," I said dully.

"And for that, they are all worthy of death?" he asked gently.

"Yes." If it had been in my power, I would have killed them all myself.

There was a contemplative silence for a few moments. "I have said once before that Fate is a fickle yet harsh mistress, but I do not believe she is completely heartless."

The fact that Luc thought of fate as a female entity almost made me smile. "Fate cares less about us than I do about the traitorous meat sacks. It doesn't have a heart at all."

Now I pictured Luc with an eyebrow raised. "If that is so, then how am I still able to communicate with you?"

"Because you're not real. I've conjured you up so I don't go completely insane." Of course, there was a good chance that that ship had already sailed. Only crazy people had conversations with dead people, even if it was just in their minds.

"How do you know that I'm not real? You haven't even tried to find me."

I heard reproach and sadness in his tone and fresh guilt hit me. Before I could respond, my senses detected a group of humans approaching the mausoleum. My hallucination disappeared, leaving me feeling more bereft than ever.

My chosen abode was in the heart of the Toowong Cemetery in Brisbane. Four stone sarcophagi were my silent roommates. They were so old that their writing was almost illegible beneath layers of dust and cobwebs. No one had ever visited the tomb before, let alone a whole group of people. Hardly anyone came to this section of the graveyard at all.

Curiosity, my old nemesis, drew me back to my resting place again. Still in particle form, I didn't bother to re-form my body to listen in on the group. I now had the ability to pluck thoughts directly from the minds of anyone I chose. Kokoro would be proud of me if she'd known of my new talent. Or maybe she'd be angry because I could now do what she no longer could.

The first mind that I delved into belonged to a sixteen year old girl. *This place is giving me the creeps!* I sensed a shiver run down her spine. She'd agreed to accompany her boyfriend on the trip, but she really didn't want to be there.

The next mind I touched on told me what they were all doing here. *Just one more year of dragging these gullible saps through the supposedly haunted cemetery and I'll finally be able to move to the UK.* The thought came from a fifty year old man. He was almost rubbing his hands together in glee at the prospect of moving overseas. He'd always wanted to live in the UK and now his dream was almost within his reach.

*Ugh, it's one of the ghost tour groups.* Now that I knew who and what the group of humans were and why they were here, I wasn't happy about it at all. My curiosity was satisfied, but now I was annoyed. They'd never come this close to my resting place before, but they seemed to be heading directly towards me this time.

*This is so awesome,* an excited teenaged boy thought, breaking into my reverie. He was the kid that had dragged his reluctant girlfriend along with him. *I thought this was going*

*to be bogus, but I can actually feel evil emanating from that tomb!*
His enthusiasm reminded me of Geordie and added to my
general misery. I missed all of my friends, but I missed
Geordie most of all.

I wasn't surprised that the humans were picking up on
the malevolence that I felt towards their kind, but it was
irritating to have them flocking around me to soak up the
gloomy atmosphere. Any second now, they'd be invading
my inner sanctum. The thought of my particles being
trampled on by human feet propelled me into re-forming
my body. The blanket fell to the filthy ground as I stood.
Weathered but still sturdy, the wooden door had a keyhole,
but the key itself was missing. Taking two steps forward, I
placed my hand against the door just as the tour guide
tried to push it open.

"Huh. The door seems to be stuck." Disgruntled, the
tour guide put his shoulder against the door and struggled
to shove it open.

"Is it locked?" the young female asked. All up, over a
dozen people were in the group. They were eager to gain
entry so they could gawp and take photos of my home.

"I guess it must be," the tour guide said after straining
with all of his might to force the door open. A bright flash
of light filtered through the cracks as someone took a
photo of the mausoleum. More shots followed, leaving
bright spots dancing in front of my eyes. I moved aside
slightly when a tiny shaft of light pierced the dimness
through the keyhole. The tour guide shone his torch
through the opening and attempted to peer inside. "It's
too dark to make out anything inside."

A guy in his mid-thirties pushed his way through the
group. "Stand back, I'll get it open. I paid good money for

this tour and I'm not going home until I see a ghost." His name was Tom and he was half drunk. I could smell beer fumes wafting off him even through the door.

"You can't kick the door in," someone protested. "That's vandalism! Have some respect for the resting place of the departed."

"Do I look like I give a shit about the departed?" Tom sneered. His foot thudded against the door, which I easily held shut with one hand. Dust sifted to the floor and one of the boards creaked alarmingly. It would only take one more kick to snap the wood and I wasn't about to let that happen.

As insidious as smoke, I invaded Tom's mind. I sent him a picture of a rotting corpse rising out of one of the sarcophagi with its arms outstretched and bodily juices dripping to the ground. Faltering as the image filled his mind, his second kick missed the door and he lurched forward. The thump of his head connecting with the wood was followed by his unconscious body falling to the ground.

*Wonderful,* thought the ghost tour guide in dismay, *this isn't exactly going to be fantastic for business.* "Give him some room," he urged as the entire group surged forward to help the unsuccessful vandal.

"He should be ok," someone decided. "He didn't split his head open and it looks like he's already coming around."

"What happened?" Tom groaned as he came to. Several pairs of hands helped him to his feet.

"You tried to break the door down and conked your head," the male teen told him.

"I hope you have a good lawyer," Tom said to the tour

guide. "I'm going to sue your arse off for this."

"No one held a gun to your head and forced you to try to break in," another man pointed out.

Embarrassed at knocking himself out, Tom took a swing at the offending man. A short scuffle broke out before the two men were separated.

"I paid to see ghosts, not to watch grown men acting like children," an elderly woman sniffed.

"This tour sucks," the frightened teenage girl declared. "I vote we leave." Her vote was seconded and the group straggled back the way they'd come.

Peace descended and I lay back down on the hard and uncomfortable ground. The threadbare blanket settled over me once more and I subsided back into a semi-sleep. I searched for Luc, hoping to resume our imagined conversation, but he remained stubbornly absent.

# Chapter Three

As my sleep deepened, I fell into a familiar and disquieting dream. It had plagued me even before my friends and I had managed to make our way from Viltar back to our home world.

Even before I opened my eyes, I knew I was on a boat. The rocking motion was a dead giveaway. Salt and fish were usually the predominant odours, but they were conspicuously absent this time. While I was lying on a bunk bed, it was smaller than the ones I'd dreamed myself into before.

Rolling out of the bunk to my feet, I scanned the wall for a porthole, but it was missing. Stepping through a hatch into a narrow hallway, I began to suspect that I wasn't on a normal boat at all.

A man appeared through a doorway ahead and hurried towards me. He wore a dark blue uniform that looked naval to me. Looking right through me, he made no effort to avoid a collision and passed through me as though I was a ghost. I caught a hint of his frightened thoughts as he hurried away. He wasn't sure what they'd been sent to investigate, but his captain was nervous about their mission. A worried captain meant a worried crew and everyone on board was tense.

Feeling the hands of destiny settling on my shoulders, I debated about ignoring the dream and trying to wake myself up. Gregor's intuition that fate would try to force me to fulfil the role that it had set for me hadn't left my mind. *Just see this dream through and find out what everyone is so worried about,* my inner voice suggested.

Gone was my alter ego's snarky, sarcastic attitude and now it sounded almost humble. Ever since it had instigated the breakup between Luc and me, I'd had little time or patience for my subconscious. Frankly, I wished it would die a long and painful death. Even a short, painless one would do, just as long as it didn't screw anything else up for me again. Not that there was anything left to screw up. I'd hit rock bottom and my life couldn't possibly get any worse than it currently was.

My curiosity had always been difficult to resist and it was no different this time. With great reluctance, I trudged after the sailor. Entering a high-tech command centre, I finally realized I was in a submarine. I'd seen enough movies that involved the submersible vessels to recognize the consoles and equipment. The periscope in the centre of the room was also a telling sign.

A man in his fifties with prematurely white hair, a greying beard and weathered skin was in charge. The crew's eyes darted to him regularly, gauging his mood to see if they should be frightened or not. A quick sweep through the minds of the crew told me they were on edge. As I'd already figured, they'd been sent out to investigate the disappearances of sea creatures. They were English, so I assumed we were in the waters somewhere near the UK.

"Sir, I've just picked up something on the radar," a young sailor said and indicated the screen in front of her. Unseen, I crossed the room to examine the screen. It was mainly dark, but a few bright green dots were scattered across the monitor. A far larger dot had appeared at the top of the screen.

The captain hurried over to peer over the sailor's shoulder. "What is it?"

Shaking her head, the young woman shrugged. "I don't know, sir. Whatever it is, it's big." Her tone was ominous and the mood in the room plummeted even further.

Straightening up, the captain debated about his choices for a few moments before heaving a quiet sigh. He'd been sent to learn everything that he could about the depletion of aquatic life in the area. He'd also been ordered to search for several boats that seemed to have vanished. He had little choice, but to investigate the blob that had been picked up on the radar.

At their captain's orders, the submarine changed course and headed towards the object that was moving slowly towards us. As the captain reached the periscope, I sent my consciousness into him and looked out through his eyes. Blinding light swept over the deck, then flowed towards the stormy sea. A lonely lighthouse sat at the end of a distant promontory, doing its duty to keep ships safe from harm.

The light flashed in a full circle before repeating the

journey. The third time that it made the trip, it fell on a shape that hadn't been there the first two times. Whatever it was, it was darker than the clouds that stormed overhead. It was so vast that I could barely comprehend what I was looking at.

"Mother of God," the captain breathed. Panic seized his insides and he froze as the creature cut swiftly through the waves.

"Sir, the unknown object is gaining speed," the young sailor advised. Her voice had gone high as panic set in. "It will be on us in less than five minutes!"

Snapping out of his paralysis, the captain issued orders for them to retreat. Laboriously, the submarine turned around and prepared to dive, but it was far too late for them to escape. Even if they'd been able to dive, I doubted that would have saved them from this particular adversary.

I watched through the captain's eyes as the dark mass approached. It towered over the submarine, which probably looked like a toy in comparison. A shudder ran through the vessel and my stomach tried to fall to my feet when we suddenly rose into the air. Sailors were thrown to the ground and screamed in shock, pain and terror. Still watching through the periscope, the captain clenched his teeth to hold in a scream of his own as a gigantic split appeared in the black mass.

With a tortured screech of metal, the vessel was torn in half. Several sailors fell through the opening and were snatched out of the air by dextrous appendages. They were tossed into the maw of the beast and the two halves of the submarine followed them. The captain's screams became impossible to contain when several rows of teeth formed and closed around us.

Snapping awake from the dream, my suspicions of what was causing the depletion of ocean life were confirmed. Just before the Viltarans had fled from their home world, I'd sensed several familiar life forms on board their vessel. I'd sensed them again when we'd crash landed our stolen spaceship in one of the rivers near Manhattan. I now knew what it was that had stowed away during the ride to Earth in the hope of making a new life on a far more hospitable planet.

*So, now that you know what the danger is, are you going to join up with your friends and work out a way to stop them?* I didn't ponder on the question that came from somewhere deep within my psyche. My answer was immediate and firm. "Nope," I said out loud.

Baffled astonishment met my words. *Why not?*

"You don't get it," I said out loud to the voice inside my head. "I don't care if they eat all the humans. In fact, I kind of hope they do."

*But...but...* Distressed by my uncaring attitude, my alter ego floundered for an argument that I might listen to.

*You do not have a choice.* I frowned when a different voice spoke inside me. It was vaguely feminine, but it didn't sound like me at all. *You are my creation, Mortis. I have given you a purpose and you must fulfil your destiny.*

If it had been able to beat, my heart would have been thundering inside my chest. Unless I'd gone completely crazy, and that was a distinct possibility, Fate itself was talking to me.

A grim smile tilted the corners of my mouth up slightly as I realized that I had Fate by the proverbial short hairs. It clearly expected me to get off my butt and come to the rescue once more, but I wasn't going to cooperate this time. I had nothing left to lose and I wasn't about to let myself be used again.

"Screw my destiny," I said. "You killed Luc, you bitch. You're deluding yourself if you think I'm going to rush to help the walking blood bags just because you want me to."

My inner voice gasped in horror at my temerity at being so disrespectful to the entity that was in charge of our futures. When Fate responded, it held a touch of amusement in its tone. *God isn't the only one who works in mysterious ways. I allowed you to think that Lucentio was dead so that you would be able to develop your talents further. You now have the skills that will be necessary to face the adversaries that threaten not just humanity, but your own kind as well.*

A spark of hope raced through me at the possibility that Luc might still be alive. "Tell me the truth," I said to the new voice inside my head. "Is Luc ok?" I was tempted to send out my senses immediately and discover the answer for myself. Dread that this conversation was just another figment of my imagination stopped me.

*Lucentio is alive, Mortis,* the voice responded. *But he is gravely wounded. You are the only one who can heal him and restore your beloved to his full health.* I sensed the voice fading and then there was silence. Even my subconscious remained quiet while I thought over the information that I'd just been given.

Clutching the ragged dog blanket to my chest, I closed my eyes and readied my consciousness. With a deep mental breath, I sent out my senses in search of Luc. Expecting him to still be somewhere in France, I found only our five companions in the small country.

Sweeping my senses out further, I found a group of

strange vampires somewhere to the east of France. I sensed a vaguely familiar presence in their midst, but it was faint and I couldn't latch onto it. My hope increased, but there was no way to tell if it was Luc or not until I saw him for myself.

Gathering myself to teleport, I hesitated and took a moment to scan the minds of the strange vampires. They were all expecting me to appear and none of them were planning on offering me their hands in friendship. Instead, I'd be more likely to receive a spear in the back. I didn't know who they were, but they knew me and they'd planned for treachery.

As stealthily as possible, I slid into the mind of one of the guards and used his eyes to peer around the room. It wasn't really a room at all and appeared to be a cavern. The guards stood in a circle with their backs to whatever or whoever they were guarding. I desperately wanted to turn the vampire around to see if it really was Luc in the centre of their circle, but I didn't want to give my presence away.

Somewhere below the guards, I sensed dozens more of my kin. They were dead to the world. Most were barely a few months old, in vampire years. Others were even younger than that. While I'd been mourning my loss, someone had been busy building an army. There were far too few of them to attempt yet another vampire invasion, but instinct told me they were up to no good.

I found nine more undead on the same level as the guards and attempted to scan their minds. Six were asleep and were beyond my ability to read their minds. The other three were awake. I'd met one of the vampires before and knew him to be honourable. Hopefully, he would be able to give me some useful information so I wouldn't have to barge into a situation that I didn't fully understand.

Before I transported myself halfway across the world, I figured it would be a good idea to find some clothes. I wouldn't be very intimidating if I arrived in the nude.

# Chapter Four

It was the middle of the night in Brisbane and the streets would thankfully be mostly empty in the centre of the city. For the first time since finding myself in the cemetery, I left the mausoleum, but not by the door. With the blanket wrapped around me, I teleported directly into the clothing store that I'd once been the manager of.

Over twelve years had passed since I'd last been inside the store. I'd spent ten years floating around in space as a vampsicle. Not much had changed in the shop since I'd become a creature of the night. Jeans were even tighter, if that was possible, but the shirts and blouses still seemed to be the same. I was both surprised and glad to see underwear was also available in the store now. I wouldn't have to waste time trying to find a nearby place that sold them.

I quickly picked an outfit. Being slender and average in

height, I had no trouble finding jeans to fit me. I went with black and picked out a t-shirt and leather jacket to match. The dark colour would help me blend into the shadows. My feet were still bare, so I moved over to the window to see whether the shoe store was still across the street. It was, so I popped inside and found socks and a pair of black boots in my size.

Finished shopping, I materialized outside the store and prepared to teleport myself to Europe. The dark alley across the road caught my eye. It was the very spot where Silvius had snatched me from so long ago. Drawn by my morbid curiosity once more, I crossed the road and stepped into the mouth of the alley.

Used syringes, broken bottles and puddles of vomit decorated the length of the passageway all the way up to the white door at the far end. This bathroom was where most of the store owners and staff in the area took their infrequent toilet breaks.

I'd once been afraid to use the facilities after dark for three different reasons. Firstly, it was dark and spooky and the only illumination came from a single bulb at the mouth of the alley. Secondly, the alley was a haven for rats, which I'd been deathly afraid of back then. Thirdly, junkies, muggers, rapists and other lowlife scum frequented the area. They sometimes used the narrow laneway to conduct their various businesses in.

My fear of the dark had fled when my life had been taken from me. So had my terror of rats. As for criminals, they no longer held any danger for me. I was the monster creeping through the shadows and now I was the thing to be feared.

Remembering back to the last time that I'd used the

bathroom, I'd had a close encounter with a rat and had very nearly peed my pants in fright. Right on cue, two rats squeezed out from a hole in the bathroom door that hadn't been there the last time I'd seen it. Huge and bold, they were river rats that had left the Brisbane River behind and had headed for the comfort of city life.

One stopped beside me and stood up on its hind legs in an attempt to intimidate me. I bent, picked it up and stared into its beady eyes. "Who is afraid of whom now?" I asked it as we examined each other from a few inches away. With a squeak of anger, it sank its teeth into my hand. Surprised by the attack, I dropped the critter. The tiny tear in my hand healed even before the rat hit the ground. My brow wrinkled in puzzlement when, instead of the usual black crud that passed for my blood, a bead of fluorescent yellow blood stained my skin.

The rat had doomed itself to death by biting me. Heaving for air and squeaking in pain, it tottered a few steps, fell onto its side, twitched a couple of times and died. Usually when I was bitten, the offender's mouth and insides were melted by my highly acidic blood. Hunkering down beside the deceased vermin, I saw no evidence that my blood had eaten through its flesh this time.

"That's strange," I said then started back and almost landed on my butt in a pool of vomit when its eyes snapped open. A red glow emanated from them, illuminating the passageway around us. *Uh oh,* I had time to think before the rat opened its mouth and squealed with hunger. Its eyes latched onto the other rodent that was now frozen in fear. Scrambling to its feet, the newly risen rat streaked towards its kin. Fur and blood flew as the critter fed on its companion. The second rat didn't go down without a fight and sank its teeth into its attacker.

Mouth hanging open in amazement, I watched as the second animal died and was almost instantly reborn as the undead. *Holy shit, they've turned into vampire rats!* Both rodents turned towards the bathroom door, no doubt with the intention of feasting on their kin. Picturing a vast horde of vampire vermin sweeping through the city, I leaped forward and snatched them both up an instant before they reached the hole.

Neither of the rodents made a move to bite me and both went quiet in my hands. Their beady, fiercely glowing eyes latched onto my face. While I could understand and speak every language known to man and intelligent aliens, I seriously doubted I'd be able to communicate with animals. To test the theory, I tried to read their minds. Apart from a few pictures of their newly awakened thirst for blood, I couldn't really grasp the thoughts that were going through their tiny brains.

I'd never sired another vampire before and I was at a loss of what to do with the rats. I was both immortal and capable of healing any wound, no matter how dire. *What if the rats are just like me?* If so, then I had a serious problem on my hands.

There was only one way to find out just how much alike we were. I wanted privacy to perform my experiment and it was possible that a human might stumble across us if we remained in the alley. I didn't want to leave any evidence of myself behind, so I popped back into the clothing store long enough to grab the blanket that I'd dropped. Eventually, the store manager would figure out that some of their merchandise was missing, but hopefully they wouldn't be able to pin it on me. I hadn't seen any cameras inside either of the stores, so I hoped I was in the clear. I already had a bad enough reputation without being labelled a thief as well as a monster.

Returning to the mausoleum, I made sure the door was still firmly closed before setting the rats down on top of one of the stone sarcophagi. Sitting up on their haunches like dogs begging for food, they watched my face without blinking. Suddenly reluctant to harm them, I forced myself to pick up the rat that I'd inadvertently sired. It stared at me trustingly as I gripped it in both hands. With a twist of my wrists, I tore it in half and felt a small pang of regret as it immediately broke down into a puddle of goo. It was easier to destroy the second rat, since it was my minion's minion rather than my direct descendant.

While my blood was now fluorescent yellow, the rats' blood had still been red. I wasn't sure when my blood had been transformed. It had probably happened after I'd been infused with the barrage of nanobots. It seemed that they'd altered me far more than I'd realized.

Thinking back on all of the horrible situations that I'd gotten myself into, most had resulted in my dismemberment, or at least in intense pain. I came to the realization that each episode had ended up with me receiving a new type of power. Luc's apparent death had caused me mental anguish rather than physical pain, but I could now read the minds of every being on the planet, if I so chose.

Fate had pushed, prodded and bullied me to where I was today. It had created the legend of Mortis and it had made sure that I was equipped to deal with, and to destroy, any threat to humanity. In a way, it made sense that most of my kind had been culled. Even the vampires who didn't have aspirations of taking over the world still needed to drink human blood to survive. We could all be considered a threat to our former species.

Vampires were obviously a lesser race to the powers that ruled the universe. Like it or not, I'd been created to serve humans. The thought rankled and rebellion rose. *Why don't you rescue Luc first and worry about saving the humans next?* It was a sound suggestion and I couldn't fault my inner voice for making it. Fate had told me that only I could save my beloved and I took that as encouragement to try to help him. If he really was still alive, that was. I wouldn't believe it until I saw Luc for myself.

It would still be daylight in the northern hemisphere, but I couldn't wait any longer. Sending my senses to the caverns, I pinpointed the only vampire who wasn't an enemy and transported myself into his room. It was small, cramped and had an ancient wooden bed against the back wall. It was so old that the mattress was made of straw. Age had made the wood fragile and it would no doubt collapse if I attempted to sit on it. The prisoner hadn't been given the option of using the bed and was chained to the wall. Rusty, yet sturdy manacles pinned both of his wrists.

Sensing that he was no longer alone, Danton opened his eyes. "Hello, Natalie." He was completely unsurprised to see me. His master must have foreseen my coming, but I wasn't yet sure why Danton was locked up.

"Hi, Danton. How is the Prophet?"

Chained tightly, he managed a worried shrug. "I can only hope that my master is still alive." He didn't seem to be surprised that I was speaking to him in his native tongue.

"He's alive," I reassured him. "He's asleep at the moment." It was more like a state without animation rather than sleep, but he knew what I meant.

Relieved, Danton nodded at the manacle on his right wrist. "Do you think that you could free me?" Much stronger than a normal vampire, I wrenched the shackle from the wall, then freed his other arm. He inclined his head. "Thank you."

With a fringe of white hair on his otherwise bald head and wearing a stained, torn white robe, he looked like a monk, but was actually the prophet's main protector. The five other men in nearby cells had once guarded their leader as well. I assumed they were all that was left of his personal retinue.

"What's going on? Who locked you in this cell?"

"We have been imprisoned at the behest of a lesser vampire who has risen high during the past few months. He calls himself Magerion."

"Sounds pretentious," I said with an inner snigger. "What's his real name?"

"Melvin," Danton replied and smiled at my eye roll.

"What's Melvin's story?"

"It is the classic tale of an insignificant man with delusions of grandeur. One of Vincent's servants, Melvin spent the past few centuries snivelling at his master's feet." Vincent had been in charge of the mountain lair in Romania where the prophet had made his home. As evil as he'd been ugly, he'd been the first vampire that I'd tested my holy marks on. "With Vincent's demise," Danton continued, "Melvin was freed from his servitude. He pledged his allegiance to the Prophet and was amongst the few of us who survived the purge."

The purge had been instigated by General Sanderson, back when he'd still been a colonel. He'd wiped out as many of our kind as he could find, but he'd kept a few alive. I wished I could resurrect the Comtesse so I could kill her again for ratting out her own kin just to save herself and her courtiers.

"What gave this guy the right to lock you all up?"

"The Prophet woke from his coma shortly before the aliens invaded Manhattan and predicted that you would return. He decreed that you would rule over all of the remaining vampires. Melvin had gathered a few followers and one of his lackeys was present when the Prophet made his pronouncement. Unfortunately, the Prophet spoke quite clearly, for once."

The oracle had been stricken with visions over two thousand years ago and had foreseen my coming. The visions had scrambled his brain, so he usually spoke in gibberish. The few times that he was lucid, his prophecies had been dutifully noted down by his followers.

"Melvin and his henchmen had secretly begun to build a small army of fledglings," Danton said. "After the Prophet's vision, he changed his name to Magerion and declared himself to be the new ruler of the European vampires. His supporters agreed that you do not have any authority over us because you aren't European."

"Gee, and it's just the job I've always wanted; Empress of the European undead." Danton smiled slightly at my sarcasm. "How does Magerion plan to stop me from usurping him?"

"The fool believes he can change fate itself. He sent his lackeys to France to find some kind of leverage that he could attempt to control you with."

While I winced at his choice of words, since I'd also been a fool who'd attempted to control fate, wild hope clutched at my dead heart again. The possibility that someone had kidnapped Luc's bits and pieces had never even occurred to me. Maybe he hadn't died at all, but had instead been stolen from me.

"They found it," I told him. "They took Luc." My fists clenched in fury that my one true love was being used as a pawn.

Compassion and understanding shone from the monk's black eyes. He rested his hand briefly on my shoulder. "I am sure that Lord Lucentio is still alive and well."

"Actually," I responded, "he's in about a thousand pieces and is hovering on the brink of death." Danton blinked in wordless astonishment. "It's a long story, but a few of us are kind of immortal now. Luc was blown apart, but he hasn't broken down into slush yet. Apparently, only I can heal him."

"Is your blood by any chance now yellow?"

Now it was my turn for astonishment. "How could you possibly know that?" Even as I asked the question, I knew what the answer had to be. "Don't tell me, the Prophet saw it in a vision."

Danton inclined his head again. "Indeed. Before you rescue Lucentio, I ask that you first visit my master. He has information that you need to hear."

Knowing that Luc was so close, I didn't want to delay his rescue any longer, but Danton's urgency convinced me to see what his master had to say. My senses told me the prophet wasn't currently conscious. He'd either allowed himself to fall into what passed for their sleep, or he'd fallen into a coma again. He had a penchant for starving himself to the point of having very little energy.

I wasn't sure how I was supposed to communicate with an unconscious vampire, but I shrugged and followed the monk's suggestion. "Brace yourself," I told Danton as I took his hand. Before he could ask me why, I transported us both out of his cell.

# Chapter Five

Danton staggered a step when we suddenly appeared in the prophet's bed chamber. It was far smaller and shabbier than his previous bedroom had been. We were deep beneath the ground and the cave system was dank, dark and depressing. It was sad to realize that even this place was more welcoming than my mausoleum.

Blankets were piled on top of the slight figure in the bed. The smell of cinnamon wafted from the wizened vampire. The prophet was in even worse condition now than the last time I'd seen him. Wispy white hair floated around his wrinkled face. His mouth was sunken, as if he'd lost most of his teeth. Black bags crouched beneath his eyes. Starvation was never a pretty sight. For creatures like us, it was downright hideous.

Turning in a circle, Danton came to a stop and stared at me. "How did you bring us here so quickly?" He spoke barely above a whisper so the two guards standing outside wouldn't hear us.

"Teleportation. I've learned a few new tricks since I saw you last," I whispered back.

Motioning me closer to the bed, he checked on his master. "I hope one of your new 'tricks' will serve to revive the Prophet."

"I only just found out that my blood is yellow a short time ago," I warned Danton. "I have no idea what will happen if I feed it to another vampire." I knew what happened when I fed it to rats, but I wasn't about to divulge that embarrassing episode to him.

"My master's vision foretold the healing powers of your blood." From the disturbed glance he shot sideways at me, I guessed there was more to the story than he was telling me.

"What else did his vision tell him?" It was obvious he didn't want to tell me, but I wasn't about to attempt to heal his master until he filled me in. I could have scooped the knowledge directly from his mind, but that was a trick I wanted to keep to myself for the time being.

"The Prophet foresaw that, while your blood has become a great blessing, it also has the potential to become a great curse."

Raising my eyes heavenward, I was completely unsurprised. "Of course it does. Why wouldn't it? I'm Mortis, so everything about me is cursed." I said this bitterly and he flinched when my voice rose slightly.

On the other side of the crude wooden door, the guards halted their conversation. "Did you hear something?" one of them asked.

"It was probably just a rock falling somewhere," the

other one replied.

Apart from these two guards and the ones who were keeping watch over Luc, the bulk of Magerion's force was in the caves beneath us. It seemed prudent to dispatch these two before I tried to heal the prophet. "I'll be back in a second," I said to my companion and teleported out into the hallway.

Dressed in ragged clothing that had to be several decades old, the guards gaped at me when I appeared before them. Before they could reach for the swords at their hips, I grabbed them both by the hair and bashed their heads together. Their skulls split apart, but their brains never had a chance to leak out. Dead instantly, their empty clothing fell to the ground and their bodies joined them with a wet splatter.

Fishing keys out of one of the puddles, I wiped them clean on a shirt, unlocked the door and pushed it open. Danton relaxed slightly when he saw it was just me. "There is little point in trying to rouse my master while daylight still shines above," he said. "I suggest we free the Prophet's guards from their confinement."

Shrugging, I handed him the keys. "You're the boss."

He grinned, but his tone was solemn. "No, Mortis, *you* are the boss."

"What do you think sounds better, Empress or Queen?" I mocked.

"As long as you use any title other than Comtesse, no one will complain," he said and shuddered. The praying mantis had been well known and well hated. I doubted anyone would be sad that she was dead. I was kind of surprised that no one had given me a medal for taking down the entire Council single-handedly. Granted, I'd killed most of them while they'd been asleep, so it hadn't exactly been a fair battle.

Almost narrow enough to cause claustrophobia, the tunnel had been roughly hewn through dense rock. The ceiling was low and water seeped through minute cracks in the walls and pooled on the ground. I had a feeling we weren't far from the prophet's former mountain home. He'd probably been sent a vision centuries ago that he would one day need a safe haven to retreat to. Someone had carved out this secret retreat and I doubted it had been made by humans.

Danton stopped at the first door, but I pointed further down the hall. "Your men are about halfway down the corridor."

Slanting me a curious look, he continued down the tunnel until I stopped at a door. It took him a few tries before he found the correct key. By the time we'd freed all five unconscious guards from their chains and carried them to the prophet's bedchamber, the sun was readying itself for bed.

Taking another count of the fledglings in the caves below, we would be badly outnumbered once the sun faded from the sky completely. "Watch over them," I told Danton. "I'll be back in a minute."

"Where are you going?" he asked as he cleaned vampire goo from the sword that he'd picked up in the hallway.

"To destroy Magerion's minions."

Nodding grimly, Danton saluted me with his borrowed weapon. "Until you return."

Zapping myself downward and into the centre of the unmoving fledglings, it took a second for my eyes to adjust to the dimness. Up above, gas lamps lit the hallways.

Down here, there was only one source of light. A small fire sat off to one side and shed flickering shadows on the wall.

Gathering the power of the holy marks, I mentally marked each newly made vampire for death. With less than a hundred targets to annihilate, it wasn't necessary to let the power build up until the floor was shaking. Once all in the room were caught within my mental crosshairs, I released the holy marks and winked myself back into the bedchamber above to avoid the carnage.

Keeping my senses on the targets below, I felt them all explode into nothingness. "It's done," I told my new companion.

The sun fell and the five warriors roused before Danton could voice the questions that were foremost in his mind. Their confusion was short lived and they adjusted to their freedom quickly. "Guard the door," their leader told them as they stood.

"Yes, master," they replied. With a curious glance at me, they began filing out into the hall. It had been over a decade since they'd seen me last, but they recognized me. They either remembered me from my brief visit to their mountain retreat, or they'd watched the video footage that had been taken of us during the alien attacks in Manhattan or Las Vegas.

More than one of the soldiers had surreptitiously filmed us in action and had leaked the footage to the press. I hadn't seen the videos myself, but had seen them in the minds of many of the humans when I'd been learning how to use my telepathy. If my friends and I hadn't been famous before, we were now. *Don't you mean* in*famous,* my alter ego said slyly.

Trusting Danton, his men didn't protest at leaving me alone with him and the prophet. A couple of them gave me a respectful nod before leaving. Speaking of the prophet, the cinnamon stick hadn't woken with the advent of night and still remained trapped in his coma.

"What do you want me to do?" I asked Danton. For all I knew, the monk might have an elaborate ceremony planned. His mind was a confusing whirl of emotion and thoughts that were difficult to sift through.

"You could try cutting your flesh and dribbling a small amount of your blood into the Prophet's mouth." Danton seemed as uncertain about how to proceed as I felt.

I held my hand out and he handed me his sword. Knowing how quickly I healed, I leaned over the ancient vampire and held my hand just above his lips. They were parted slightly, as if waiting for me to feed him. I barely felt the sting as the rusty metal sliced into my palm. Only a few drops of fluorescent yellow escaped. They dripped into the wizened vampire's mouth as the cut healed.

Danton leaned over the bed opposite me and watched his master in apprehension. The prophet's eyes snapped open a second later. I let out a mental breath when they were the usual black rather than scarlet. I'd been worried that he'd somehow become my servant just from drinking my altered blood.

Focussing on my face, the prophet spoke in a language that sounded like gibberish to anyone but me. "Mortis, is it time for you to take up your rightful place as our absolute ruler?"

"Not just yet," I replied in the same language. "I have a couple of things to take care of first."

"Ah, yes. You must first restore Lord Lucentio, then

save humanity from the creatures that are about to cause great harm to our world."

Sensing humour in his words, I voiced a complaint that I'd kept bottled up inside since I'd first been created. "How many times must I save the flesh sacks? Haven't I done enough for them already?"

"Not quite," he said and reached out to take my hand. "You still have several tasks to perform before Fate will allow you to rest."

His grip on my fingers was weak and his hand looked like a mummified claw. My first instinct was to make a sound of horror, leap away and wipe my hand clean, but I resisted the urge. Then his message filtered through. "I have *several* more tasks ahead? Seriously?" My dismay was profound. I'd already saved the Earth three times from an invasion of one kind or another. Now I was faced with an unknown number of quests to perform before it would all finally be over.

"Some tasks will not be as daunting as you fear," the prophet soothed.

His hand fell out of mine as his strength failed him. Danton leaned over and tucked the blankets around his master as I furtively wiped my hand on my jeans. *Now I smell like a cinnamon stick,* I complained mentally. "Danton told me you have information that I need to hear," I said.

"You have seen what happens now when creatures feed on your blood." It wasn't a question and I nodded as I suppressed a small shudder. "You must be vigilant and keep watch over your home, Mortis."

I could understand what he was saying, but his words were still cryptic. My home was a mausoleum. If I could manage to save Luc, I'd never return to its damp confines again. Sunken black eyes watched me, waiting for a response. "I'll keep watch," I promised and that seemed to satisfy the aged vampire. His eyes slid shut, but I believed he was simply resting rather than subsiding back into his coma. My blood wouldn't sustain him for long and he'd need to feed, or risk death. His life force was flickering dangerously on the edge of being snuffed out.

Danton gestured for me to follow him and we left the bedchamber and traversed through the narrow hallways. The monk stopped when we were out of earshot of his master. "What did the Prophet say?"

"He told me to be vigilant and to keep watch over my home."

"That is all?" Danton's brows rose in surprise.

"Pretty much," I shrugged. "Now, if you'll excuse me, I have a rescue mission to perform."

Danton and his five warriors hurried after me. "I believe I would like to see Magerion humbled before the true ruler of our kind," Danton said to my back. I didn't mind having an entourage, just as long as they didn't interfere when I fought my way through Magerion's minions to reach Luc.

# Chapter Six

It would have been far quicker to simply teleport into the large cavern, but I didn't want to deprive Danton and his men from the carnage that was about to be unleashed. I followed Danton's directions as we made our way through a series of passageways to a final, far larger tunnel. Light flickered at the end of the path, illuminating the cavern where my beloved was supposedly being kept.

Facing the opening, one of the guards spotted me and raised the alarm. At his shout, more vampires spilled into the cavern from several other passageways. Our small group was now outnumbered by three to one, but none of Danton's warriors seemed perturbed. They formed a small shield around their leader with me as the spearhead. They'd stopped long enough to arm themselves with swords, but I hadn't bothered to find any weapons. I'd tear these henchmen apart with my bare hands if I had to.

Drawn by the shouts, another vampire scurried towards the main cavern. I sensed him slowing down to a walk just before he reached the opening, then he sauntered nonchalantly into sight. Strutting through the opening his underlings made, he stopped in the centre of the room beside a wooden box. I sensed the semi-familiar remains inside that I was now pretty sure belonged to Luc.

"Ah, Mortis," the short, rat-faced vamp said, "how nice of you to join us." He spoke in Romanian and I answered him in kind.

"You must be Magerion." Looking him up and down through the crowd of armed lackeys, I didn't hide my sneer. "You're a lot shorter than I expected." He wore a black cloak that was several inches too long for him and dragged on the ground. I suspected it had once belonged to Vincent. His thin, pale face was framed by stringy brown hair that hung to his shoulders.

Rage twisted his rat-like features into an even uglier mask. "Get me a torch," the self-declared ruler of the European vampires snarled to one of his men.

Hurrying over to the fire, a henchman pulled a flaming chunk of wood out of the pile. Our kind tended to be extremely flammable and he held the wood gingerly as he made his way back to his leader.

Magerion took the torch and held it threateningly over the small box. "Choose your words carefully, Mortis. The fate of your precious Lord Lucentio lies in my hands."

Cunning and a jealous hatred shone from his eyes. Living beneath Vincent's rule would have been enough to drive anyone mad and Magerion appeared to be certifiably nuts. Yet he was lucid enough to have planned the kidnapping of my most favourite companion. *I'll have to be careful dealing with this little psycho.* Then again, being careful wasn't something that I was very good at. "What do you want from me?" I asked him bluntly. Finesse had never been one of my strong suits, either.

"Pledge your loyalty to me and become my concubine."

His supreme confidence almost made me laugh even as I mentally threw up at the idea of having his grimy hands on me. He wasn't the first insane vampire to think he could force me into his bed. "And if I refuse?"

Lowering the torch towards the box, he chuckled and even that sounded like a rat squeaking. "Then Lucentio will burn."

Pretending to ponder his offer, I wished I knew whether Luc was impervious to fire or not. My friends could now heal wounds that would be fatal to our kind, but they had yet to test their capacity to heal to its fullest extent. "What do you plan to do if I pledge myself to you?"

Thrown by the question, he stared at me blankly. "Do you mean what specific acts will I require you to perform in bed?"

Mentally vomiting again, I shook my head. "What is your plan for our kind?"

"Ah." Wrenching his mind out of the gutter, Magerion puffed out his narrow chest. "My plan is to turn as many humans into my slaves as possible. I have already begun to build my army and I will soon take control of Romania." His grin revealed ragged yellow teeth that any rodent would have been proud of.

"I have some bad news for you, Melvin," I said with false regret. "I kind of destroyed your army."

"My name," he said through clenched teeth, "is Magerion." He drew himself up to his full five feet four inches of height and tried to stare down at me imperiously. Since we were exactly the same height and I was wearing boots with a three inch heel, he failed miserably. Then my message filtered through his rage. "What do you mean you have destroyed my army?"

"They're dead." I drew my thumb across my throat to illustrate my point. "That *is* why I was created, you know." Still trying to comprehend that the bulk of his undead army was gone, he had trouble understanding my meaning. "It's my destiny to stop psychos like you from attempting to take over the world," I explained.

Magerion's narrow face hardened. "We all have a choice, Mortis. We cannot be forced down a path that we do not choose to take." He was very wrong about that. Every time I'd tried to thwart my destiny, my course had been forcibly corrected for me. "As a consequence of your choice, Lucentio will now die." The grin he sent me was full of malice. "Say goodbye to your lover forever."

As he turned to drop the torch into the box, I willed myself to stand right in front of him. I caught the torch as it fell and hurled it at the closest group of his minions. One immediately caught on fire and bright blue flames flared. Screaming, melting and flailing his arms, he managed to set two of his cohorts alight. The rest scattered to avoid the flames.

Roaring a command for his warriors to attack, Danton drew his sword and went on the offensive. He was well skilled in combat, as were his men. Magerion's lackeys were far less competent with their weapons and were being slaughtered.

Turning to flee, Magerion's feet left the ground when I grabbed him by the back of his cloak and lifted him into the air. Scarlet light from my eyes bathed his face when I turned him around to face me. Gibbering in terror, he clawed at my wrist, but he couldn't break my hold. "Do you know what I do to anyone who tries to harm my loved ones?"

Feet flailing, he choked out a reply that sounded more like a plea. "No."

"Let me show you." Dropping him, I grabbed him by the throat before he could try to run. My free hand became a swirling mass of particles that were almost too tiny to see. Magerion began to scream even before my molecules invaded his skull through his mouth, ears and nasal passages. Once deep inside his head, my hand became solid again. The self-proclaimed ruler's eyes bulged and he made a strangled sound as my hand closed around his brain.

I could have squeezed the organ to a pulp, but decided to try an experiment instead. Concentrating on my hand, I willed it to reattach itself to my wrist. An instant later, my arm was whole and I held a soggy grey lump in my hand. Bereft of his brain, Magerion's body instantly turned to ooze. The organ in my hand broke down to coat my fingers in goo as well.

With a grimace of disgust, I knelt beside the now empty cloak and wiped my hand clean. Danton and his warriors had taken care of most of Melvin's men. I caught sight of one sprinting down the tunnel that led to the prophet's bedchamber. Before I could race after him, a pair of minions attacked me.

Empty handed, I wasted a few seconds dodging their wild sword swings before grasping them both by the face and unleashing the holy marks. I had full control of the dark power that resided in me now. It came when I called it and their heads popped simultaneously. Their bodies disintegrated into mush, leaving the usual puddle behind.

Snatching up their dropped weapons, I teleported into the prophet's bedchamber just in time to see the shrieking henchman straddling his withered body. Gathering myself to leap the short distance to the bed, I staggered a step when the prophet spoke directly into my mind. *No, Mortis, you cannot save me. My end was foretold on the night that I was sent my first vision over two thousand years ago. Remember my warning; remain vigilant and watch over your home…* His words trailed off as the lackey's sword punched through his chest.

"No!" Leaping forward, I beheaded the henchman, but I was too late to save the prophet. His eyes were closed and he was smiling slightly. Apart from the sword sticking out of his flesh, he almost appeared to be sleeping peacefully. The dark watery stain of the dead henchman soaked into the bedding, overpowering the smell of cinnamon.

A strangled sound behind me announced the arrival of Danton. "I'm sorry," I told the monk as he dropped to his knees beside the bed of his former master. "I wasn't fast enough to save him."

Sparing me a grief filled smile, Danton attempted to absolve me of my guilt. "I was aware that the Prophet's end was near. You are not responsible for his demise. We all must face our end sometime." His gaze slid away from mine when he remembered that I was essentially immortal. For me, there probably wouldn't be an end.

Reverently, he grasped the sword that was sticking out of the bundle of sticks that had been his master and pulled it free. With a dry crackling sound, the prophet collapsed into dust rather than into a puddle of sticky goo. His essence had been severely drained from his self-imposed starvation. Apparently, we needed blood in our system to turn into a moist sludge.

Apart from Danton, his five warriors and me, the caverns were now empty of life. It was time for me to inspect the contents of the box and determine whether Fate had been telling me the truth about Luc.

# Chapter Seven

Leaving Danton and his men in the prophet's chambers to grieve for their loss, I willed myself back into the main cavern. Sitting in the centre of the cave, the plain pine box looked far too small to contain an entire person. I vividly remembered the state that Luc had been reduced to and knew that his chunks would easily fit inside.

Steeling myself for crushing disappointment, I walked over to the container and looked down. I'd been in this condition myself many times now, but my stomach tried to flop over at the sight of blasted flesh that had been reduced to the consistency of dog food.

It wasn't until I spied a familiar hand that was whole and unmarked before I finally allowed myself to believe that it was Luc inside the box. Picking the appendage up, my own hands trembled. "Is that really you, Luc?" I whispered.

Without a mouth and larynx to answer me, the best he

could do was to wiggle one of his fingers. Then I felt his mind connect with mine, just like it had when I'd been dreaming. *What took you so long?* The question was asked with a mixture of relief and exasperation.

"Sorry," I responded out loud. "I was too busy wallowing in self-pity to come to your rescue. I thought you were dead."

*I'm still alive and you're here now,* he whispered in my mind. *I have tried to piece my flesh back together countless times, but I do not know how.* His frustration and fear came through loud and clear.

"I'll show you how, but first I have to get you out of this box."

Picking up the container, I found a spot that was clear of the sludge of the fallen and tipped his remains out onto the ground. I placed his hand on top of the pile, then stepped back to give him some room.

Thinking about the process that my particles went through each time I managed to break myself down then re-form again, I sent the picture to Luc. It took him a while to sort through the images and grasp what he needed to do. *I think I understand,* he said doubtfully. *I shall try to put myself back together again now.*

He'd been in this condition for months and his flesh would be weak. Fate itself had told me that I would need to heal Luc before he could become whole again. I stripped off my jacket and held one of my borrowed weapons over my left arm. "I'm ready when you are," I said to my one true love.

When I felt him gathering his will, I made the first slice. Bright yellow blood splattered onto Luc's remains and they began to quiver. With each slice that I made into my flesh, the quicker his bits and pieces began to move. It was fascinating to see them trying to realign to their natural positions as the fluid that powered me rained down on him. His flesh sucked up the liquid like thirsty ground that was in dire need of water.

Shivering, dancing and squirming into place, the outline of Luc's body rapidly became more pronounced until he resembled a jigsaw puzzle that just needed to be connected. A final splash of my blood landed on him and was absorbed beneath the skin that was suddenly whole and unmarked.

Sitting up, Luc examined his body then, stared up at me in wonder. Stark naked, he was as perfect as I remembered. Our minds were still joined and his love swept over me. It enfolded me even before he stood and his arms did the same.

"I thought I'd lost you forever," I told him in a small voice that was muffled by his chest.

"I knew you would find a way to restore me," he said with complete faith in my abilities.

"I guess you aren't mad at me anymore?" I asked.

Leaning back slightly, he cupped my face with his hand. "I was more disappointed than angry with you." Disappointment was somehow worse than his anger would have been. "How could you have believed even for a second that my love for you wasn't real?"

"Don't blame me," I said crossly. "Blame Fate. She's the one who arranged all this."

With our minds linked, he could see that I was telling him the truth. "So," he mused, "I was right all along. Fate really is female."

"It looks like it," I said very grudgingly and felt his mind beginning to recede from mine. When they separated, I found I couldn't delve into his thoughts as easily as I could with everyone else. *That's probably a good thing,* my inner voice said. *Would you really want to know what he's thinking all the time?* I had to concede that my subconscious was right again. I'd hate it if Luc knew every thought that was going through my head and I was sure that he'd feel the same way.

Picking up a jacket that wasn't too badly stained, Luc tied it around his waist in a makeshift skirt. It gaped open on one side, revealing his muscled thigh. My flesh hunger stirred at the tempting sight, but I forced it away as Danton and his retinue arrived.

"Lord Lucentio," the monk said and offered Luc his hand. "It is good to see you again."

Shaking the vampire's hand, Luc's nod was grave. "I would like to offer my condolences for your master's demise." He'd gleaned all that he'd missed since he'd been blown up by General Sanderson directly from my memories.

"As I told Natalie, the Prophet foresaw his death long ago." He may have known that this night was coming, but Danton's grief for his master would remain sharp for a long time. Unlike many of our kind, he'd loved his master dearly. The prophet might have spoken in gibberish most of the time, but he'd treated his people well. Only when Vincent had been placed in charge of their domain had trouble started. Luc and I had taken care of that when we'd killed most of the damned that had been overtaken by their sentient shadows. Magerion was to blame for this latest upheaval, but I'd set things to rights once more.

"Are you aware of the disappearances of both aquatic

and human lives during the past few months?" Luc asked the monk. It was an added bonus that he'd witnessed everything that I'd seen and heard during the months that we'd both been locked away in our confinement. I wouldn't have to explain anything that he'd missed.

Danton nodded. "This cave system is far cruder than our previous home, yet we do have some modern amenities. I have seen the news broadcasts regarding the disappearances."

"I'm pretty sure I know who, or what, is behind the missing fish," I told the small group and became the centre of attention. "You already know about the Viltarans that invaded Manhattan and Las Vegas?" I received nods all round. "Well, they inadvertently brought some stowaways along with them when they left their home world."

"Are you saying that another species of aliens is responsible for the depletion of aquatic life?" Danton asked. I wasn't sure what visions the prophet had been sent, but apparently they hadn't been very detailed. That wasn't really much of a surprise. Most of the visions he, Kokoro and I were sent were vague at best.

"Yep and I'll tell you all about it, but I don't want to have to tell this story twice." We would require help to battle these new enemies and I knew just the bunch of vampires to bring into the fold.

"Can you transport all of us at once?" Luc asked.

I had no idea whether I could or not and shrugged. "There's only one way to find out. Let's all join hands."

Nervous, but obedient, the warriors slid their weapons into their sheaths and clasped hands. I didn't have a sheath, so dropped the sword to the dirt. Luc and Danton offered me their hands and I grabbed them, closing the circle.

Sending my senses westward, I concentrated on the small group of vampires that I recognized to be our friends and teleported all eight of us to France.

Expecting to find myself in the safe house that was our usual haunt, we were instead in a large library. Twin brown leather couches faced each other across an antique coffee table. A smaller, daintier couch sat before a fire. The room was large, but somehow cosy and welcoming.

"This is Gregor's mansion," Luc said even as I recognized the room.

Along with our five closest friends, I'd also sensed the presence of several unfamiliar vampires. "Someone else is here," I told the others. Scanning the minds of the dozen strange vamps, I frowned. While they weren't overtly hostile, the strangers weren't exactly friendly either. I hadn't even met them yet and they already seemed to be haughty and pompous. "I think they might be a few courtiers that survived the First's call to his cavern of doom."

Luc seemed glum that some of the courtiers might still be alive. While he'd been a part of the Court for his entire undead life, he hadn't particularly liked any of his peers. Most had been rounded up by the First and had then been converted into imps. Any that had survived had been destroyed by me when I'd taken down the Comtesse and her lackeys. "They must have fled from the Court when the Comtesse began sending her courtiers to Russia," Luc surmised.

The praying mantis' shadow had ascended and had been in charge for a while. It had started funnelling the courtiers to Russia, where the First had his lair. Upon the First's death, the Comtesse's shadow had returned to normal. My own silhouette had been sentient for a time and it had also lost its intelligence, not that it had been particularly smart to begin with. I'd had a small entourage of shadows following me around everywhere at one stage. That was another story that I didn't want to dredge up right now.

"Shall we accompany you?" Danton asked politely.

"We're all part of the same team now," I reminded him. "We few are the remnant of our species. We kind of have to stick together." I wasn't happy about adding a dozen snobby European vampires to our team, but I had no cause to end their lives. Yet. Being haughty wasn't a killing offence. *I can always kill them if they start harbouring thoughts of world domination,* I told myself.

"I can only imagine how Geordie will react when he sees you," Luc said as we headed for the door.

"It should be memorable," I joked, but I was feeling pretty nervous. Geordie would either be overjoyed to see me, or he would be furious that I'd been gone for so long. My fingers were crossed for the first choice.

# Chapter Eight

Luc led the way, since he knew the mansion well. He and Gregor were good friends and he'd lived here for a while after becoming a Lord. He'd been tempted to leave the Court entirely, but had decided to become a deliverer of justice instead. That way, he still had ties to the Court, but could leave for extended periods of time.

I'd picked up on this knowledge the one and only time that I'd tasted his blood. Only now could I appreciate his self-sacrifice. He'd stayed to attempt to make life better for the servants and underlings like Igor and Geordie. Luc's innate kindness and ability to care for others was just one more reason for me to love him.

We walked down a hallway that sported several paintings that were probably very expensive, and stopped at an open door. Elegant furniture predominated inside what appeared to be an old fashioned sitting room. The delicate and antique royal blue couches and settees had been arranged into a rough circle. Half of the visitors were seated, the rest were standing strategically near the exit to another room. None seemed to be armed, but I remained suspicious of them anyway.

Our friends sat directly opposite from their guests. Kokoro and Gregor were side by side with their hands clasped together. Igor lounged beside Gregor and Ishida had taken the spot on his former seer's other side. Geordie sat slightly apart from the others. Slouched down in his chair, his arms were folded and his lower lip was pooched out in a pout.

Luc sensed my surge of emotion at seeing our friends again and slipped his arm around my waist. Only a few short hours ago, I'd been trying to will myself to die. Now I had everything to live for again. Luc was back, he was whole again and he didn't hate me as I'd feared. He loved me as much as he ever had.

After delving into his mind, I knew that the emotion hadn't been forced upon him by destiny. I'd selfishly abandoned my friends and had convinced myself that I was keeping them safe. *I hope they can forgive me for being a coward and for walking away from them.*

With his uncanny knack of sensing emotion, Geordie looked up and saw Luc first. The teen's jaw dropped open and his eyes bulged as words stuck in his throat.

"I believe there is something wrong with your servant," one of the visitors said in a snotty, upper crust British accent. "He appears to be having some kind of fit."

Usually the height of diplomacy, Gregor's brows drew down into a frown. "I have told you on more than one occasion that Geordie and Ishida are not our servants."

Luc and I shared a glance at that news. *I bet Ishida loved being mistaken for a lackey.* He may have abdicated this throne, but that didn't make him anyone's flunky.

Lifting a hand, Geordie pointed with a finger that trembled. "It's Luc!" His eyes focussed on me as the visitors turned to see what all the fuss was about. "Oh, look," the teen said with false enthusiasm, "Nat is here, too." *So much for him being overjoyed at my return*, I thought sadly.

"Good lord," the snotty female said to the others. "Her parents named her after an insect!"

"Her name is Natalie Pierce," Gregor said sharply to the quietly sniggering bunch of strangers, "but you might know her better by her title of 'Mortis'." Their sniggers cut off at that and they turned assessing gazes on me.

"Australians tend to shorten their names," Ishida said with a fond smile at me.

"I'd heard the rumours that the dreaded one was an Australian," drawled the British vamp. "I'd so hoped they were incorrect. Our reputation is already bad enough without having someone who comes from a penal colony as our supposed leader."

Standing, she turned and her attention went straight to Luc. Her eyes dropped down to the gap in his makeshift skirt and she smiled languidly. "Lord Lucentio, you are looking very well indeed."

I caught the image she had of stripping off the jacket Luc had tied around his waist and pulling him down on top of her. I forced it out of my mind before I could leap forward and punch my fist through her heart.

Taller than me by several inches, she was buxom enough even without the corset pushing her breasts up to just beneath her chin. Her dark red hair had been meticulously arranged into artful curls. They fell over one shoulder and nestled in the valley of her impressive cleavage. Her dress was sapphire blue and had gone out of style several hundred years ago.

"I am well, Lady Millicent, thank you." Luc offered her a bow as she glided over to him, eyeing his near naked form with a sultry smile. She offered him her hand and he automatically lifted it to his mouth.

For a second or two, I struggled against the urge to rip Millicent's lips off and make her swallow them. I'd never felt jealousy like this in my life before and I wasn't sure how to deal with it. I had no doubt that Luc had been forced to service this creature more than once in his distant past and that she'd enjoyed their liaisons immensely. I struggled not to read her mind again. If I saw even one more image of her in Luc's arms, I'd end her life. It seemed prudent to find out what they wanted before I killed any of them. For all I knew, they might turn out to be vital to our cause.

Dropping the snotty cow's hand, Luc put his arm around my shoulder, clearly staking his claim. Only then did I realize most of the male guests were undressing me with their eyes, as well as with their thoughts. As we'd suspected, they were refugees from the former Court. Scanning their minds, I gleaned that they'd returned to France after they'd learned of our victory over the Viltarans. They fully expected me to form another Court. They believed they would be given places of honour due to their former status as lords and ladies.

Taking in how cosy Luc and I were, Millicent's mouth tightened slightly. Every inch as arrogant as the former

Comtesse, she managed to thrust her breasts out further and gave my far less impressive chest a contemptuous sneer. "It is a pleasure to make your acquaintance, Natalie," she said with a false smile.

"Actually, Millie, this isn't the first time we've been acquainted with Natalie," drawled another of the strangers. Tall and lean, his hair was an artfully tousled mess of dark brown curls. "I distinctly remember the night she and Lord Lucentio graced us with their presence." His smile was far too warm and familiar and his eyes dropped down for a slow perusal of my body. He remembered the night that I'd been forced to strip down to nothing at the praying mantis' order all too well and with startling clarity.

"Don't call me Millie, Thaddeus, and I won't call you Teddy," Millicent said peevishly. Both were thousands of years old and came from lands far away. They'd taken on the pretence that they were of British aristocracy, mainly to gain ascendency over the other courtiers. I could have called them on their subterfuge, but I didn't want to admit my telepathy just yet.

Ishida and Geordie rolled their eyes in unison at the courtier's snarky comment and I couldn't help but smile.

"You find us amusing?" Thaddeus queried. His mouth hovered on the edge of a laugh. A quick peek inside his mind told me he wasn't averse to being the brunt of a joke. He was the kind of guy who liked attention and he didn't care how he got it. He and Geordie would probably get along famously.

"I find you all annoying," I replied and my smile disappeared. "What are you doing here?" I knew the real reason why they were here, but I wanted to hear the lies that they'd carefully concocted.

"Why, we are here to join you," another Brit, a male this time, blustered. He truly had been born in the UK and his accent was genuine. He was far from aristocratic and had once been a peasant. He'd gladly left his life of toil and hardship behind for a new life of glamour and riches. He'd quickly become as jaded as the others beneath the dictatorship of the Council. He'd still been a servant, just a cleaner and better dressed one.

"Really? Join us in what?" I read his thoughts easily enough and a picture of the old Court was clear in his mind. "Because, if you think we'll be forming another Court, you're dead wrong. There are no more Lords or Ladies." I flicked a glance at Geordie, who was staring at me broodingly. "Or servants," I added and the teen's lower lip trembled as he came close to bursting into sobs. "We're equals now and no one has any right of lordship or dominion over anyone else."

"That is not quite true, Natalie," Danton stepped forward to say.

"What do you mean, Danton?" Gregor asked. He and the others remained seated. They were still in shock that Luc wasn't only alive, but that he'd also been restored to his full health.

"My master made one last prophecy before he was murdered." Murmurs swept around the room at that news. "He proclaimed that Mortis would become 'the absolute ruler and that all would unknowingly bow down before her'."

Geordie's expression was as confused as mine. "What does that mean? How can we 'unknowingly' bow down before her? We already know she is in charge."

Danton shrugged. "I do not know. I am certain that it

will become clear in time."

Standing, Gregor gestured for his guards to come forward and addressed the courtiers. "If you will leave us now, we have some catching up to do."

Millicent and her crew weren't happy at being dismissed, but they took their leave as graciously as possible. Luc gave Thaddeus a narrow stare when he stopped to take my hand and kissed it. "I am ready to bow down before you now," the cheeky courtier said, then trailed out after the others.

"I am ready to bow down before you now," Geordie repeated in a high pitched, girly voice when they were out of earshot.

Ishida doubled over in laughter and I broke into giggles. "I missed you, Geordie," I said when I managed to regain control of myself.

"Then why did you not contact me?" Unhappiness made him look even younger than his fifteen mortal years.

"Because I was too busy sulking and wallowing in misery," I said honestly.

"Are you back to stay?" he asked.

"If you guys will have me."

Geordie met my eyes and his were so vulnerable that a lump lodged in my throat. Luc gave me a light shove and I walked over to the teen. Geordie rose and his thin arms wrapped around me tightly. "I am so glad you are back, *chérie*. I have missed you, too." I'd hurt him horribly by running away, but he'd already forgiven me. His mind was wide open to me and I read only love and support for me inside.

Ishida's hug was shorter, but no less affectionate. Igor graced me with a fond squeeze of my shoulder and then

Gregor and Kokoro enfolded me in a double hug.

Then it was Luc's turn to be greeted. "I knew you would be able to put yourself back together," Igor said and gave his old friend a quick hug. Neither seemed to feel the least bit awkward about hugging while Luc was nearly naked.

"Without Natalie's help, I would still be in pieces," Luc said as he received the same twin hugs from Gregor and Kokoro that I had. Ishida and Geordie were next.

Another lump came to my throat at the sight of Europeans and the last two remaining Japanese vampires united in friendship. Their nations had been at war for thousands of years and they'd once felt compelled to kill each other on sight. *That's one good thing I've accomplished as Mortis,* I conceded. I'd forged peace between them and their old prejudices had been destroyed.

Danton and his retinue had moved to the far side of the sitting room to give us a chance to catch up. Outside, I sensed Gregor's guards patrolling the mansion grounds. Our little reunion had been as private as possible and I was grateful for the monk's consideration. I was also very glad that the party of strangers were gone.

None of them had cared for anyone but themselves. They'd been taught that our kind cared only for food and sex and that love was forever beyond our reach. That wasn't true at all. It was a lie told by masters who preferred to oppress their servants rather than to treat them with dignity and respect.

Luc left long enough to change into some borrowed clothes. He came back wearing black trousers and a tight black sweater that was a size too small for him. It showed off his physique almost too well. "How long have Millicent and her cohorts been here?" he asked as he took a seat on the couch beside me. Danton and his warriors joined us, but only their leader took a seat.

"They arrived last night," Gregor said. His expression hinted that he was less than pleased about their arrival.

Kokoro stirred uneasily. "They claim that they wish to join us, but I see nothing but trouble ahead if we allow them to be a part of our group."

Ishida looked at her in surprise. "Have your visions returned, Kokoro?"

Her smile was fond and I was pretty sure she came close to ruffling his hair. "No. It is simply women's intuition."

"I agree," I interjected before any of the menfolk could laugh at her. "My intuition went into overdrive after we munched down on that second Viltaran." We'd drained the creature to death and I'd been so full of his blood that I'd been sloshing with it. "It's telling me that they can't be trusted."

"They are a bunch of snobs," Geordie grumbled. "Millicent refers to me as 'servant boy'."

"She refers to me the same way," Ishida said with a dark glance at the hallway that they'd disappeared down.

"I take it they're staying at Isabella's estate?" Luc asked.

Gregor nodded. "I did not want them staying here and Isabella's mansion has remained unoccupied since her death. It seemed like the logical place for them to stay."

"But, she died twelve years ago," I said. "Her mansion must be in pretty bad shape by now." Poor Isabella, who I'd never had the chance to meet, had been a victim of the Japanese warrior that had pretended to be me. Acting on Ishida's orders, my imposter had done her best to eradicate the Council. I'd killed her before she could do the job. In hindsight, I wished I'd let her cut them all down. It would have saved me the trouble of doing so later. Of course, Fate had had another plan in mind all along.

"I arranged for both of our estates to be maintained during our absence," Gregor explained. "I suspected that General Sanderson would turn against us at some stage and that, when he did, we would be gone for some time. Of course, I did not expect to be gone for an entire decade."

Most of his guards had either been exterminated, or had been rounded up and sent into outer space. I was confused about who had been following his orders. "Who maintained the estates while we were vampsicles floating around in space?"

"I arranged for humans to manage the properties. I found a reputable business that specializes in maintaining vacant estates," Gregor explained. "Once word spread that we were back, my surviving guards returned." There were only a small handful of men left to watch over him now where there had been dozens previously. Unlike the other lords and ladies of the Court, Gregor didn't believe in creating servants. He employed vampires who had no masters or homes of their own. By treating his people with respect and dignity, he'd ensured they would be loyal to him even in his absence.

His guards were few, but they would come in handy when we tackled our next task. Speaking of which, it was time to let them all in on what I'd learned. "I have some news for you," I said to the group.

"Have you finally sent out your senses and figured out what is eating all the life in the ocean?" Ishida asked with one brow raised. It was a subtle dig at my earlier refusal to help them discover the cause of the disappearances.

"Yes," I said primly and the child king cracked a smile. "I sensed something familiar on board the Viltaran ship just before it fled and now I know exactly who they are."

Gregor's eyes widened as he realized what it had to be. "It's the octosquids, isn't it?" I nodded and he told everyone the theory that he'd instantly formed at this knowledge. "They knew the Viltarans would head to our planet when they were in danger of becoming extinct. They stowed away on their ship in the hope that Earth would contain enough food and water for them to survive in." It was a statement rather than a question.

"That would be my guess." I remembered one of the aliens asking how much water our planet contained. I'd blithely replied that we had plenty. "Remember when they told us they could grow to roughly the size of the Kveet cave?" Everyone except Danton nodded. He had only a vague idea of what we were talking about, but he'd catch up quickly enough. "I don't think he was talking about that one particular cave. I think he was talking about the entire cave system."

Igor looked as if he'd been hit in the stomach. "If that is true, then they have the capacity to be almost unbelievably gigantic."

"I saw one in a dream last night," I told my stunned friends. "It was big enough to swallow a submarine like it was a cocktail sausage."

Gregor sank back against his seat as the implications set in. "I think our planet might be in serious jeopardy this time. I am not sure that we will be able to defeat these enemies as easily as we have our previous ones."

Earth had been threatened more than once already and we'd managed to prevail. If Gregor thought we were in deep trouble, then things had to be even worse than I'd imagined.

# Chapter Nine

"I have a few questions," Danton said. "What is an octosquid?"

Geordie fielded that one. His hand was firmly tucked into mine and I felt his slight shiver as he pictured the hideous aliens. "That is the name Nat came up with. They are as black as ink, have a body that looks a bit like a jellyfish and hundreds of slimy tentacles that are covered with tiny mouths." His other hand mimicked a mouth that opened and closed, gnashing the air in an endless quest for food.

"They were relatively small when we saw them," Igor said. "They were roughly the size of an average human. Except for the one that had been transformed into a Viltaran clone. Its body alone was the size of this room. Its tentacles would have stretched the entire length of the mansion."

Danton and his guards took in the size of the large room and couldn't hide their incredulity. "Now I have even more questions." The deceased prophet's protector was taking the news as well as could be expected. "Could someone please explain what happened to you on this alien planet?"

All eyes turned in my direction, so I figured it was up to me to fill him in. "After the governing powers decided to kick us off Earth, our ship drifted into deep space. We were frozen into ice cubes and fell into a kind of hibernation. I woke up after what turned out to be ten years of sleep."

"So, that is why you were gone for so long," Danton mused.

I nodded and continued the tale. "I broke into the cockpit and managed to get the emergency power to the console working for a short time. I called for help and the Viltarans heard me and turned up a few days later. They captured our ship and took us back to their planet."

"You'll never guess who they really were," Geordie said to the monk. Humouring the teen, Danton raised his brow in silent query. "They were our ancestors!" Geordie declared and grinned at Danton's astonished surprise.

Gregor offered an explanation. "The Viltarans were a warlike people whose goal was to conquer other planets. Their technology far exceeds ours and they'd created nanobots that had the capacity to turn other species into clones of themselves. They'd conquered, then destroyed all of the habitable planets within their reach. They then began sending out Seeker ships to search for new planets to destroy. One crash landed on Earth."

Understanding flickered across the monk's face. "It was

an alien that fathered our species?"

"Actually, a robot minion turned the First into a monster," Ishida corrected. "He carried a vial of his master's blood, which contained the nanobots. He fed it to the First and our species was created. Gregor suspects that the nanobots were faulty, which is why we weren't instantly transformed into Viltaran clones."

"Where do the octosquids come into the story?" Danton asked.

"We were captured by a race called Kveet, who became our allies," Kokoro replied. "The octosquids had taken refuge with the Kveet in the cave systems, where there was still water to be found."

It was Igor's turn to continue the tale. "We banded together with the Kveet and began hunting down the Viltarans. The last few fled to Earth, inadvertently bringing the black sea monsters with them."

"Now that they are here, they have enough food and water to grow to their full potential," Luc finished the tale.

Danton mulled over what we'd told him. "How many of these creatures are we facing?"

"Ten," I answered.

He grimaced at my reply. "What is the best way to kill them?"

"I managed to explode one of the clones with these," I held up my hands to expose the crosses that were embedded on my palms. "But it was much smaller than these ones. It would be like comparing a tick to a horse." The analogy shocked everyone. It would be difficult to grasp just how gigantic these things were until they saw them with their own eyes. I'd just seen one in a dream so far, but my dreams were rarely wrong.

"We're going to require weapons," Gregor said bleakly.

"Lots of weapons," Geordie added.

"And plenty of manpower," Igor said. "We will not be able to tackle these monsters alone."

"I am not sure any government will be willing to ally themselves with us this time," Luc said as diplomatically as possible.

"Why?" I said with mock innocence. "Just because I turned the US President into a meat suit?"

Geordie's delicate stomach betrayed him and he almost dry heaved at the reminder of what I'd done to President Rivers. Ishida patted his friend on the back in sympathy. I felt no remorse for exploding the woman from the inside out, but the picture on both of their minds wasn't pretty. I'd reduced myself down to particle form and had invaded her body. When I'd re-formed, her body had burst apart and I'd been clothed in her blood and skin.

"Humans will have difficulty fighting the octosquids in deep water," Gregor said when the silence stretched out. "If the aliens retreat below the surface, the human armies will be rendered all but useless."

"Will we be affected by the pressure if we follow them into deep water?" Geordie asked curiously.

"Perhaps, but not to the same extent that humans would."

Luc contemplated his old friend, knowing that he'd formed a plan, yet he didn't want to voice it. "There are fewer than forty of our kind left." He'd gleaned that information from me. "We may be able to survive in deep water, but I do not think that we alone will be able to defeat our new adversaries."

Gregor's gaze shifted from Luc to me and back again.

"Are you suggesting that we must create more of our own kind? It would take months before they could regain enough control to become useful."

"Not 'we'," I replied. "Just me. And I'm pretty sure my servants won't be the same as normal fledglings." It was just a hunch, but since I was so different, I believed my minions would be as well.

Geordie looked at me in confusion. "But your blood is fatal to anyone who drinks it. I thought you were unable to sire our kind."

Luc came to my rescue before I could explain myself. "The nanobots changed Natalie's blood. It now has the capacity to heal rather than to destroy." One thing he hadn't gleaned from me was the vampiric rats. That unfortunate episode was locked deeply away in my psyche, but I wasn't going to be able to hide it for much longer.

Danton nodded in support. "A few drops were enough to rouse the Prophet from his coma." We both remembered the oracle's warning that I had to remain vigilant, but neither of us brought that part up. It would probably just confuse everyone even more.

"Have you tried to sire another vampire yet?" Geordie asked. I sensed his jealousy at the mere thought that another vampire might become more important to me than he was.

I shifted my gaze away from his and found everyone staring at me expectantly. "Kind of," I said with great reluctance. This was a tale that I'd hoped I wouldn't have to tell. Unfortunately, there could be few secrets between us now if we wanted to survive through this latest disaster.

"What happened?" Ishida demanded.

"I was bitten by something and it, um, turned."

"What bit you?" Geordie asked. Laughter danced in his eyes as he sensed my embarrassment at divulging this story.

"It was a rat, ok?" I snapped. "A rat bit me and died and a few seconds later it turned into the undead."

I had to give the two teens credit, they manage to control themselves for a full three seconds before they broke down into shrieks of laughter. "You sired a v-v-vampire rat?" Geordie stuttered while pointing at my mortified face.

Kokoro turned away, but not before I saw her smile widely. *Only Natalie could manage to get herself into a situation where a rat would become the undead,* she thought in affectionate amusement.

Gregor and Igor were far better at controlling their expressions, but Igor's shoulders heaved in silent mirth a couple of times. Luc showed his support by pulling me to his side. He kept his thoughts tightly in check, but the look he slanted at me spoke of silent laughter. I grumpily leaned against him until everyone finally managed to regain their decorum.

Waiting for the teens' final giggles to fade, Gregor spoke. "So, we know you can turn animals into our kind, but you haven't yet tested your blood on humans."

Igor raised his hand in a silent threat when Geordie's face screwed up in laughter again. The adolescent cringed against me and kept his giggles on the inside.

Frowning at the kid, Gregor continued. "If you can indeed create our kind, you just might be able to generate an army to help us combat the octosquids." No one suggested any of the others should begin creating minions of their own. Their surface thoughts were enough to tell me that none particularly wanted to sire an army of their own. As Gregor had already pointed out, it would take too long for their servants to gain control of their hungers to be of any assistance to us.

"That sounds like a good idea, except for one thing," I said. No one seemed to realize there was a fundamental flaw with this plan. "I was created to cull our kind and to make sure our numbers don't grow out of proportion. What do you think Fate will do if I make an army?"

"I do not think we have much choice," Ishida told me frankly. He might look like a twelve year old kid, but he'd been an emperor for ten thousand years and he was well versed in war. "Once the threat is over, you can simply destroy your army."

Remembering the pang of regret that I'd felt when I'd killed the rat, I wasn't so sure it would be that easy for me to dispatch even one true vampire, let alone an army of them.

Igor sat forward to make a point. "Before we make too many plans, I think we should test your ability to sire our kind."

Gregor nodded briskly. "I agree. We need to choose a human for you to try to turn."

"Who do you suggest?" I asked dryly. "I don't even know any humans."

Geordie's response was sly. "You know one. That soldier who was following you around in Manhattan and Las Vegas seemed to be very attached to you."

"Higgins?" I remembered the soldier well. He'd been one of the few walking blood bags that hadn't tried to kill me. He and a couple of hundred other soldiers had temporarily become my slaves. They'd helped to contain a group of officials that I'd decided to slaughter in order to teach the rest of humanity not to mess with vampires. I hadn't given any of them another thought since that night. *You were kind of busy sulking,* my inner voice reminded me. *Shut up!* I waved a mental fist at it and it quickly retreated.

Several steps ahead of me already, Gregor stood. "I suggest you try to locate Corporal Higgins. While you do, we'll search for a place to contain him in the event that he manages to survive the transition from mortal to vampire." Fledglings rose with an insatiable hunger for blood and we didn't want him to go on a killing spree.

Ever practical, Igor made a suggestion. "You should also find some food for your Corporal and bring it back with you."

We all stood and I slanted a look at Luc. "Do you want to come with me?"

"Of course. Where you go, I go." His tone was implacable and I caught a fleeting glimpse into his mind. He didn't want to be parted from me again after spending so much time alone and in pieces. I had the impression that he knew I could delve into his thoughts and he guarded them tightly.

I offered my beloved my hand and he threaded his fingers through mine. An instant before we teleported, I caught Geordie's wistful thought. *I wish I could find someone to love me like that.*

## Chapter Ten

My connection to Higgins helped me to locate him amongst the billions of people that populated the planet. The hypnotism had forged a link between us that I followed halfway around the globe.

When Luc and I appeared before him, Higgins started back hard enough to smack his head against the wall. Ordinary in looks, he had brown hair and eyes and a medium height and build. He was sitting on a small cot and was wearing orange coveralls. They were the brightest thing in the small, cramped room.

"Hi, Higgins. How are you?" As small talk went, it was kind of lame.

Standing, the corporal rubbed the back of his head and stared at us with wide eyes. "I'd feel a lot better if I wasn't locked up in this cell," he said after he'd gathered his wits.

I'd noticed the plain grey walls and lack of furniture, but

only when I turned and saw the bars did I realize that we were in a prison. We were surrounded by the other humans that I'd once bamboozled and I'd erroneously figured we were in an army compound. The bright orange jumpsuit should have been my first clue that Higgins had been incarcerated.

"I am surprised your government did not execute you for treason," Luc said to the former soldier.

Higgins crossed his arms and smiled wryly. "A shrink examined us and determined that we couldn't be held accountable for our actions, since we'd been hypnotized into following Natalie's orders. Besides, they don't believe in execution nowadays."

I admit I was confused. "If you've been cleared of all blame, then why are you all in here?"

"We stood by and did nothing when you murdered our President," he explained. "No one is ever going to be able to trust us again. They don't know whether we can ever re-enter society after being beneath the control of a vampire."

They hadn't just watched idly as I'd turned their leader into chunks of flesh. They'd shot the guests and dignitaries in the legs to prevent them from fleeing from the Kveet imp feeding frenzy. It would have been cruel to mention that, so I didn't remind him of the actions I'd forced them all to take.

"How long do they intend to keep you imprisoned here?" Luc queried.

Higgins' shoulders slumped in dejection. "We'll be locked up here forever."

The despair in his tone plucked at my conscience. I'd thought that I was done with humanity and that I lacked the ability to care what happened to them. It appeared that

I'd merely suppressed the emotions beneath my rage at their treatment of my friends and allies. Not all mortals were bad. Some, like the corporal, were honourable and only wanted to serve their people and to protect their country.

"Have you heard about the mysterious fish disappearances?" I asked.

Higgins shrugged carelessly. "I've heard. What about them?"

"What if I told you it was caused by aliens who hitched a ride here on the Viltaran ship?"

His interest was piqued enough for him to straighten up slightly. "Then I suggest you talk to someone who is still enlisted in the army and try to become their allies again." His tone suggested that I'd have a hard time pulling that off.

"I am afraid that humans will be less than effective in this war," Luc told him.

Suspicion narrowed the corporal's eyes. "Why are you here, exactly? What do you want with me?"

There was no point beating around the bush so I decided to tell him the bald truth. "I want to turn you into a vampire so you can help us fight them."

Blinking at my statement, Higgins was momentarily speechless. I could have transported him back to France and turned him against his will, but that had been done to me and I still resented it. I didn't have the right to decide someone else's fate for them and I wasn't going to force him into this.

We remained silent as the soldier thought over my offer. It didn't take him long to reach a decision. He was only twenty-six and he'd be spending the rest of his life behind bars. Alternatively, he could accept my invitation to join the ranks of the undead and become a free man. Kind of. "Ok. Count me in." Now that the decision had been made, he was eager to commence his transition. "Are you going to make the same offer to the other guys?"

He indicated the man staring at us from across the wide hallway. I recognized him instantly. Sergeant Wesley hadn't changed much since I'd seen him last. He was still short, with wide shoulders, sandy blond hair and a pug nose. His expression was both curious and guarded. We were speaking too quietly for him to be able to hear us, so he had no idea why we were here. "That depends on how turning you goes," I said.

Higgins regarded me uncertainly. "What do you mean?"

"I've never turned a human before. You'll be my first."

His chest puffed out in pride that he'd been my first choice. "It's a risk I'm willing to take, ma'am."

Luc turned his head at the sound of several guards approaching. Cameras were probably watching each cell, so they knew we were here. "We should leave," he suggested.

"One more thing," I said as the guards rapidly closed the distance to the cell. "Who is the worst criminal in this jail?"

"That would be Danny McCredie, otherwise known as Diabolical Danny," Higgins replied and threw a worried glance through the door of his cell where the guards would shortly appear.

"Let's pay him a visit." Taking both men by the hand, I searched the jail. There were several men called Daniel or Danny, but there was only one man who was truly diabolical. Just before the guards sprinted into view, I teleported us down two levels and into McCredie's cell.

Lying on his bed with his back to us, Danny stared dreamily up at the ceiling. He gave no indication that he knew we were there. I'd read enough about the criminal from Higgins' mind to know he was indeed the worst of the worst. Nicknamed 'Diabolical Danny' by the press, he preyed on boys between the ages of five and twelve.

Molesting them would've been bad enough, but he hadn't stopped there. Once he was done with them, he chopped them up and ate them to hide the evidence of his heinous deeds. A neighbour had become suspicious of his tendency to burn things in a pit in his backyard late at night and had called the cops. The police had caught their suspect shovelling human remains into his homemade pit. The final nail on his coffin was when they'd found containers of human flesh in the fridge and freezer. Each had been labelled with the dead kids' names.

Naturally bald, Danny's skull sported a tattoo of a demon's face. More tattoos covered his arms. All depicted images of monsters straight out of hell. He was a large man, with muscles that bulged against his orange jumpsuit. I shuddered at the mental pictures of the poor kids that had suffered at his hands. If anyone deserved to be torn apart by a fledgling vampire, it was this guy. "We're taking him with us," I told my companions.

Luc stepped over to the bunk as shouts came from out in the hall. We'd just been spotted by the camera lurking in a corner of the cell. Lost in his memories, Danny's eyes remained vague as he was dragged off the cot and to his feet. He towered over Luc by several inches. A small smile played around the criminal's mouth. It would be a pleasure to see it replaced with a scream.

We'd only been gone for a short while, but Gregor and the others were waiting for us when I dragged my companions across the globe again. Higgins' knees wobbled and Luc steadied him while keeping a firm grip on our prisoner when we arrived.

Our friends had gathered in Gregor's library. "I believe we should move to another location to discuss our plans," Gregor said and nodded significantly towards the sitting room down the hall. My senses told me that Millicent and her retinue had returned. "The catacombs should be a suitable location to perform our experiment in."

"Join hands," I told them all quietly. Once they'd complied, I zapped us all directly into the remains of what had once been a beautiful mansion. A fire had ravaged both the main building and the separate building that had once been a barracks for the guards. Old rubble and ash were piled to one side and the place hadn't been touched in years. No one had made any attempt to rebuild it so far. Regret flickered across Luc, Igor and Geordie's faces. Their stay in the mansion might not have been pleasant most of the time, but it had been their only home for centuries.

Blinking slowly, as if rousing from a dream, Diabolical Danny swept his muddy brown eyes across the group and settled on Ishida. The teen would have been sickened by the thoughts that passed through the inmate's mind. Geordie drew back, picking up on the malevolence that emanated from the man who would shortly become a snack for Higgins.

Ishida would be insulted if I asked him to remain behind, so I shut out the images that were coming from the convict and scanned the ground beneath our feet. I sensed no life in the catacombs. For all I knew, they'd been discovered by the humans and might even have been filled in.

"I did not realize the mansion had been destroyed," Gregor said softly and with regret. "I should have ensured that it was also protected during our absence."

"It was not your responsibility," Luc assured him. "Perhaps it is for the best that the mansion no longer stands." He for one wouldn't miss the place and he'd never intended to live here again anyway.

"I'll just check to see whether the catacombs are still intact." I said then teleported several levels beneath the ground.

Little had changed since I'd last seen the dozens of cells where humans had been kept as cattle for the courtiers and Councillors. The bars of the cells were rustier than I remembered, but they would be sturdy enough to contain a couple of prisoners. I quickly popped upwards to check the servants' quarters and the courtier level. They were all fine, if dusty. The staircase that had once led to the mansion was clogged with dirt and debris. It would take an excavator to stumble across the opening and I doubted the humans had plans to build anything on the grounds.

By the time I reappeared on the surface, Igor held a makeshift torch of a length of wood and a few scraps of fabric in his hand. When we were all touching again, I zapped us beneath the ground. The light from Igor's torch only stretched for a few yards around us. It wouldn't last long, but that was ok. Pretty soon, everyone who was still alive in the catacombs would be able to see in the dark anyway. Night vision was just one of our many perks.

Gregor fished a key from his pocket and indicated that

we should deposit our inmate inside. He'd stolen one of the prison keys decades ago and even he hadn't been sure why. It came in handy now and Luc propelled McCredie through the door.

"Let's do this before I change my mind," Higgins said. A nervous tic started up in his jaw as he clenched his teeth. He was about to leave his mortal life behind and he would never be human again. Briefly, second thoughts rose, but he manfully squelched them down.

"I'm going to cut my wrist," I said and took the small dagger that Igor offered me. I was glad he hadn't handed me the machete that was hanging at his waist. While cutting myself didn't hurt all that much, I preferred a small cut to a large one any day. "I heal very quickly, so you'll have to be fast."

The corporal looked ill at the thought of drinking my blood. "Don't you have to drain me before I drink your blood?"

"I don't think so." To be perfectly honest, I had no idea what I was doing, which was the story of my life. "I seem to be different from my kin." That was an understatement and a half. "Let's just try this and see if it works."

Bracing himself, Higgins moved closer until he was standing only inches away. I sliced deeply into my left wrist and he took hold of me, bent and put his mouth to the wound. He managed two swallows before the cut closed, but two were enough.

Snapping upright, his back arched and his mouth opened in a silent scream as agony ripped through him. His hands flailed and caught mine in a grip that would have crushed a mere human. He fell to the floor and I knelt beside him as he writhed in agony. Linked to his mind, I felt him dying as my tainted blood coursed through his veins, spreading like the malevolent virus that it was.

Gasping for air, his breathing slowed and his chest heaved twice before going still. A few seconds passed before I felt a new kind of life infuse the corpse of the fallen soldier. Higgins' eyes snapped open and his grip on my hand made my bones creak. Scarlet light washed over me as he examined my face. I helped him to his feet and he turned to study the others. He went still as he spied Danny and I felt the blood hunger rise up to twist his insides. His instincts kicked in as he identified the only source of food in the room.

Gregor opened the cell door as my first ever human servant lurched forward with his hands outstretched. The door was locked once he was inside. Higgins' brand new fangs descended and glinted in the torchlight. Awareness of sudden and immediate danger filtered through Diabolical Danny's psychosis. He tore his gaze away from Ishida and turned towards the fledgling vampire that was about to eat him. Right on cue, Igor's torch began to fail. It winked out just as the inmate backed into the bars and realized that he had nowhere left to go.

Shrill screams rent the air as the glow from my minion's eyes became noticeable to his prey. Higgins was far smaller than McCredie, but he easily overpowered the larger man and bore him to the ground. He sank his fangs deep into the shrieking criminal's neck. Clawing at my fledgling vampire's face, Danny thrashed in terror. His struggles became weaker as my servant drank his fill. With a final burst of energy, he gave his attacker a taste of what he was suffering by biting him on the shoulder. *Uh oh.* I hadn't anticipated the possibility that the inmate might ingest Higgins' blood.

Blood coated Higgins' mouth and chin when he was done. Crawling away, he sat with his back against the bars and covered his face with his hands.

I hadn't told my friends about the second rat, so what was about to happen would be a surprise to everyone. We watched as Danny clutched at his chest as his newly tainted blood reached his heart. Just like Higgins, he gasped, writhed and his chest heaved. His feet twitched a few times and then he expired.

"Is he about to turn into your second generation fledgling?" Geordie asked me shakily.

"Um. Yes," I replied and was unsurprised when all gazes briefly turned to me.

When Danny's eyes opened seconds later, they were blazing red instead of muddy brown. Climbing to his feet, he swept his scarlet gaze across us and settled on Ishida. His grin was hungry, but not for the black ooze that ran through Ishida's veins. His deeply ingrained mental illness had mingled with his blood hunger and had catapulted him directly to a raging flesh hunger.

"Did you know that this might happen?" Gregor asked.

"I should have warned you that it might," I admitted. "The rat that bit me wasn't alone. The second rat took a chunk out of the first one when it was being munched on. It turned as well."

Ignoring us, McCredie was fixated on Ishida. "Come inside and play, little boy," he crooned in a deep, gravelly voice that was enough to give any child nightmares. "I have a present for you." He grabbed his bulging crotch meaningfully.

Geordie made a sound of profound disgust when he realized what the inmate wanted to do to his friend.

"I would be most appreciative if you would allow me to destroy this…creature, Mortis." Ishida's tone was offhand, but his voice trembled slightly.

Sickened by the new images raging through Diabolical Danny's mind, I nodded my agreement. Igor offered the teen his machete. Ishida took the weapon and waited for Gregor to unlock and open the door. His expression was inscrutable as the criminal leaped towards him.

Size meant nothing when you were facing an opponent that was highly skilled in weaponry. Danny crashed into the bars as Ishida sidestepped his lunge. Looking down, he roared in rage when he saw his intestines spilling out of a wide gash in his orange prison outfit. Whirling around, he screamed when one of his hands was hacked off and thudded to the ground.

Piece by piece, Ishida reduced my second generation minion into a quivering pile of severed flesh. With a final swipe of his borrowed machete, he cut the monster's head off. "That is for all the children you violated, then murdered," he said to the slushy remains that had been a notorious killer only seconds ago.

"I take it you've heard of Diabolical Danny?" I asked when he exited the cell.

"I saw him on the news several months ago," Ishida replied as he returned Igor's weapon with a bow of thanks.

"He molested, slaughtered and ate over thirty kids," Geordie told me solemnly. "I would have been too old for him, but even I'm glad that he is dead."

Too proud to show his emotions, Ishida stood with his head held high. He wasn't about to admit that he'd been frightened of a mere fledgling vampire.

"I'm sorry I brought him here. If I'd known about his history, I wouldn't have."

Luc added his apology to mine. "Neither of us was aware of his infamy." We'd both been indisposed during the past few months and hadn't kept up with the news.

"It's my fault," Higgins said. His words were muffled behind his hands. "I knew who and what he was and I didn't warn you about what he'd done."

Gregor and Kokoro shared a look of surprise. Apart from me, every other newly made vampire that had ever been created was born with an uncontrollable thirst for blood. Our kind were little better than zombies when we first rose. We were compelled to feed until we'd sated our blood hunger. Once that happened, the need for sex became just as overpowering. Only when we'd satiated both hungers were we able to function. Generally, this took several months. Higgins shouldn't even have been capable of coherent thought yet.

Probing my new minion's mind, I read his guilt at mauling a man to death and only a faint need for hunger. "Huh. That's weird."

I didn't realize I'd spoken out loud until Geordie queried me. "What's weird?"

"Higgins isn't a mindless feeding machine like a normal fledgling."

"What do you mean?" Danton asked.

"He feels remorse for turning Danny." He shouldn't, since the criminal had been an abomination and had deserved to die painfully.

Kokoro looked at me suspiciously. "How can you know what your servant is feeling?"

If I'd been human, my face would have turned red in embarrassment. My secret was out, but I knew I wouldn't have been able to keep it to myself forever. "I can sort of read minds now."

As I'd guessed, Kokoro felt a spike of jealousy that I'd somehow attained the gift that she had once possessed. Proving herself to be my staunch friend, she willed the emotion away and offered me a smile. "It can be quite annoying at times, but the ability can also come in very handy."

"You mean you know what we're all thinking all the time?" Geordie was aghast at the idea.

"Only if I concentrate on someone specifically. Otherwise, I hear this continual background noise of thoughts. I've learned to shut it out, mostly." The teen wasn't reassured by my explanation. "I promise I won't rummage around inside your head." He was slightly mollified by my vow. I didn't mention that I couldn't help but skim their thoughts on a fairly constant basis.

Gregor made a sensible proposal. "Now that we know Natalie has the ability to turn humans into her servants, we should retire back to my estate to discuss our plan."

Stricken by Gregor's words, Higgins rose and turned to face me. "Is that all I am to you? A servant?"

"No," I told him honestly. "You're a soldier in my own personal army now. You'll have command of my troops during the times when we're separated."

He was mollified by my answer and offered me a nod of acceptance as we gathered into a circle. A soldier was all he'd ever wanted to be and I'd just given him back his dream. *Just how big will my army become,* I wondered silently. We had ten monsters to destroy and each one was gargantuan in both size and appetite. I wasn't sure that even two hundred vampires would be enough to stop them from eating their way through the entire population of our planet.

# Chapter Eleven

I'd forgotten about Gregor's unwanted houseguests, but I remembered them quickly enough when we materialized in the library and I heard Millicent complaining from the sitting room. "Well really! How rude of them to sneak off and leave us to sit here and twiddle our thumbs! I thought Gregor was more refined than this."

"He *is* consorting with the Japanese dogs and an Australian bumpkin now," muttered another snotty female.

*Bumpkin?* I came close to laughing out loud at that, mostly because it was true. Compared to the sophisticated and jaded courtiers, I was just a simple country girl, even though I'd lived in large cities all my life. "What are we going to do about them?" I asked Gregor quietly and pointed towards the sitting room.

He shook his shaggy blond head. "I do not know. It

would be undiplomatic to send them away. I fear we may need every vampire that we can locate for the battles ahead."

"How many of your comrades are locked up in that prison?" Ishida asked Higgins.

The corporal's eyes had stopped glowing and had returned to their normal brown. His pupils were much larger than normal and his face was still coated in blood. Apart from that, he looked like a normal man. "Just under two hundred," he replied.

Gregor sent an appraising look at the teen. "What do you propose, Ishida?"

"I assume that most of the soldiers are honourable men rather than disgusting reprobates like Danny McCredie. We need men and women with fighting skills who will wish to assist us in our battles. These soldiers would be our best candidates." It made sense and it was pretty much what I'd been thinking as well.

"It will take time to convert nearly two hundred soldiers into vampires and each one will need to feed," Ishida pointed out. "If we work together, we can set up a production line of sorts and convert the soldiers quickly. Natalie can determine who has the moral fortitude to join her army and we can dispatch any of the inmates who might accidentally rise as our kind."

Gregor's pride in the young ex-emperor was obvious. "That is a very good plan, assuming the soldiers will wish to join us. Now, we just have to convince Millicent and her friends to assist us."

"Let me handle that," I said and marched out of the library and down the hall to the sitting room. I could be very persuasive when I needed to be. Having deadly crosses embedded on my palms helped. Even a glimpse of them would have most vampires willing to follow my orders.

Thaddeus grinned at me when I entered and offered me an elegant seated bow. I caught an errant thought from Luc along the lines of tearing Teddy's head off and using it as a bowling ball. Stifling a grin of my own, I kept my expression chilly.

Millicent's back went stiff as she realized we'd returned, but she didn't deign to turn around and face us. She clearly expected to be treated like royalty and she was going to be sadly disappointed. "Gather around, troops," I said. "We have a job to do and we need your help."

Standing, Thaddeus snapped me a salute. "Major Thaddeus reporting for duty, mistress!"

I couldn't help but smile at his enthusiasm. Millicent reluctantly stood as the rest of her retinue joined Thaddeus in a neat line. "What help do you require?" she asked as she pushed her way through to stand in front of her companions. As the oldest, she thought of herself as their leader. None of them disputed her right to do so.

"We're going to a jail in the US to convert a couple of hundred criminals into fledglings," Geordie told her brightly.

"I was not talking to you, servant boy," she said coldly without even glancing at the teen. "I was speaking to Natalie."

"We're going to a jail in the US to convert a couple of hundred criminals into fledglings," I told her. "By the way, his name is Geordie. I don't want to hear you call him, or Ishida, 'servant boy' again."

"They are abominations that should have been

destroyed long ago," she huffed. "It is known to anyone who possesses sense that children should not be turned into our kind. Their minds and bodies are not equipped to deal with our hungers."

My reply was almost frigid enough to raise frost. "They aren't children, they are teenagers, and they deal with our hungers just fine. They are also my friends and they've helped save the world three times. Where were you when the First was converting our kind into imps? Where were you when the Second and his brothers rose and created a horde of slaves? I don't remember seeing you anywhere when the Viltarans landed and started changing humans into their clones."

Millicent dropped her eyes beneath my accusing stare. "We did not know that our help was required," she said stiffly.

"It's required now," I told her. Looking her up and down, I switched my examination to her entourage. "Find some normal clothes to wear. We're going to a prison, not to a ball."

He might be a grownup version of Geordie, but Thaddeus managed to put aside his mischievousness. "We will, of course, aid you in any way that we can. Unfortunately, we don't possess normal clothing. We erroneously presumed that we would return to Court life." While Gregor wore one of his hand tailored suits, the rest of us were dressed casually. The courtiers were overdressed and out of place.

"There should be spare clothing in the servants' quarters," Gregor told them. "One of my men will assist you to find something suitable." Hovering nearby, a guard snapped to attention and led the way down the hall.

Millicent glanced down at her beautiful gown, ruby red this time, then straightened her back. With a grudging nod in my general direction, she glided after the others towards the back of the mansion.

Luc turned to Gregor. "I assume you have a plan on how we're going to accomplish this task?"

I wasn't the least bit surprised to hear that the smartest of us all had already devised a strategy. "I propose that Natalie should visit the prison warden first. She can convince him not to interfere with our proceedings."

By 'convince', he meant bamboozle. No prison warden in their right mind would allow us to squirrel any of their convicts away. I wasn't sure whether they'd care if we fed the worst of their inmates to the fledglings or not. His feelings weren't really a factor, since the only reason I was even contemplating doing this was to save their world yet again.

While we were waiting for the courtiers to change, I took Luc with me to scout out the prison. It took less than a second to travel halfway around the world. We appeared a short distance away from the maximum security complex that was surrounded by arid land. Wherever we were, there were no other signs of civilization in the area.

Bright lights blazed inside the buildings and exercise yard. Two of their prisoners had gone missing and they had to know that something supernatural was behind their disappearances. Scanning the minds of the guards, I garnered that the video had been too grainy for them to make out our faces. They didn't realize we were vampires and assumed we were some kind of aliens.

I located the warden and found him to be alone. Linking hands with Luc, I willed us into the man's office. He was tall, broad shouldered and African-American. The nameplate on his desk said 'Warden Jeffries'. Standing with his back to us, he studied a bank of monitors. One of the screens had been frozen in place and showed Luc and me talking to Higgins. Luc was blocking most of me from sight and only part of his face showed on the screen. Of me, I could see my butt and one leg and nothing else.

"The camera really does add ten pounds," I observed quietly.

Whirling around, Jeffries fumbled for the gun at his hip. He made the mistake of meeting my eyes and all resistance drained out of him. My hypnotism worked a lot faster than it once had. One quick glance was enough to ensure that any human would fall beneath my control. I could also control vampires, but I didn't use it against them unless I had to. I had a feeling that my powers had become far stronger than they used to be.

"Warden Jeffries," I said to my temporary slave, "gather your men together in a room where they can be safely contained."

"Do you want me to call in the guards on outside patrol as well?" He might be beneath my spell, but I hadn't stripped him of his intelligence like some vampires did when they took control of a human's mind.

"Just the guards in this cell block should do," Luc told me.

"What he said," I said to the warden.

With a nod, Jeffries sat down at his desk and picked up his radio. With a few terse words, he ordered his men to gather in a meeting hall. We watched one of the monitors as guards began filing into a large room a couple of minutes later.

"That's the last one," the warden said as a final man stepped through the door then closed it behind him.

"Lock them in," I instructed. Jeffries stood and walked to the console to the left of the monitors. He pushed a button and the penned guards immediately started shouting in panic and reaching for their radios to call for help.

"Tell them that the prison has been invaded by aliens and that they're safer where they are," Luc advised.

I smiled at my one true love, glad that he was more than just a pretty face and a hot body. "Good thinking."

The guards calmed down once Jeffries conveyed the lie, but they remained uneasy. "Sit tight and wait for further orders," their boss commanded them then switched his radio off and turned to me expectantly.

"Good job. Now wait here." Now that the cell block had been secured, it was time to visit with the prisoners. Leaving the warden behind, Luc and I left the office and appeared near Higgins' vacant cell.

Sergeant Wesley gave me an appraising look as we approached him. "Ma'am," he said with a polite nod. "It's good to see you again."

"I'm sorry you were thrown in jail, Sergeant Wesley." He accepted my apology with a guarded nod.

Up and down the hallway, imprisoned soldiers watched our interaction. None asked questions or begged for us to release them. They'd fallen beneath my spell previously and almost seemed to have an inkling as to why I was there.

"I'm here to make you an offer," I said loudly enough for most of them to hear me. "A new threat is coming that makes our fight with the Viltarans look like a game of tag."

My words were repeated to those who were out of range.

"What is this threat?" a soldier asked from halfway down the hallway.

"It's another type of alien," I responded. "Unlike the previous adversaries that we've faced, these aliens don't intend to try to take over your world." I paused for a moment to add weight to my next words. "They intend to eat it."

"What do you need us to do, ma'am?" someone called as several expletives were uttered.

"These creatures survive in water. Fairly soon, they'll run out of food and will head for land. They'll most likely retreat to the water again as soon as we attack them. Humans won't be able to battle them if they sink deeply beneath the surface." I let them come to their own conclusions.

"You want us to become *vampires*?" one brave soul called out then laughed incredulously.

"You've got to be kidding," someone else objected. "We'll be turned into monsters that'll rip people apart and will feed on them!" Anger and fright quickly spread through the group.

Sergeant Wesley reached for my arm through the bars. "Is that why you took Corporal Higgins away? To be converted?"

"Yes. I wasn't sure I could turn anyone and had to test my ability."

"Did it work?" His eyes searched mine, looking for a lie.

"Yep. He's one of us now."

"Is he a blood crazed monster?" It was a well-known fact that fledglings woke ravenous for blood and lacked the ability to control their hungers.

"No. My fledglings are different from normal. You'll need blood to survive, but you'll be able to control your hunger and you won't lose who you are in the process."

Luc made a suggestion. "Perhaps you can discuss your options while Natalie and I collect the Corporal. Once you see his condition for yourselves, it might help you to make up your minds."

"Good idea. We'll need a few minutes to talk it over," the soldier said.

I zapped Luc back to France in time to watch as Millicent emerged from the servants' quarters in a borrowed guard's outfit. While it was far too long in the arms, it barely fit across her buxom chest. Folding the sleeves up, she'd already done the same for the pants. She looked ridiculous wearing the outfit with a pair of bright red high heels, but I kept my smirk to myself. None of the courtiers were happy about wearing normal clothing, but at least they weren't complaining out loud.

Higgins had washed his face and had changed his shirt while we'd been talking to his comrades. He was far more presentable without the bloodstains. I also noticed that his looks had already improved. Instead of being merely average, he was now handsome. His jaw was squarer, his eyes were slightly wider apart and his nose was thinner. They were subtle changes that were a result of becoming the undead.

People were more inclined to become bamboozled by an attractive vampire rather than an ugly one. The ugly ones had other tricks up their sleeves to snare a meal. My maker had been hideous in the extreme, but he'd been able to change his appearance at will. I'd been suckered into thinking that he was a frail and harmless old man. That illusion hadn't lasted long, but he'd already ensnared me by then.

I wasn't sure how many people I could transport at once, but knew I could handle up to a dozen. Trying to shift more and failing would be too embarrassing, so I opted to shift our team in stages. Gregor left a few of his men behind to keep watch over his mansion. Danton's warriors weren't about to leave him unguarded, so they would have to come as well.

"I'll take you guys first," I said to my closest friends and Higgins. "I'll be back for you next," I said to Danton and his men. The monk nodded and his warriors seemed appeased that they wouldn't remain behind. "I'll come back for you lot last," I told Millicent's crew.

"We shall await your return with bated breath," Thaddeus quipped.

Geordie bristled, but a stern glare from Igor kept the teen from voicing his complaint. He always reacted badly when other men attempted to woo me. Luc wasn't particularly happy about it either, but he merely rolled his eyes. There was no contest between Luc and Thaddeus. Luc was far more attractive, but it wasn't just his looks that captivated me. I had witnessed his memories and I'd also been inside his mind. He was a man of honour and principles and my heart belonged to him. No one could ever compare to him or have a chance in hell of stealing me away from him. He seemed to read my expression and winked.

"Are you ready?" I asked the group as they joined hands. At their nods, I whisked us back to the prison.

# Chapter Twelve

A mini riot was raging between the soldiers. They'd split into two camps; one team was on board with the idea of becoming my undead servants and the other was less certain. If they hadn't been locked in their cells, they would have been brawling.

Higgins listened to the debate for a few moments before striding down the hallway. The shouting died down when his comrades realized the person they were arguing about had appeared.

"Corporal, how are you feeling?" a soldier asked.

"I'm fine, Charlie."

"Did she really turn you into a vampire?" Sergeant Wesley asked.

"Yes. It hurt like hell, but it was over quickly."

"How come you aren't trying to eat us?" Charlie asked.

Higgins flicked a glance back at me. "Because Natalie

turned me herself. She's not like other vampires and we won't be, either."

"How do we know you're really undead?" someone shouted.

Stepping over to the inmate's cell, Higgins reached inside and grabbed the soldier by the front of his shirt. The man squawked in alarm when he was lifted several inches off the ground with one hand. "Is that enough proof? Or do you want me to feed you some of my blood and see what happens?"

"You mean, if we turn, we can also change others into vampires?" the soldier asked when he was placed back on his feet. The thought seemed to horrify many of the men.

I stepped in to answer that question. "This is why I'm not simply turning you against your will. I don't want anyone to join my army unless they want to." I met their stares and turned in a circle until I'd caught the eye of as many of the men as I could. "A war is coming that makes everything else that our planet has suffered so far pale in comparison. If you don't step up and fight to save the humans, who will?" That got through to them and a short, but thoughtful silence descended.

"I'm in," Sergeant Wesley called out so everyone could hear him. "Given a choice between sitting around doing nothing, or saving our planet, I opt to be a hero, even if people will think we've been turned into monsters!"

Spoken so starkly, his words helped the others to reach their own decisions. Not all of the soldiers stepped forward to join our ranks, but most did. I would make sure that anyone who refused to side with us would be set free anyway. They didn't deserve to remain locked up forever just because I'd hypnotized them into following my orders.

Gregor drew me aside as the shouts of agreement began to fade. "We'll see about getting their doors open and rounding up meals while you return for the others."

Luc took a step towards me, then visibly stopped himself and gave me a strained smile. "I won't be gone long," I told him and went up on my toes to give him a kiss. My flesh hunger rose as soon as our lips touched and so did his.

Ishida slanted a look at us. "Is now really the time for that?"

It wasn't, but it had been so long since Luc and I had been together that it was hard to deny our needs.

"Ishida is right," Luc said softly and trailed a fingertip across my bottom lip. That small touch was enough to make me shiver in anticipation. "Now is not the time."

"We'd better find the time soon," I muttered darkly. If we didn't, I'd be in danger of spontaneous combustion.

Danton, his warriors and a few of Gregor's men were ready to go when I returned, but they weren't alone. Thaddeus gave me a sunny smile and offered me his hand. "I'm ready to go, my Liege." His attempt to charm me was laughably easy to see through. Nicholas, a gorgeous but overly muscled vampire, had been fond of calling me by the same title. He'd been a double agent sent by the Comtesse to infiltrate our ranks. He'd done his best to cause dissent and to worm his way into my bed. It had been my pleasure to finally carve his heart out.

I didn't waste time in protesting, but I didn't insert my hand into his and instead took Thaddeus by the wrist. Danton took my other. Moments later, I deposited the small group in the prison hallway, then went back to make one final trip.

Millicent made sure she didn't have to touch me as her retinue gathered into a circle. I took two of the courtiers by their wrists as the rest joined hands. They were justifiably nervous at the thought of being at my mercy. I was tempted to pop over to the Sahara Desert and dump them in the middle of it, but we really did need every vampire that we could scrounge up. I had a feeling that the octosquids would leave the oceans in search of more food soon.

The doors to the cells opened as we arrived and soldiers lined up in the hallway uncertainly. "Who doesn't want to join our ranks?" I asked. Scanning the minds of the men, I identified a few who had homicidal tendencies. Most hadn't acted on their urge to murder anyone, yet. If I turned them, they wouldn't be able to contain their baser instincts. Pointing at them, I crooked my finger. All up, nearly twenty men wouldn't be joining our army.

It took two trips to carry them a safe distance from the prison. I deposited them in an empty field near a large town somewhere in the mid-west. It would be up to them to secure their own freedom now.

"You five, hold up for a second." I pointed at the men that had the dubious mental strength to suppress their killer instincts before they could sprint away.

"What?" one asked with a sneer. "We're good enough to be part of your private army, so what do you want with us?"

I looked deeply into his eyes and he went quiet as he fell beneath my spell for a second time. I repeated the act with the other four men. They stood quietly, eyes glazed over at the strength of my hypnotism as they waited for orders. "You no longer feel the desire to murder people," I instructed them firmly. "You will not hurt anyone else, unless you're protecting your own life or the lives of others," I added as an afterthought. "Create new identities, find decent jobs and be productive members of society."

"Yes, ma'am," they said as one.

I hated the idea of turning anyone into my permanent puppets, but I couldn't set trained killers loose without putting some kind of leash on them. I released the mental hold I had over them and they blinked, as if coming out of a dream. "Can we go?" one of the men asked.

I scanned his mind quickly and found no trace of homicidal tendencies. "You can go." The other four had also been purged of their darker thoughts. My command was embedded in their subconscious so deeply that no one would ever be able to reverse my orders. It was chilling to realize that my hypnotism had grown so strong. I didn't want to risk their bamboozlement being wiped out by being turned into my undead minions and I also didn't want to restrict the wills of my servants. This seemed like the best solution.

By the time I returned to the prison, meals had been readied for the first ten men who were about to become new recruits in my army. Geordie handed me a sharp dagger and held up a plastic cup that he would presumably use to catch my blood in. "I didn't think you would want all those strange men biting you."

Personally, I thought *he* didn't want the men to put their mouths on me, but it was a good idea. It would be much faster to feed the men from cups rather than from the wounds I'd have to inflict on myself. "Thanks, Geordie," I said and he smiled shyly at my praise.

Luc was on my right and Geordie was on my left as I

approached the first candidate. Luc's hand came to a rest on my shoulder in support. Geordie winced in empathy when the blade bit into my flesh. Bright yellow blood squirted into the cup that he held beneath my wrist. I dug the blade in deeper, slicing from my wrist down to my elbow. I moved the blade slowly and didn't stop until the cup was full. The wound healed quickly and there was no trace of a scar when I was done.

"Did that hurt?" Ishida asked as he stepped up with another cup.

"Not as much as it used to." Since feeding from our ancient ancestors, I was less pervious to pain and discomfort in general. Still, the sight and sensation of cutting myself open was far from pleasant.

"Two small swallows will do, gentlemen," Gregor advised the men who were nervously waiting their turn to be transformed.

Geordie handed the cup over to Sergeant Wesley and he took the required sips. The teen retrieved the cup an instant before the soldier convulsed. Igor eased the man to the ground, displaying a compassion that few knew he possessed as the human left his mortal life behind. White faced and holding onto his composure by a thread, Charlie took the cup that Geordie offered next.

As Wesley's eyes snapped open to bathe Igor in a red glow, Thaddeus stepped forward with a terrified convict held firmly in his grip. The inmate's screams rang out as my newest minion feasted. As the sergeant finished his snack, Charlie awoke as the undead.

It didn't take long before I felt like a cow that was being milked, but for blood rather than for milk. The production line worked surprisingly well and we had an efficient system in place. One person would step up to catch my blood while someone else took their cup to feed to a new set of prisoners. Others brought convicts forward to feed the newly made monsters.

Millicent handed me a cup and kept her face a blank mask. I read the revulsion of what we were doing from the surface of her mind, but beneath that something darker lurked. I couldn't quite probe into the thought, she held it closely guarded. I knew she hated me and all that I stood for. She was envious of my fame and wanted Luc for herself. Her eyes met mine and I gave her a knowing smirk. Her mouth tightened and she marched off without a word as soon as her cup was full.

Losing so much blood would have killed a normal vampire. Even I had to feed several times to replenish what I was giving to the men who were now my servants. I'd felt a connection between us when they'd simply been beneath my spell. Now that they belonged to me body and whatever souls they had left, I could feel them on a whole new level.

Dawn was dangerously close when the last man became a vampire. He fed from a final petrified inmate, then one of Danton's warriors led the partially drained snack away. Swords and daggers had pierced half a dozen hearts of the inmates that had fought back. We didn't want to chance one of the cons rising as the undead.

From the way my new fledglings were swaying on their feet, I didn't think they would share my ability to remain awake during daylight hours. While they had some of my traits, they obviously didn't share them all.

"You should begin transporting your men to the catacombs," Gregor suggested. "It is daylight back in

France," he reminded me. "They will fall asleep as soon as they arrive."

It was the logical place to store them, so I nodded. I'd just fed a few minutes ago and felt chock full of energy again. "I'm going to try to shift more than a dozen at a time." The only way I'd be able to learn what my limitations were was to experiment.

Luc motioned twenty men to step forward. They formed two neat rows and the ones in back put their hands on the shoulders of the men in front. I reached out to take Higgins and Wesley by the hand and pictured the courtier's level of the catacombs. Moments later, we appeared in the dark, yet opulent rooms. Just as Gregor had predicted, my men fell asleep the instant we appeared. They thudded to the carpet and lay in an unruly mess.

Thirty men waited for me when I returned to the prison. Fifty waited the next time and then only eighty remained. Feeling just how close the sun was to rising, I mentally crossed my fingers that my talent wouldn't fail me. It would be difficult to make sure all of the slumbering fledglings were touching if they were unconscious. Hopefully, I could take them all before the sun showed up.

"Gather in close," I instructed my soldiers. They obeyed and we all winked from one side of the world to the other. I felt no fatigue from shifting so many people at once and figured I still hadn't reached my limit yet. I briefly wondered how it was possible that I could do the things that I could do. I'd been designed by Fate and it had decided what my capabilities would be. There was no use questioning things that I would never have an answer for.

I couldn't leave my men sprawled all over each other, so I spent a few minutes lining them up neatly so they wouldn't wake up in compromising positions. Being unholy creatures of the night, they all now possessed night vision, so it wasn't necessary to leave a light burning for them. Even so, I wasn't about to leave them alone down here deep beneath the ground. They were mine now and I was responsible for their well-being. That included their mental as well as their physical health.

I'd never imagined that I would become the ruler of an army of vampires, but I was now and I had a duty and an obligation to these people.

# Chapter Thirteen

Now that we knew I could transport a large number of people at once, everyone was waiting for me in one group when I returned to the prison. "I'll be back in a second, I just have to talk to the warden," I told my waiting friends and new allies.

Millicent huffed impatiently and crossed her arms. Geordie shot her a glower. *I hate that snotty cow.* I smirked at his petulant thought and willed myself into the warden's office. He sat at his desk, staring at the monitors bleakly. The bodies of the few dead inmates were stacked off to one side. He was still beneath my spell, but he felt responsible for their deaths anyway.

"Jeffries." He roused at my voice and turned to face me. "Alert the police, the army or whoever you think needs to know, that I have turned these soldiers into a small army of vampires. Tell them that we have no intention of trying to take over your world. I'm going to use them to attempt to stop a bunch of aliens from eating everyone on your planet."

"Why were those six men killed?" he asked and pointed at the monitor that showed the deceased. My bedazzlement of him had been light and it was already wearing off on its own.

"Do you really think anyone will miss them?" My tone was dry and he half shook his head before he could stop himself. "I chose to turn these soldiers into my own private army for a reason. They're all good men who were locked up simply because they were forced to follow my orders. All new vampires have to feed, even mine. Our blood is highly virulent and those six men were accidentally infected. They were all unfit to live amongst humanity even when they were still humans. They'd be far worse as the undead."

Nodding grudgingly, he reached for the phone on his desk. "I'll pass on your message to the authorities."

Leaving the distressed warden, I zapped myself back to the others then shifted us all to Gregor's mansion. As our group broke up, Geordie either accidentally, or purposefully jostled Millicent. From his insolent smirk, I guessed he'd done it on purpose.

"Did your parents not teach you any manners, serv-" Millicent cut off her insulting title of 'servant boy' before she could finish it and her eyes slid over to me to judge my reaction.

"No," the teen replied with a glare. "They were peasants, *milady*. We didn't live in a mansion and eat off silver platters. Five of us lived in a one room shack and wore sacks for clothing. We didn't exactly have much of a chance to learn any manners."

"It comes as no surprise that you hail from peasant stock," Millie said with a contemptuous sneer. "I cannot imagine what use you could possibly be to anyone, let alone to the great and venerable Mortis." She turned her sneer on me and my fury rose. The pompous vampire flinched and stepped back when a red glow began to emanate from my eyes. Anyone who knew me knew that this was a bad sign.

Gregor wisely drew my friends and true allies away from the twelve cowering Brits as I stalked closer to them. "I think the real question is what possible use *you* could be to me," I said in a steely tone that made them flinch again. "You are not, and will never be, welcome here. I'll give you five minutes to gather your belongings, then I'll transport you to a location of your choice. I don't care where it is, just as long as it is far away from here."

Thaddeus, with his jacket folded over one hand, lifted his other hand to protest. I turned my scarlet eyes on him. Swallowing his plea to remain with us, he bowed and hastened after the others as they fled. None of my friends approached me as I counted down in my head, which I was grateful for. I doubted I'd be able to carry on a conversation and continue to count down at the same time. *I really have to find a watch soon.* The errant thought fled before I could lose track of the count.

The courtiers returned within the allotted time, carrying the clothes they'd left behind. I wasn't going to give them time to change or to return to Isabella's estate for whatever other possessions they'd brought with them. Millicent marched over to stand in front of me and stared down her nose at the top of my head. I didn't deign to tilt my head backwards to meet her icy stare. "Have you chosen a destination?" I asked her.

"Yes. Take us to China. Anywhere in the country will do, as long as you don't leave us out in the sun to burn to death," she said acidly.

*Now that's a tempting thought.* For once, I managed not to voice my sarcasm.

"Bye, bye," Geordie said in a mock sad tone and gave them a wave. "We'll really miss you." His insincerity made me smile inwardly even as Igor's hand connected with the back of his head. "It was worth it," the teen muttered as he staggered forward a step.

The unwanted visitors jostled together and I took Millicent by the wrist. With the picture of an underground area foremost in Millie's mind, it was easy enough to hone in on the exact location that she was aiming for. Wide eyed at what was a familiar underground parking lot for her when we teleported, she stared at me suspiciously. "How do you know about this place?"

"You have no idea what I do or don't know," I said with a cold smile. Thaddeus flinched and hunched over the bundle he was carrying. I flicked a curious glance at him, but was distracted by Millicent thrusting her chest towards me. She used her breasts like weapons. I wasn't a man and they held no power over me, apart from slight jealousy that she was far bustier than I'd ever be.

"Well," she said briskly. "I can't say that it was a pleasure to meet you, but I'm sure this will not be the end of our alliance. You will have need of us again one day and perhaps you'll be more courteous next time."

"Don't bet on it," I responded, then whisked myself away before she could say anything to anger me further.

They'd had their chance to become part of our team and she'd blown it for all of them. Our numbers were small, but we'd have to make do. I needed people who could work together, not a bunch of superior snobs who looked down on everyone else. My tolerance levels were far lower than they'd once been. To be truthful, they hadn't been all that high to begin with.

Geordie's eyes were shining with admiration when I returned. He lurched forward to hug me as soon as I appeared. "Thank you, *chérie*. I know I can always count on you to stand up for me." He gave me a hearty kiss on the cheek, then stepped back.

Igor gave his apprentice a sardonic look before turning to me. "I am surprised you did not just kill them," he said to me.

"I thought about it," I replied honestly.

Luc was studying me closely. "Why didn't you?"

Uncomfortable beneath the scrutiny of so many, I shrugged. "I'm supposed to be the leader of our kind. What sort of ruler would I be if I killed everyone that I didn't like?"

Ishida answered that question. "You would be a tyrant. My people suffered beneath many such monsters before my maker began to choose our Emperors." He slanted a sly look at Kokoro.

She looked at her former ruler in surprise. "How long have you known that I am your maker and that I was the one to choose our rulers?" she asked the teen. She was as close to being aghast as I'd ever seen her. Even when she'd still been able to read minds, she hadn't known that her closely guarded secret hadn't really been a secret at all.

"I have always known that you were my creator," Ishida

said with a shrug. "I remember well the night that I lay dying from a fever. You came to me and told me you would save me and that I would become the next Emperor."

"I did not think you remembered that," she said quietly. "You have never once let on that you knew my true relationship to you."

"As for you choosing the rulers before me, I overheard you speaking to the elders one night," the teen said. "You thought your meetings were a secret, but my guards knew and alerted me to them. I attended one of your gatherings in secret to ensure that you were not plotting against me. When I saw you were merely concerned about our people as a whole, I decided not to interfere."

Gregor couldn't have been prouder of the child king's deviousness if the teen had been his own son. He gave Ishida a quick hug and Ishida allowed it. Their small family had grown stronger while Luc and I had been absent.

"Have you come up with a plan to deal with these aliens, Gregor?" Danton asked.

No one was surprised when Gregor nodded. "We have yet to see the actual size of our adversaries and can only rely on Natalie's dream. Her vision gave me an idea that I would like to try, but it will require some preparation."

"What equipment will we need?" Igor asked.

"I believe explosives would be our best bet." That was the answer I'd been expecting. We couldn't fight the octosquids with our bare hands. "We will need to find a large number of weapons," Gregor elaborated. "We will also require suitable transportation."

"You mean a boat," I deduced and received a nod of confirmation.

"Can you sense where the aliens are right now?"

"They're spread out all over the place. The closest one to land is lurking near the UK." The dream of being on the submarine as it was being torn in two was still fresh in my memory. I wondered if the vessel had already been eaten by the octosquid, or if the sailors were still alive.

Gregor's fist came to rest beneath his chin as he thought through his plan some more. "We need to locate appropriate weaponry first," he decided. "The boat will be fairly simple to organize." He turned to me. "Do you think you will be able to locate someone who can help us?"

"Yes, but it might take a while. It'll be easier to do if I go into dust mote mode." Geordie sniggered at my phrasing, then started when my clothes dropped to the floor in an empty pile.

Teleporting to the UK was the easy part. Finding someone who could direct me to a cache of suitable weapons was harder. Performing a quick sweep of London, I found some soldiers and scanned their minds to see if any of them knew more about the type of weapons that we needed. Jumping from mind to mind, I narrowed the list down further and finally came to a stop.

Coalescing behind my target, I studied him without his knowledge. The physical requirements for soldiers must have slackened while my friends and I had been in outer space. He was maybe two inches taller than me, which would put him at five feet six inches. His mousy brown hair was rapidly receding, making him look ten years older than he actually was. Skimming his mind, I found he was thirty-one and had been hired due to his intelligence and knowledge of weaponry rather than for his fighting skills. I also gleaned his name.

Leaning forward, I tapped him on the shoulder. Letting out a startled shriek, he swivelled his chair around and goggled at my misty body. My head was the only thing that remained solid. "Are you a g-ghost?" he stammered.

"No, Steve."

His eyes went even wider that I knew his name. "Are you an alien?"

"Technically, yes." I'd started out as human, but the alien nanobots in my veins had transformed me into something far stranger. "I need your brain." Steve's hands went to his head and he shrank away from me. "Calm down," I said and rolled my eyes. "Your brain on its own won't do me much good. I need the knowledge it contains."

Before he had time to scream, I whisked him back to France. Falling to his knees, he stared up at the group surrounding him. "Everybody, this is Steve. He's going to tell us all about the neat weapons they've been stockpiling in England."

"B-b-but I can't," our captive whispered. "That would be treason."

Luc reached down and hauled the terrified human to his feet. "You do not have a choice," he said as he stared deeply into my captive's eyes.

Going limp, Steve nodded jerkily as he fell beneath my beloved's spell. "Yes. I'll tell you anything you need to know."

Danton's brows rose. It was almost unheard of for us to be able to bamboozle someone of our own sex, unless they were sexually interested in us. All seven of us that had returned from Viltar had changed in several ways. Being able to hypnotize any human we liked was just one of the perks.

Luc guided our informant to a chair and the others took seats on the couches as I poured my particles back into my clothing. I took a spot on a couch between Luc and Geordie as the question and answer session began.

# Chapter Fourteen

Steve turned out to be a font of information. The Americans weren't the only ones who had created weapons which could be used against our kind. The Brits had also designed guns that could rapidly fire explosive rounds. They were more powerful than ordinary grenades and could be fired at a much faster rate.

They hadn't yet had the chance to use them in the field. We'd nipped both vampire invasions in the bud before the fledglings could increase their numbers enough to take over the world. The military in Russia, Africa and the US were the only ones that had been involved. This time, the threat wasn't going to be contained to a small part of the world. Everyone was going to be affected.

It was a good thing the Brits had remained wary even after we'd been kicked off the planet. They had stockpiled enough weapons to stop another hostile vampire takeover attempt. The weapons would have come in handy when we'd been battling the droids and Kveet imps in the United States. But that war had also been halted before other countries could become involved.

"Where are these weapons stockpiled?" Gregor asked our compliant captive.

"In an underground facility on the outskirts of London," Steve replied.

"Is the facility under constant guard?" Igor enquired.

Nodding, Steve elaborated. "Soldiers are on perpetual patrol around the grounds and cameras have been set up to watch every entrance."

"What about inside where the weapons are stored?" Luc asked.

This time, Steve shook his head. "There is no need to have guards inside. It's impossible to enter without the proper authorisation. Only three men have access to the facility and you'd need their eyes and fingerprints to use as verification of their identity." Then he remembered that I was able to transport myself to another location in the blink of an eye. "Then again, I guess you could just pop inside the place any time you want."

"How many of these weapons were made?" Gregor asked.

"Several thousand guns, plus hundreds of thousands of rounds of ammunition," was the prompt reply. "There are also other types of explosive devices, similar to the ones the Americans designed, as well as a few other fairly standard weapons."

Leaving the bamboozled human to sit quietly on his own, we drew aside to discuss our options.

"We need to know more about our adversaries," Gregor

said and turned to me. "Have you tried to read their thoughts?"

I hadn't yet because I didn't want to tip them off that we were aware of their presence. It was necessary now, so I sent out my senses. We knew practically nothing about the octosquids and how their bodies worked. I had no idea whether these weapons would be powerful enough to kill them or not.

It took only seconds to locate the behemoth that was slowly making its way towards the UK. Its thoughts were so different from ours that it was difficult to sort through the barrage of information. I caught images of its home world, when it had been stolen as an infant. Far larger than Earth, its planet was predominantly made of water and had once teemed with aquatic life. Considering the size the octosquids grew to, even their planet could sustain only so many of the creatures at once. They tended to stake out a territory and defend it to the death. Any infringement on another's turf resulted in an inevitable battle.

"That's interesting," I murmured.

Geordie was nearly dancing on the spot in anticipation. "What did you learn?"

"They're a bit like feral dogs. They each pick a spot and attack any rival that dares to encroach on their turf."

Gregor factored that information into his plan. "That *is* interesting and this knowledge might come in useful. What do you know of their physiology?"

That required another trip into the mind of the mammoth. I grimaced when I found what we needed to know. "They are really, really hard to kill. They heal almost as well as us, if more slowly. They have the capacity to grow back any body parts that are destroyed, but it takes time. They don't have a respiratory system like we do. They don't have a heart, lungs or any other vital organs to destroy. It seems that they're really just a big stomach with hundreds of arms." My report didn't exactly lift anyone's spirits.

"What about their brains?" Ishida queried. "If they can think, surely they must have a brain."

"They do, but it is located above their stomach and deep inside their bodies. We'd have to carve our way through their flesh to reach it. Also, I'm pretty sure their brains are roughly the size of a large city block."

Danton blinked and shook his head. "You mean their brains aren't just the size of a building, but an entire *block* of buildings?" At my nod, trepidation filled him. "How can we possibly prevail against creatures as large as this?"

"By strategically using the weapons that will soon be at our disposal," Gregor responded. "Did the Prophet give you no warning of this threat at all?"

The monk shook his head slowly. "He did not mention this particular danger." Our gazes locked for a moment as we both remembered what Danton's master had warned me about. *Deal with one problem at a time,* I told myself. The problem was, while one disaster was playing itself out, another always seemed to be lining itself up. *What could be worse than ten gigantic aliens that are intent on eating everything on the planet?* My inner voice was morose and I had no answer for it. If there was something worse than this ahead, I wasn't sure I even wanted to know about it.

"We should return our informant to his workplace before anyone notices that he is missing," Luc suggested. "We should also begin to retrieve the weapons while Natalie's soldiers are still resting."

Steve came at Luc's call and we gathered into a circle and joined hands. I transported us all to an underground building that was at the forefront of our captive's mind. The massive warehouse contained countless rows of metal racks that stretched twenty feet into the air. Large silver boxes in various shapes and sizes lined the shelves. Igor cracked one open to reveal guns similar to the ones that General Sanderson and his men had used. These ones were smaller, lighter and could hold more ammunition.

While the others began hauling containers down from the shelves, I whisked Steve back to his office. Sitting him down on his chair, I stared into his eyes and felt Luc's hypnotism fade and mine take over. "Go back to work and forget you ever saw my friends or me," I ordered.

Nodding jerkily, Steve swivelled his chair around to face his desk and returned to the task he'd been performing when I'd so rudely kidnapped him earlier. He began whistling cheerfully even before I disappeared.

The others had stacked an impressive number of boxes in neat rows on the floor when I returned. I'd never tried to shift anything inanimate before and I wasn't sure that I'd be able to pull it off. Given how many boxes there were, I decided to try to move them directly into the cells in the catacombs. There wouldn't be enough room for them on the courtier level. Putting my hand on one of the stacks, I concentrated on taking the containers with me. A second later, I appeared in one of the cells. Grinning that the boxes had made the trip with me, I teleported back to the UK.

Geordie was waiting for me when I returned and he was also grinning at my success. He held up his hand and I high-fived him. He didn't flinch away from the direct contact with my holy mark. The teen trusted me implicitly and knew I'd never hurt him.

I turned to the next stack and Igor made a motion for me to hold off on transporting them. "Let's try something." He and Luc nudged two of the rows together until the boxes were all touching. I was willing to try shifting them all at once and placed a hand on both rows. It was just as easy to move both bundles into the cells.

Everyone was smiling at my success when I returned. "I believe this will go much faster than I'd anticipated," Gregor said.

By nightfall, we'd appropriated as many weapons, ammunition and explosives as our small army would be able to carry, plus some extras. Igor, Geordie and Ishida disappeared into a tunnel that led further into the catacombs. They wanted to test the weapons, but they needed to move far enough away that they wouldn't accidentally bring any walls down beneath the main area.

The rest of us climbed up to the upper levels. My minions would be waking soon and I wanted to be there when they did. They would be hungry and we'd have to find them food before we embarked on the risky plan that Gregor had thought up. He'd kept it from everyone so far, but he was unable to shield his surface thoughts from me. As always, his scheme was brilliant and I wasn't about to ruin the surprise that he had planned.

# Chapter Fifteen

Higgins was the first of my servants to rouse. Unlike a human, he didn't wake up groggy. He was fully alert and on his feet in an instant. Several lamps let out a soft glow that was far more welcoming than oppressive darkness would have been. The others began to wake as a distant explosion made the floor tremble.

Reaching for a weapon that he didn't currently have, Higgins looked around in alarm. "What was that?" His senses had become enhanced with his death and the blast sounded much closer than it actually was.

"That's just Igor and the two boys trying out the weapons that we'll be using against the octosquids," I told him as his comrades began to wake.

"Oh." Relaxing, Higgins examined his temporary home. "Where are we?"

"We're in France. We're in the catacombs where the

vampire Court used to be located." *Before most of them had been lured to the First and I'd killed what was left of them,* I added mentally. The rest of the men were awake now and listened in on my explanation. "There used to be a mansion above us, but it was destroyed. This level is where the courtiers lived. The servants' quarters are on the level below this one and beneath that is where the food was kept."

"*Was* kept?" Charlie complained. "I was kind of hoping for breakfast." Several of the men laughed then seemed surprised that they still could. This was all very new to them and they weren't going to get much of a chance to settle into their new roles as the undead. We had battles to attend and instinct told me we'd be deep in the middle of our first skirmish with a gigantic alien soon.

"Don't worry, we'll find you a meal before we embark on our boat ride," Gregor reassured the men.

"Ugh," someone complained. "I hate boats. I puke my guts up every time I step on one."

"Our kind are unable to vomit," Kokoro informed the soldier. "You will find that a great many things have changed now."

"I'd noticed," said Charlie. "Higgins looks like a movie star now." His dry tone made some of the others chuckle. Exclamations of surprise were made when they noticed changes in their comrades. Charlie was tall, skinny and had bright red hair and matching freckles. He hadn't improved much in the looks department so far and could be considered average looking at best.

Luc bent to whisper in my ear. "They'll be asking for mirrors so they can preen like teenage girls soon."

My laugh was huskier than usual as a shiver of lust

bolted through me. My minions stilled as they felt my flesh hunger rise. "What is that?" Higgins asked.

Gregor caught the panicked look I sent his way. If my flesh hunger became any stronger, it might make my servants' hunger rise as well. Gregor came to the same conclusion. "I will watch over them and perhaps explain a few things while you and Lucentio attend to your needs."

Kokoro flashed me a saucy wink as I took Luc's hand. I zapped us to the one place where I knew we'd be safe. Most importantly, we'd be alone and could proceed to become properly reacquainted without being interrupted.

Standing in the bedroom of the safe house that had been our haven more than once, I expected Luc to tear my clothes off and ravage me. Instead, he drew me into his arms and simply held me. Sinking against him, I wrapped my arms around his waist and held onto him as a tumult of images flashed through his mind. Luc was recalling being blown apart by the traitorous General Sanderson and he didn't block the images from me this time.

He'd been aware on some level as we'd gathered up his remains and had transported him to this very bedroom. I'd stayed with him, holding the hand that he'd so desperately tried to move to show me that he was still alive. He'd been unable to stop Magerion's men from stealing him away and had spent the past few months in a pall of despair that I'd never be able to find him.

The telepathic contact we'd had during my dreams had helped to keep him sane. Knowing that I loved him enough to lose my will to live had spurred him to hold on. His joy at finally being rescued and healed paled beside the love he felt for me.

I let out a tearless sob and his arms became crushing.

"Don't cry, Ladybug. Be happy that we're together again."

The nickname that I'd once found so annoying tugged at my dead heart. "I *am* happy. I just wish you hadn't suffered so much."

Tilting my head back, he stared into my eyes. I felt myself falling beneath his spell once more, but it was love, not hypnotism that claimed what was left of my soul. "I would suffer it all again, and more, as long as I knew we would be together again," he said.

Before I could descend into sobs, his mouth came down on mine. Our flesh hungers flared and lust took over. I didn't bother to undress, but simply went into dust mote mode from the neck down. Luc looked down as my clothes dropped and my naked body re-formed. "Well, that is certainly a convenient way to disrobe." One corner of his mouth quirked up in amusement.

"Your turn," I told him and pulled his too tight sweater over his head. His eyes began to glow, matching the scarlet light that was blazing from mine. His pants hit the floor then he tackled me to the bed.

Pinning my hands down, he tortured me with his mouth. Luc knew that I preferred hard and fast to slow and languid, but I wasn't about to protest. He needed to show me how much he loved me and he used his body to convey his message.

His mouth was cool as it closed over my breast. He moved to the other only after my back arched in need. Teasing me with his tongue, he slid his way down my torso. He moved lower and lower until he hovered over the juncture between my thighs. My hands were free now and they clasped his shoulders and hauled him back up. "You can do that later," I told him then flipped him onto his back. "I need this now." He barely had a chance to brace himself before my flesh enclosed him and I began to ride.

Luc's hands gripped my hips and it was his turn to arch his back. I was still secretly amazed that he was mine. He'd entertained hundreds of desirable courtiers and he'd chosen me above all of them. It was a fact that I still had trouble believing sometimes.

Reaching my utopia, I was tumbled onto the mattress as Luc continued to pound himself into me. I went over the edge of ecstasy a second time and he joined me in what was pretty damn close to bliss.

Rolling onto his side, he took my hand. Nearly as strong as me now, none of his bones had broken during our bout of horizontal gymnastics. Once, I'd caused him pain nearly every time we fed our flesh hungers. Now, he felt only pleasure. I wasn't sure who I had to thank for making my friends all but indestructible, but I sent the thought out there anyway.

*You're welcome,* a female voice whispered deep inside my mind. A tinkle of laughter came at the shock of hearing Fate take the credit. My life as a vampire had been mostly crappy, but it was a destiny that I couldn't escape from. Studying the perfect face of the man lying at my side, I wasn't sure that I would have changed any of it, if it meant that we could have a chance at happiness.

"What are you thinking?" my beloved asked.

"That it's time I stopped trying to fight my fate."

Dark eyebrows rose in surprise. "What is your fate?"

"To keep the humans safe, to be the leader of whatever vampires are left and to have mind-blowing sex with you as often as possible."

Lifting my hand, he brushed his lips across my knuckles. "You can count me in. Especially on that last point."

My laughter cut off when he slid his way back down my body. Luc was a determined vampire and he was intent on finishing what I wouldn't let him start before. "Oh, ok. If you insist," I mock grumbled.

"I do insist," he responded before my ability to think disappeared as his head lowered once more.

# Chapter Sixteen

We found the courtier's quarters empty when we returned to the catacombs. We took the stairs down to the cells below, passing the equally empty servants' quarters. Our friends had been busy while Luc and I had been satiating our hungers. Every soldier was now armed and all were familiarizing themselves with the foreign weapons and explosives. Igor strode amongst the men, making sure they all knew how to operate the guns. Few required help, since they'd used guns very similar to this already.

Geordie and Ishida were placing small explosives inside brightly coloured bags. From the luxurious and bright silk and satin fabrics, I figured some long dead courtier's handbags had been pilfered for the job.

Wearing their orange prison jumpsuits, my army didn't stand a chance of blending in on the streets. They needed to feed, but I couldn't take them anywhere dressed as they were. *Unless I dump them in another prison and let them munch down on the inmates,* I mused. Hopefully, my men would have better control this time and could watch over each other as they fed. We didn't need to accidentally add any axe murderers to our ranks.

Gregor had already considered the problem and crooked his finger at me. Since he was the brains of our operation, I felt no anger at being ordered around. *If I ever become an arrogant bitch, make sure you tell me,* I said to my inner voice. *No problem,* was the immediate and almost eager response. I could always count on my subconscious to point out my faults. The possibility that I might one day end up like the Comtesse had sparked my concern. She'd been hated by pretty much everyone. I didn't feel the need to be universally loved, but I'd prefer not to inspire actual hatred.

Luc stayed by my side as I walked over to Gregor. Having him so near was a comfort of its own. I'd never imagined that I'd ever fall in love and hadn't really believed it existed outside of fairy tales. Now I knew it was very real and I didn't ever want to lose it again.

"There is a prison nearby where your army can feed," Gregor said when we reached him. It was nice to know that we thought alike. "Once they've fed, we should head for the boat that our informant described."

The boat in question was hidden from public view. Even Steve had only caught a glimpse of it once. He'd heard that the vessel contained stealth capabilities so it couldn't be picked up on radar. That would be handy to keep us hidden from humans as we travelled to do battle with the first octosquid. Once the humans figured out who and what we were, they'd most likely try to kill us. Then we'd have two enemies to fight rather than just one.

Danton, his five warriors and half a dozen of Gregor's guards would be accompanying us on our journey. All up, our army consisted of just over two hundred vampires. What my fledglings lacked in experience as the undead, they made up for with their military training. No one yet understood just how pitiful a force we would be against the colossi that we'd be facing. I'd tried to describe the new and improved octosquids to them, but seeing would be believing.

"Ishida and I have something for you, *chérie*," Geordie said. The pair approached me with their hands behind their backs. Not wanting to spoil the surprise, I deliberately stayed out of their minds.

My smile of anticipation turned into a grin when they revealed my samurai swords. Forged on Viltar by our Kveet allies, they were replicas of nearly identical swords Ishida had given to me as a gift. My original swords had been destroyed by General Sanderson, but these had proven to be excellent replacements. I'd left them behind when I'd slunk back to the mausoleum in Brisbane to wallow in grief. I was both glad and surprised that they'd brought them along.

"Thanks, guys." My appreciation was heartfelt and Geordie immediately choked up.

"Have a look at the blades," Ishida urged.

Sliding one free of its plain black sheath, a dragon was revealed on the blade. It had been etched into the metal with exquisite detail and was an exact replica of my original sword. The other blade held a lion that was also identical to the original. Now I was the one who was having trouble controlling my emotions.

Dull silver in colour, the swords had proven to be sharp and deadly and were worthy replacements for the first pair that I'd owned. "Thank you. They're beautiful." I gave Geordie a wink and Ishida a deep bow to show my gratitude of what had to be his own work. There were no Japanese craftsmen or women left to carry on their traditions. He and Kokoro were all that remained of what had been a small, but vital nation of our kind. Ishida himself had painstakingly etched the designs, showing a true artistic talent that I hadn't even known he'd possessed.

Donning the sheaths, my swords crisscrossed my back and I finally felt that my world had returned to as close to normal as it could get. "Is everyone ready?" I asked as my friends, allies and soldiers gathered around.

"We're ready," Higgins replied on behalf of my men.

"We're heading for a nearby jail," Gregor informed the group. "We seven can take care of the guards," He indicated those of us who'd been to outer space and back, "while the rest of you concentrate on feeding. Pair up, watch each other and make sure your meal doesn't ingest any of your blood. If they do, kill them." The order should have been chilling coming from a sophisticated man who was wearing a civilized dark brown tweed suit. Instead, it drove home to everyone that this wasn't just a drill. This was real and our actions could have deadly consequences.

Following the mental directions that I'd gleaned from Gregor, I found the jail and transported us all to it without any trouble. I still hadn't reached my teleportation limits. Again, I was glad that no one had handed me a Mortis manual when I'd first been created. Not knowing what was or wasn't possible meant that I wasn't constrained by rules that might not even apply to me.

Instant pandemonium erupted when we appeared inside a mess hall. It was feeding time for the inmates as well as for us. Hardened criminals screamed when we appeared like ghosts. My friends and I moved to intercept the guards as my army and allies paired up. As instructed, they fed one at a time. Choosing victims willy-nilly, they subdued the convicts and bit into their throats. No one was savaged to death and most of the paired men even drank from the same victim, if from opposite sides of their necks. It was a tightly controlled operation that went off without a hitch. No one needed to be dispatched this time.

Among the prisoners, I found four men who had previously been in various forms of law enforcement or the armed forces. They'd instinctively bunched together and none backed away when I approached them. While afraid, they weren't terrified to the point of being unable to function. They recognized my soldiers as being military men, despite their new status of also being blood suckers.

"You're the vampire who stopped the alien invasion," one of the men said in heavily accented English, giving me an appraising look.

"That's right and now we have to step up and do it again," I replied in French.

"There's a new threat?" one of the others asked. Skimming his thoughts, I saw he was in for manslaughter and that he'd be spending the next few years behind these bars. He was suffering from a post-traumatic stress disorder after being deployed overseas for two tours. Someone had taken a swing at him in a bar and his training had taken over. That man had paid with his life and this soldier had paid with his freedom.

"Unfortunately, yes. We're facing another species of aliens, but these ones are far bigger and hungrier than anything we've seen before."

"Hungrier than you guys?" asked the ex-soldier sardonically as he watched my men feast.

"We look like kittens and fluffy bunnies next to these things," I said dryly.

"What do you need from us?"

"I'd like you to join us, but I won't force you to."

"You want to turn us into vampires?" one of the others asked more calmly than I'd expected.

"Yes."

Longing to be a part of a unit once again was universal for all four candidates. Now that they'd served time, even after they were released, they'd never be able to join the army or police force again. I knew what their answers would be before they gave them. Receiving four nods, I rolled back my sleeve and pulled one of my swords free. "Drink fast before the wound heals," I advised the first man to step forward.

All four drank, died and then were reborn. Several of my soldiers stepped forward, dragging fresh victims to offer to feed their new kin. They might come from different countries, but they'd all been sired by me and that made them brothers, of sorts.

Luc offered me a handkerchief to clean the yellow stain from my sword. He didn't question my decision to turn these new prisoners. He knew that I was able to see within the hearts of all men and women now.

My four newest recruits wouldn't have much time to settle into their new roles as vampires either. Still shaky after their first meal, they joined the crush as Gregor gestured for them to gather around. The guards we'd bamboozled had only been put under our spells lightly and would snap out of their daze soon. We locked the cons in the mess hall and left the guards safely in the hallway. I didn't want them to be torn apart by the terrified inmates.

"Is everyone ready?" I asked.

"No," someone muttered and Geordie's shrill giggle came from somewhere in the middle of the group.

This next shift would be tricky. I knew the rough location of the boat that we needed to borrow, but not exactly where it was. It was so secret that only a few hundred people even knew it existed. It was only taken out on test runs in the dead of night when it wouldn't be seen by the public.

Using the images that I'd pilfered from Steve's mind, I transported my army into a heavily fortified compound. High concrete walls were topped by razor wire and guard towers stood at all four corners. Bright spotlights flashed to life and humans shouted in alarm when we were spotted. One of my soldiers saw the boat at a small dock and pointed. It sat low enough in the water that I could barely see the top of it above the crowd.

Borrowing Sergeant Wesley's eyes, since he was on the outskirts of the group, I examined the craft. Long and sleek, it had been painted black, all the better to blend into the dark, I assumed. A name had been painted on the side that seemed fairly apt; Shadow. It would be almost invisible out on the water, especially at night. I whisked us all inside before any shots could be fired by the sailors who were swarming from a long, low brick building towards us. Hopefully, the Brits would be reluctant to shoot at their prized vessel.

Standing in the cockpit of the boat, I saw that we were floating in a small stretch of water that was surrounded by a fence. A large metal gate barred our escape. We'd have to get it open before we could leave.

Igor took a quick look at the array of buttons, searched for a way to power up the boat and shook his head at me. I'd have to find someone who could pilot this thing before we'd be going anywhere. Probing the minds of the men who were racing towards the boat, I located the man in charge. He was inside the main building, advising his government that they were under attack. The phone slid out of his hand and thumped to his desk when I appeared in his office before him. An angry voice demanded answers until I placed the phone back in its cradle.

"What do you want?" the sailor asked. His hand stealthily shifted towards the gun at his hip.

"To borrow Shadow." I halted his protest by capturing him with my gaze. "Open the gates," I ordered. Standing jerkily, he marched over to a console and pushed a button. Just as I'd hoped, none of his men had opened fire on the boat. Probably because it was worth half a billion dollars. One of his men frantically called for orders through his radio. "Tell your men to stand down and not to attack." Returning to his desk, the commander did as ordered. A captain in his own right, he had the capacity to pilot the boat, but I didn't want to take a fragile human along for the ride. It was easier to skim the information that I needed and to leave him behind.

Returning to the craft, I popped back into the cockpit. "Take the wheel," I told Igor and the crowd shifted to allow him to comply. Following instructions that I'd picked up from the commander, I pushed a few buttons, pulled a lever, then pushed a final button that was hidden beneath the console. The boat rumbled to life and surged towards the gates. Igor smoothly piloted us out into the dark water. If I'd been behind the wheel, I'd probably have scraped the boat against the gates on the way out. The gap was fairly narrow and I had limited experience in piloting boats. The one and only time that I'd ever used one had resulted in a messy and painful shipwreck.

Sorting through the information that I'd skimmed from the captain, I flicked another switch and a radar screen came to life on the console. It had a wide range and picked up on several nearby vessels, as well as the octosquid.

Our target was still moving slowly, but inexorably towards land. I knew it was capable of moving much faster when it was hunting for food. Sometime in the next couple of hours, we would have our first encounter with an alien behemoth.

# Chapter Seventeen

Thanks to the knowledge that I'd picked out of the captain's head, I knew we'd have more than enough fuel to reach our quarry. Shadow had been built for both stealth and speed. Being all black, it vaguely reminded me of the Viltaran seeker ship that had carried us back to our home planet.

There wasn't enough room for everyone in the cockpit. We were crammed in so tightly that there was no room to move. There was room to store cargo down below. The boat had been designed for a crew of thirty, not two hundred. *Some of the men will have to move below.* Gregor had the same thought as me. He directed two thirds of the soldiers to file down the short flight of stairs to give us some more room.

Extra weapons had been brought along and were handed over to my four new recruits. Higgins quickly gave them a tutorial on how to use them. I'd noticed some of the men carrying rectangular silver containers, but I didn't ask what was inside. Igor had overseen the distribution of their gear, so they were no doubt weapons of some kind.

It was a tense voyage with little small talk being exchanged. It was storming and lightning occasionally gave bursts of blinding white light that seared my eyes. The sky was low and heavy rain made it difficult to distinguish between the clouds and the ocean.

Everyone was tense and unsure of exactly what we'd be facing. We seven survivors of Viltar were the only ones who'd ever seen an octosquid. Even when they'd been roughly man-sized, they'd been terrifying to behold. I'd seen two of them after they'd been converted into imps and they'd become much uglier with their transformations. The ten that we'd be battling would be much larger in size than the octosquid imps.

From what I'd garnered from the mind of the behemoth that we were approaching, it wouldn't consider us to be a threat. We were simply too small and too few in number to be of any concern to it, or so it would think.

Their planet had been discovered by the Viltarans after the war mongers had come close to destroying their own home. Mostly made up of water and with little land, it was useless to the invaders. They'd opted to steal some young, then blast the entire planet apart rather than attempt to conquer a species that was so immense in size.

Ten of the captives had escaped and had grown to maturity in the caves of the poisoned planet of Viltar. Adult in mind only, their size had been limited by the small pools of water that had been available. They had only been able to grow to their true potential after making their way to Earth. Now that they finally had access to food and water, they'd rapidly increased in size.

With their larger size, their appetites had become prodigious and they required vast quantities of food. They'd doomed not just us, but also themselves by choosing our planet to be their new home. They were aware of this, but they were reluctant to attack their few allies. It would only take another few weeks to completely deplete the water of food. Then they would have to change their minds about sharing the planet. They knew food could be found on land, but none had ventured forth into the coastal towns or cities yet.

Passing a vaguely familiar lighthouse that sat on the tip of a promontory, a chill of recognition raced down my spine when Kokoro pointed at a vessel in the water to our left. Light swept across the submarine from my dream. Their radar would shortly pick up on the creature that was gliding towards us both. The octosquid rapidly grew larger on the screen in front of me and the blip that belonged to the submarine quickly fell behind us as we motored past them.

I didn't need to send out my senses to track the beast, the radar did the job for me. Our quarry felt no alarm when we came within whatever passed for its senses. The alien lacked eyes, but seemed to rely on its own version of radar. It knew that, within the shell of this boat, a bunch of tasty treats awaited.

What it didn't know was that the tasty treats were armed and were ready to blast it apart, or to die trying. It also had no way of knowing that we weren't edible at all. Most of us would disintegrate upon death, leaving it unsatisfied and as ravenous as ever.

Kokoro was the first to spot the distant colossus. She made an incredulous sound that drew my friends forward. Curiosity had me peering through the rain lashed window. The storm made it difficult to see anything. Then lightning flared, helpfully illuminating our prey.

Geordie's mouth dropped open in dismay as he squinted up at the creature. "It's…" Lost for words, he trailed off.

"Gargantuan," Ishida said on behalf of his friend.

*I'm not sure our current weapons will be enough to destroy a creature that large,* Gregor thought and my spirits plummet. Gregor was adept at estimating our odds of success. If he didn't think we'd be able to take the monster down, then we were most likely doomed.

*Have some faith,* my inner voice said with a large dose of scorn. *Fate believes you can win, so don't give up before you've even tried!* Once again, my alter ego was correct. I had a job to do and I had to trust that Fate knew what it was doing by putting us in this situation. We weren't alone this time and we had a small army to back us up. "It might be big, but it's still made of flesh and blood," I reminded everyone.

Taking heart from my calm encouragement, the mood changed from despair to cautious optimism. I was their leader and they looked to me for inspiration. For a moment, I had to resist the urge to cackle wildly. I'd once been a clothing store manager and now I was Queen of the Undead. The only thing I'd ever been able to inspire people to do before was to buy an extra shirt along with their new jeans.

Picking up on my mood, Geordie grinned uncertainly. He blinked in surprise when I pulled him in and gave him a kiss on the cheek. "What was that for?"

"Just because I wanted to."

Instantly sentimental, he hugged me hard. "I am so glad that you turned out to be Mortis, Natalie."

Again, I felt the urge to shriek with laughter. "Why?"

"Could you imagine what our lives would have been like if the Comtesse had been Mortis?" he said darkly.

I wasn't the only one to cringe at the thought. "Mucia would have made the entire planet an utter misery to live on," Luc said.

I smiled at his audacity to use the name that the praying mantis had hated so much. To do so in her presence would have been a death sentence. I'd made very sure that no human, or vampire, would ever endure her cruel leadership ever again. As long as I was in charge, none of my kin would suffer beneath a tyrant. Of course, I wasn't sure how many of us would survive once we clashed with the colossus that was before us. I hadn't forgotten that it was only the first of ten new and dangerous adversaries.

It was difficult to predict how the octosquid would react when we came within its reach. There was a distinct possibility that it would snatch up our boat and rip it in half, just as it had done to the submarine in my dream.

My fears proved to be groundless as the monster moved down lower in the water. Several men swore beneath their non-existent breath when a split appeared in the mass of black flesh. Darkness enveloped us as we glided inside its maw. Once we were inside, I shut off the engine and we coasted to a stop.

For a long moment, nothing happened. Then the creature swallowed. Our boat tilted sharply downwards before sliding down a long throat that was so wide we couldn't see the sides of it. Shadow was buffeted from side to side and we braced ourselves as best as we could when a vast pool of liquid appeared below.

Instead of bursting apart when we hit the surface, our boat speared into the depths. Ishida was thrown against the window and grimaced as his skull cracked. Thankfully, the window was made of a durable material and didn't shatter. The vessel was watertight, so we remained safe and dry, but shouts of alarm rang out from the men below as they were tossed about.

Gregor helped the former emperor to his feet as Shadow righted itself and bobbed to the surface. Geordie screwed up his face at the quiet sound of Ishida's skull crackling back into place.

"Are you all right?" Kokoro asked the teen.

"I am fine," Ishida replied. A smear of black blood on the window was proof that he'd been injured.

"If you were human, you'd probably be dead," Higgins said in wonder.

"Then it is a very good thing that I am not human," Ishida replied. He'd left humanity behind so long ago now that I doubted he even remembered what it felt like to be an ordinary mortal.

"Can we all heal that quickly?" Charlie asked.

Gregor fielded that one. "We seven heal far more quickly than is normal for our kind, but you will all have the capacity to heal almost any wound fairly rapidly."

"Unless something is chopped off," Geordie piped up. "Then you can kiss that part of your anatomy goodbye forever."

Higgins' eyebrow went up at the teen's cheerful explanation. "That's good to know."

Silence descended as I fired up the engine again and we

motored through utter darkness. A shape appeared in the distance and Igor steered us towards it.

"Are you seeing what I'm seeing?" Geordie asked in a shocked whisper when we drew close enough to make out the numerous objects.

All around us, boats, ships and other vessels floated in various states of rust and ruin. I was pretty sure the boat from one of my dreams was to our left. Peering through the window, I could just make out decaying skeletons lying on the deck. In my dream, I'd stood among the pitiful corpses. I was glad to be distant from them this time.

"It's a ship graveyard," Higgins observed. His stare was pitying as he spied the bodies on the boat to our left. "We need to take these creatures down as fast as possible."

I agreed with my first servant, but our goal was somewhere above us and we had no easy way of reaching it. I could have tried to teleport us all directly into the mammoth's brain. For all I knew, it might be highly toxic and could strip our flesh from our bones upon contact. We needed to find a way to climb up to it and examine it carefully instead of rushing in blindly to the attack.

Igor was way ahead of me and rummaged around in a large metal container he'd had two of the men bring along. He held a pair of grappling hooks and extra-long ropes in both hands. "I thought these might come in handy." As always, his practical nature came to the fore.

"Smart thinking," I told him gratefully. He handed them both to me and I pushed open a hatch and stepped outside onto the small deck at the back of the boat. The smell of stomach juices, rotting meat and salt water hit me and I blocked the odour as well as I could. Geordie made a small sound of disgust and clapped a hand over his mouth and nose. We no longer needed to breathe, but our sense of smell had actually become heightened with our unholy deaths.

Even with my strength, I'd never be able to throw the hooks high enough to lodge them in the upper lining of the octosquid's stomach. Instead, I broke myself down into particles, keeping only my head and hands whole. Kokoro picked up my empty clothing and folded them neatly for me as I drifted upwards. Already, I could feel the airborne acid eating away at my skin. Our clothing would begin to fall apart if we remained inside the beast's gut for too long. I didn't want to contemplate the thought of being submerged in the stomach juices.

Using the air currents that swirled inside the cavernous stomach, I floated upwards until I reached the eggplant coloured stomach lining. I doubted the octosquid even felt it when I drove first one, then the second grappling hook deep inside its flesh. Several tugs anchored the hooks and I let the ropes drop. They fell far short of the boat, but I was hoping Igor would have more ropes to add to them. He did, and had them waiting for me. Taking them, I floated back up and tied them securely to the dangling ropes. They were now just long enough to reach the grasping hands below.

Returning for my clothing, I poured myself back into them as everyone lined up into two neat rows. The men below waited patiently for their turn to ascend the ropes. Fully dressed again, I settled my swords across my back, then moved to the first rope. Luc moved to the one beside me and we began to climb in tandem.

It was a far slower process to climb rather than to float as particles, but we still made it to the top fairly quickly.

Luc withdrew one of my swords from its sheath and I took the other. He made the first cut into the wall of flesh and dark purple blood sheeted from the wound. It smelled faintly like aniseed, but it wasn't caustic. We worked together to chop out a passage that was large enough for us to climb into.

Carving our way upwards at an angle, we hacked out a small tunnel through what seemed to be a mixture of blubber and flesh. In pairs, our army followed behind us. It took far longer than I'd anticipated before we reached a thick membrane. The casing was semi-opaque and I could just make out a gigantic shape through it. My sword cut through the skin easily enough and I carved out a hole that was large enough for even the tallest of us to be able to step through.

I took a moment to peer upward through the opening. The octosquid's brain towered high above us. As tall as a ten-story building, it stretched out as far as I could see to each side. A rather pretty lavender colour, it pulsed, as if moving in synch with a heartbeat. Natural tunnels ran haphazardly through the organ, reminding me of narrow alleyways in a dangerous city.

Geordie wormed his way through the crowd to stand beside me. I moved aside so he could also peer through the tear that I'd made. "Is that its brain?" His expression was awed. It looked nothing like our brains. Instead of being roughly oval in shape, it sat flat on the flesh beneath us. With irregular peaks and troughs, it reminded me of the ruined cities of Viltar. If I squinted hard enough, the quivering purple mass almost looked like crumbling buildings.

"Yep." We examined the gigantic blob through the

window-like membrane. "It's even bigger than I'd expected," I conceded after a few moments of stunned amazement from those who had joined us and had jostled in closer to take a look.

Gregor grimaced at the purple blood that had ruined his suit, then turned his attention to the problem at hand. He was hopeful that we'd be able to take down the beast by targeting the brain, but a few doubts still remained. He was careful to keep them to himself. "I suggest you carve a path directly to the centre of the creature's brain. We can then begin to blast it apart with our weapons and explosives."

It was the type of plan I liked best; simple and direct. Still holding the sword with a lion carved on the blade, Luc took the lead and stepped through the opening that I'd carved. He headed for the closest narrow pathway and I followed behind him. When it began curving away from the centre of the brain, Luc sliced into the tissue. While it looked tough on the outside, the organ was soft and squishy inside. It didn't take us anywhere near as long as we'd anticipated to reach the rough centre of the target.

Motioning us to stay back, Igor fired his gun and sent several explosive rounds deep into the tissue. They blasted out a cavity that was large enough to fit half a dozen men inside. The Russian picked several soldiers to help him widen the blast zone. Within minutes, they'd created a space that was large enough for all of us to fit inside.

Forming a circle, we faced outwards and fired almost in unison. The octosquid shuddered when a large portion of its brain ceased to exist. Hope and delight flashed across Gregor's face. He began to grin when he realized we might be successful after all. We might be small in size and number, but we'd already caused enough damage for the behemoth to be bothered by it.

Each of my warriors carried a gun and a bag of explosives, for those who preferred to throw a bomb instead of shooting. Igor gave my soldiers the order they'd been waiting for. "Let's blow this creature apart!"

Standing in a circle with our backs to each other, we followed his command.

# Chapter Eighteen

Aiming high, we blasted great holes in the purple jelly-like tissue. Another shudder from the beast knocked some of us down. We paused for a moment before resuming shooting or throwing explosives. I winced as the octosquid let out a mental shriek that reverberated inside my skull. Shutting down my ability to read minds, I concentrated on working my way deeper into the hulking lilac coloured mass.

Sudden blows rained down on the monster, throwing us all to the ground. The octosquid knew that it had been invaded, even if it didn't know by what. It was trying to tear its own flesh apart to get to us.

"It's working!" I shouted to encourage the others.

We redoubled our efforts and continued to pummel away at it. Each bullet that we fired was actually a small, compact grenade that exploded after a short three second delay. Each one blasted a twenty foot wide swathe through the soft purple matter. Multiply that by a hundred rounds per person, spread out over two hundred people and we were meting out significant damage. *I should have trusted Fate. She knew we'd be able to kill these things.* She might be harsh at times, but Fate needed us and she wasn't going to send us out on a fool's errand.

Igor and a few of my other soldiers had hauled some large silver containers up the ropes. He reached inside one and pulled out a rocket launcher. Higgins opened another container and pulled out a small, but powerful looking rocket. He inserted it into the launcher and gave Igor the thumbs up. Everyone cleared out of the way as the Russian sighted at a distant spot. Bright light momentarily stung my eyes as Igor fired. The rocket whooshed directly to its target and a wall of flames burst out from a large crater.

Several more soldiers withdrew similar devices from the containers that they also carried. Now that they had a large enough area to work in without accidentally blowing the rest of us up, they went into action.

I could no longer hear the thoughts of the octosquid, but I didn't need to be telepathic to know that it was suffering. Thrashing from side to side, it rained blows on its own body in the hope of ceasing its torment. I almost felt pity for the creature, but hardened my dead heart against the emotion. The aliens had come to our planet with the intention of feeding their insatiable hungers, not with the intention of attempting to live with us peacefully. They were invaders, just as the Viltarans had been and it was our job to destroy them.

Shrieking loudly enough for its entire body to vibrate,

the Goliath reverted to instinct and began to descend. "Hold your fire!" Igor shouted as he stumbled back a few steps. It became harder to stay on our feet as the beast zoomed downwards at a sharp angle. I braced myself as best I could and took Luc's hand when he reached for me.

Geordie lost his footing and slid past us, shrieking in a mixture of terror and excitement. He lodged inside a globule of brain. Kicking his feet and thrashing wildly in an attempt to free himself, he just forced himself deeper inside the tissue. I bit my lip to contain the laughter that welled up from his muffled shrieks. The adolescent wouldn't appreciate being laughed at. Neither would I, if I was in his situation.

Safely contained within the creature's insides, I still felt enormous pressure squeezing down around us. At last, we reached the ocean floor and the ground levelled out. Igor strode over to Geordie and dragged his apprentice free by the foot. The teen took the hand his mentor offered him and stood. He was covered in purple gunk from head to toe.

"You look like you were just birthed by a purple elephant," Ishida told his fellow teen.

Blinking jelly out of his eyes, Geordie shook his head and blobs flew off him. "That stuff is nasty." He wrinkled his nose, presumably at the smell, then turned and fired at the globule that he'd briefly been snared in. He'd matured since we'd first met, mentally if not physically. He trusted himself to handle the deadly weapon now. Still grinning slightly, Ishida also recommenced shooting. No stranger to war, Ishida was a competent warrior, even if he was used to using swords rather than guns.

All around us, my army of ex-cons worked

systematically to fulfil their objective and to obliterate their target. The rockets did the greatest damage, demolishing massive amounts of purple matter in mere seconds.

Twisting suddenly, the octosquid thumped itself against the ocean floor. One of my soldiers lost his balance and fired his rocket prematurely. Not everyone scattered in time and half a dozen fledglings were caught in the blaze. I felt their pain as they burst into flames before disintegrating. Thankfully, their agony was short lived, but I felt a distinct absence with them now gone. As I'd suspected, I felt their loss far more keenly than when I'd destroyed my undead rat.

Over and over, the creature bashed against the ground until it was finally exhausted. I cautiously sent out a probe and touched its mind. We'd destroyed enough of its brain to make thinking difficult. It barely retained enough intelligence to understand what was happening to it. All it knew was that something was inside it and that it had to get us out.

"Keep shooting," I urged my army. "It's almost finished!"

Unlike our quarry, we were undead and were therefore almost indefatigable. Reloading our weapons or readying more explosives, we resumed our attack. It was a strange sight to see ex-convicts dressed in orange coveralls dipping into their satin handbags and pulling out tiny bombs.

The octosquid made one last ditch effort to stop us by pushing itself upwards. It gathered its dwindling strength with the idea of dive-bombing the ocean floor for a final time.

"I wonder what that is?" Geordie said, unknowing that we were about to be smashed against the ground again.

Following his pointing finger, I saw a darker plum coloured mass that had just been revealed by his latest blast. "I don't know what it is, but let's shoot the crap out of it," I replied. Instinct told me that it was something important.

Gleefully following my order, the teen unleashed a barrage of bullets and I did the same. Others quickly joined in. An instant before the creature propelled itself downwards, the mass exploded in a wash of dark purple slime.

We all felt the body go limp when its mental cognition ceased to function. While the body was technically still alive, its brain and thought processes had essentially been destroyed. Since our planet didn't have life support systems large enough to sustain the creature, its body would also soon be dead. I couldn't even pretend to be sad about that. Several of my people had died to kill this thing. I was certain they wouldn't be the only casualties that we would suffer.

Probing the behemoth's mind to make sure it wasn't just faking it, I let out a whoop of victory. "We did it!"

"Is it really dead?" Geordie asked in wonder.

"Technically, its brain dead," I clarified. "But its body won't survive for long."

Surrounded by his warriors, Danton wiped purple blood off his face with a filthy sleeve. "Is the creature floating towards the surface, or sinking towards the ocean floor?"

It was hard to tell, since we were still cocooned in the membrane that had once contained a functioning brain, but my senses told me we were heading up rather than down. "We seem to be heading upwards."

"The boat worked quite well as a lure," Danton mused.

"Do you think we will be able to extract it from the carcass?"

Turning to Igor, I raised an eyebrow in query. Hefting his rocket launcher, he shrugged. "We can try to blast a way out through its flesh when it reaches the surface."

Covered in sticky purple blood and brain juice, we gathered into two groups. I transported the first group back to our boat and they quickly made their way downstairs. I shifted the second group, then went into dust mote mode to retrieve the grappling hooks. Pouring myself back into my clothes, I found the teens staring at me when I solidified. "What?" I asked suspiciously. While my clothes were still covered in goo, my skin and hair were now clean.

Shaking his head, Ishida articulated what they were both thinking. "You can do things that no other vampire could even conceive of, yet you treat your talents so casually."

"Each of my abilities came with a price, Ishida," I told him. "They weren't given to me, I had to earn them and I paid for them in blood almost every time." He lowered his eyes, mistakenly believing that I was chastising him. Putting an arm around his shoulder, I gave him a quick hug. "It might seem like I'm being casual about it, but that's because I feel like I'm living in a dream most of the time." He sent me a quick grin that I wasn't mad at him.

Geordie wrinkled his brow. "What do you mean?"

"Before I became Mortis, I was pretty much a nobody," I explained. "Then, all of a sudden, I was a creature of legend. The scourge of vampirekind, no less." I received a few smiles from the older vampires. My fledglings knew practically nothing about the legend that was me and listened in carefully. Even those below decks could hear me quite clearly. Our hearing was far better now that we were creatures of the night. "It was foretold by Danton's master that I'd bring death to the damned and that only a remnant would remain. We are that remnant and I'm supposedly in charge of you all." I shook my head in wry amusement. "I still find it hard to believe that I was chosen for this gig."

"The fact that you were chosen means you are the correct person for the task," Danton said wisely.

"You might not be the smartest vampire ever created, but you always find a way to win your battles," Geordie added.

"Thanks," I replied dubiously to his somewhat backhanded compliment.

"That's one giant jellyfish down," Igor said. "That leaves nine remaining. I wonder if they are aware that we just killed their comrade?"

Gregor sent an enquiring look at me so I closed my eyes and went jellyfish hunting. Luc's hand settled on my shoulder and I leaned back against him as I located the closest octosquid. Lurking deep beneath the waves, it communicated with the others using a form of telepathy that was similar to mine. I'd suspected that they could communicate using their minds when we'd been on Viltar and now I knew for certain. "They know," I said grimly and opened my eyes. "They think it was humans who killed their kin and they're pretty pissed about it."

Kokoro grasped the implications. "They can speak to each other using their thoughts?" At my nod, she looked concerned. "I imagine they will retaliate against this attack."

Our adversaries didn't think like us, but I'd caught the

general gist of what they were thinking. Kokoro's intuition was correct, they were going to retaliate, and I feared it would be soon. "One of them is going to attack a city," I confirmed.

"Do you know which city they are going to target?" Luc asked. His hand on my shoulder tightened a little with his concern.

Shaking my head, I turned to the radar screen. It offered a small scale map of the world and I pointed out where the remaining nine octosquids were situated. "This is where they're currently located." They were spread out all over the globe and each had staked out their own territory. "I'm not sure which one of them is going to attack yet."

"You'll have to try to monitor them all," Gregor suggested. "As soon as one of them starts moving towards land, we'll know which one to target next."

We were currently floating in the ocean near the UK and none of the mammoth sized monsters were anywhere near us.

"There's no way we'll be able to reach them in time to stop them, no matter which city they attack," Igor pointed out.

"Unless…" Gregor allowed the word to trail off suggestively and looked at me speculatively.

I wasn't on the same page as him and just stared at him blankly. "Unless what?" Then I remembered I could read his mind and skimmed the information for myself. "You've got to be kidding!" I protested.

Confused, Geordie switched his gaze from mine to Gregor's and back again. "What? What does he want you to do?"

Luc's grip became tighter on my shoulder before he

gentled it again. "I believe Gregor wants Natalie to attempt to teleport not just us, but the boat as well."

Ishida's eyes lit up in excitement. "Do you think you can do it?" Sometimes I wondered if he'd spent so much time playing computer games that he thought life itself was one big game.

Disturbed by the possibility of failing miserably then suffering from the embarrassment, I shrugged. "I don't know. I still have no idea what my limits are."

"You have to try!" the child king urged. Kokoro had chosen Ishida to be their emperor because a vision had told her to. Fate had known that the teen would have the courage and determination to lead his nation. As the ruler of the remaining vampire race, the least I could do was try to match his courage.

"Ok. I'll give it a go." Everyone braced themselves both mentally and physically as I placed my hands against the console and concentrated. An instant later, we were floating beside the colossal carcass of the dying octosquid. A few of its tentacles twitched in our direction, making some of my soldiers flinch away. None of the limbs came close enough to be a danger. It quite literally didn't have the brains left to try to coordinate its arms into grabbing hold of us.

"It worked!" Geordie crowed. "You are awesome, chérie!" He offered me his hand in a high five. Slapping it, I wobbled and almost went down. Luc caught me and the others crowded around with concern written on their faces.

"What is wrong?" my beloved asked. He and Geordie put their arms around my waist to keep me on my feet.

The teen was trembling in fear for me and I smiled

shakily. "I'm ok. I think that just took a lot out of me." I now had some idea of my limits and the kind of energy that using my teleportation would drain from me.

"Dawn is only a couple of hours away," Igor advised. "I suggest we return Shadow to the dock and have it refuelled. You can choose one or more of the sailors to snack on while maintenance is being performed on the boat."

"Once you have recharged," Gregor said, "we should return to the catacombs and rest up until one of our enemies makes a move."

It was a sensible suggestion and no one had any objections, least of all me. I rarely felt fatigued, but I hadn't used my muscles. I'd used my mind, which had been far harder than mere physical exercise. With practice, I hoped I'd become stronger. Hopefully, I'd become strong enough to be able to do whatever was necessary to take down our remaining enemies.

# Chapter Nineteen

Igor rapidly and skilfully piloted the boat back the way we'd come. We passed the submarine that had just been spared from a terrible fate. They again failed to detect us on their radar as they headed towards the now dead octosquid. The captain would report back to his superiors that the beast was deceased, but he'd be unable to offer an explanation as to what had killed it. An autopsy would determine the cause of death. I had no doubt that scientists all over the world would volunteer for that job.

The humans were still coming to terms with the fact that they weren't alone. They now knew that at least two alien species existed. I wasn't sure if they classified the grey skinned Viltaran clones as another species or not, and I didn't really care. I was just glad humankind was far less advanced than the Viltarans and hadn't yet mastered the ability to discover other inhabited planets. Once they did, they might very well turn into alien invaders themselves.

Armed sailors lined the dock when we returned. Their commander, who was still under my control, waved at them to lower their weapons and waited for me to appear. "Who are you people?" he asked when we stepped off the boat. His eyes flicked to the orange coverall clad men that formed up neatly behind me.

"We're not people, we're vampires. My name is Natalie."

"I *told* you it was her, Brian! You owe me twenty quid," someone crowed then stilled at a glare from his boss. "Sorry, sir."

"I am Commander Owens," he said once he'd turned his attention back to me. "I take it you and your people are responsible for killing the gigantic creature that is floating towards Ireland?" I skimmed his thoughts and saw that the submarine captain had reached the carcass and had reported his findings to his superiors. Word was quickly spreading around the globe about the gargantuan alien life form.

"We are," Gregor responded. "Your boat proved to be very handy, Commander."

Owens flicked his eyes over the hull. The gastric acids had stripped some of the paint off and had corroded the metal slightly. "How many more of these creatures are still out there?"

"Nine," Igor informed the captain.

"Are they a danger to humanity?" Owens already knew the answer, but maybe he needed to hear it stated directly.

I nodded, fighting down the urge to yawn. "The oceans will soon be depleted and then they'll head towards land in search of food."

The commander frowned. "How soon will this happen?"

"Very soon." I didn't mention that one would shortly be rampaging through a city in retribution for us killing one of their kind. Most humans already blamed us for bringing the Viltaran invasion down on them. We didn't need to add fuel to the fire.

"What strategy did you use to kill the creature?"

Gregor answered the question. "We used Shadow as a lure and allowed the creature to swallow us. Once we were in its stomach, we carved our way upwards into its brain and used these weapons to destroy it."

The commander's brows drew down when he noticed the guns that my soldiers were holding. "Where did you get them from?"

"We stole them from your army," Geordie said with a cheeky smile.

"Commander, I suggest you contact your superiors and advise them that nine aliens will shortly be heading for land all around the world," I said to the lightly bamboozled human. "They should evacuate any humans that are living in coastal areas and move them deeper inland until we can work our way around to killing all of them." It wasn't really a suggestion at all, but was instead an order that he couldn't refuse.

"I would advise against attempting to attack the creatures," Gregor told the commander. "They tend to eat anything that they come into contact with. I am fairly certain that humans would not survive for long inside the stomachs of these beasts."

Igor added a point. "You would not survive at all if they swallowed you then dove into deep water."

Studying us all, Owens allowed his frustration to show. "You expect us to leave the survival of the human race to a bunch of monsters?"

"Yes," I said bluntly. "We monsters have already saved your planet several times," I reminded him.

Dropping his gaze, he replied stiffly. "I am aware of that. It is difficult to trust your kind when they have tried to become the supreme rulers of our species twice."

"Well, none of us are interested in being your evil overlords," I said dryly.

"Why are you helping us, after we've shown you so little appreciation?" a brave sailor asked.

"It's our job," I replied with a shrug.

"What do you mean?"

"I was created to act as a guardian for humankind." Astonished murmurs swept through the sailors at that revelation. "I was also designed to kill anything that poses a threat to you."

"Including your own people?" the commander asked astutely.

"Unfortunately, yes. I destroyed the vampire Council and their remaining courtiers because they treated humans like cattle." A wave of tiredness swept over me and I swayed. Luc and Geordie immediately steadied me.

"You need to feed," Luc said quietly, but several of the sailors overheard him.

"Will feeding you turn us into vampires?" one of the men asked.

"No," I replied. "You'd have to drink my blood for that to happen."

Sending an enquiring glance at his commander, the sailor stepped forward. "I'm willing to donate some blood for the vampires who are going to save our arses." His sentiment was echoed by most of the others.

"My men also need blood," I told the commander. "Would you allow your soldiers to feed them?" Again, I couched it as a question, but it was really a command.

"Of course," he replied then turned to his men. "Anyone who wants to volunteer, line up. Everyone else, return to your duties." Their duty would be to repair Shadow and to make sure the vessel was operational as fast as possible.

Only a small handful of sailors went about making the necessary repairs. Everyone else lined up neatly. I approached the first man in the line and he gulped when my fangs descended. He trembled in fear when my hands settled on his shoulders, but he still offered me his neck. My teeth sheared through his skin and unerringly found a vein. I drank a few mouthfuls, enough to reenergize me, then I let him go. The small wounds on his neck would fade quickly. In a few hours, they'd appear to be as harmless as mosquito bites. He gave me a dazed smile that he'd survived the process without feeling much pain.

Feeling more alert now, I waited for my army to finish their snacks. My soldiers were becoming used to biting humans, but they weren't particularly comfortable munching on other men. I was glad there were no human women present and dreaded the rise of their flesh hungers. I cringed at the thought of unleashing them on any poor, unsuspecting females. Even if they hypnotized the women into giving their consent, it would still be wrong.

*Worry about that if and when it happens,* my inner voice advised. *What do you mean* if? My response was heavy on the sarcasm. *It's going to happen sooner or later.* I just hoped it would be later.

Dawn was only half an hour away when we'd all finished feeding. "We'll return after dark," I told the commander. "I sincerely hope we won't find an ambush waiting for us when we see you next."

It was a subtle warning and he nodded his understanding. My hypnotism would last far longer than usual, if I willed it to. I hadn't tried to make it permanent, but I would if it became necessary. As long as the sailor continued to follow my orders, he would retain the ability to think for himself and to make crucial decisions. The instant he thought of doublecrossing us, I'd turn him into my flesh puppet. Gone were the days when I'd ever be able to trust a human completely.

The boat's hull had been cleaned of the corrosive substance that'd coated it, but it would be hours before it would be ready to be used again. It was time for us to return to the catacombs to rest. At my gesture, everyone crowded around and I zapped us back to France.

Since they were still awake when they arrived at our base this time, my soldiers spread out to find somewhere to sleep for the day. There were enough beds for everyone on the courtier level and no one had to descend to the servants' quarters.

Igor rounded up the two teenagers and headed for the cells where the ammunition was stored. We'd come close to running out of ammo and we needed to stockpile some more. Interested in learning more about modern weaponry, Danton and his warriors joined them. Although useful at carving paths through flesh, blubber and membranes, their swords would be no match for the octosquids.

Kokoro joined me as I took a seat on an antique couch. Sitting beside me, she stared at the carpet pensively. Some effort had been made to make the courtier's quarters pleasant. Instead of raw dirt, floorboards had been installed and were covered in thick, luxurious carpet. The furniture was old-fashioned, but in good condition despite not being tended to in over a decade. A thick layer of dust coated most surfaces, but that could be easily remedied with a good cleaning.

Waiting for Kokoro to speak, I deliberately stayed out of her thoughts. I doubted she'd appreciate me prying, even though she'd delved into my private thoughts on more than one occasion and at highly inconvenient times. It became impossible to keep the door between our minds closed when she said my name.

I turned to her and she was staring at me strangely. "You heard that?"

"You said my name." It hadn't been with her mouth, but with her mind.

"It was a mere whisper of a thought," she said.

"I tend to notice it when someone is thinking about me specifically." That's what had drawn me to their meetings so often while I'd been sulking in the mausoleum.

"I'd like to test your ability to read minds. It might be handy to determine how powerful your ability is."

She was the expert and she'd know how to test my capabilities better than anyone. "Ok."

"We already know that you are able to read minds from halfway across the world. I'd like to see if you can pry into thoughts that someone wants to keep private." I sensed a twinge of jealousy that she quickly suppressed as she shielded her mind from me. "Try to read my thoughts," she invited.

Circling the thought that Kokoro kept hidden, I probed it and easily broke through to the meat inside. If it'd been able to, blood would have rushed to my face in embarrassment at the picture of her and Gregor naked and entwined for the first time. It was a memory that was precious to her and one that I wished I'd been unable to invade. She could tell by my expression that I'd breeched her defences.

Biting her bottom lip, she flicked a quick and guilty glance at her beloved. Gregor and Luc sat on another couch across the room, quietly discussing our chances of beating our adversaries. "I did not expect you to be able to pry that memory from me so easily."

"Has anyone ever been able to block you from their thoughts?"

"Not often," she replied. "Ishida was very skilled at shielding his secrets." He'd managed to keep the fact that he'd known all along that she was his master for ten thousand years. "Let's try again," she said as she readied another memory.

Uneasy at what I might find, I closed my eyes and concentrated. This time, she'd locked her thoughts away and they were much harder to pry free. In my mind's eye, I pictured Kokoro holding onto a treasure chest. Small and golden, it was held shut with an intricate lock. Zooming in on the lock, I examined the inner workings. I wasn't sure how I did it, but, bit by bit, I worked at the lock until the chest finally sprang open.

I received far more than just the one secret she'd been hiding. All of Kokoro's forty thousand years of memories cascaded over me. They started towards the end of her mortal life and I saw her as a human slave who had been prized for her beauty. The emperor at the time had used her to feed his sadistic hungers. He'd almost killed her when feeding both his blood and flesh hungers at the same time. He'd turned her into his creature when he realized he'd drained her too much.

He hadn't stopped using her body when she'd been reborn as a vampire. Having a pet psychic that could foresee the future and read minds added to his already overblown ego. Kokoro had eventually engineered his death, but not out of revenge. She knew her suffering would pale in comparison to what her people would endure beneath his reign. She'd chosen the next four emperors, knowing their reign would be temporary. Ishida had been the final emperor that she'd chosen to rule their small nation.

Sagging back against the couch, I put a hand to my forehead as the images began to fade. My expression was a combination of shock, fury and compassion. Kokoro's face pinched in ancient pain at having her memories dredged for a moment before her brow smoothed out. Forcing a chuckle, she patted my other hand. "That is what I get for testing the venerable Mortis."

"I'm sorry. I didn't mean to see so much."

Going still, she peered into my eyes. "What did you see?"

The memory she'd chosen for me to attempt to pry out of her was when she'd been turned into a vampire. She hadn't meant for me to see her entire history. "I saw everything," I said then covered my face with both hands as I fought down my pity and sorrow.

Her arm came around my shoulder and the two men

hurried over. "What is wrong?" Luc asked as he knelt before me.

"It is my fault," Kokoro said. "I was testing Natalie's abilities and she accidentally saw my memories."

Feet thudded on the stairs as Geordie came at a run. He'd sensed my misery from two levels down. "What happened?" he demanded.

Dropping my hands, I tried to soothe their concern. "I'm fine. I just saw Kokoro's past and it was...upsetting." My bottom lip quivered and so did Geordie's.

"What happened to you, Kokoro?" the teen asked.

Appearing in the stairwell, Ishida answered on behalf of his maker. "She suffered terribly beneath the rulers that came before me. They did not appreciate her gifts and they used her as if she were nothing more than a toy."

Everyone knew what he meant by that. Gregor already knew of his beloved's past and he put a hand on her shoulder in empathy. Geordie turned to me and his expression was fierce. "Promise me that you'll never let another vampire do that to anyone else ever again!"

It was a vow that would be easy for me to keep. "I promise, Geordie." I'd seen all too well the cruelties that our species were capable of. None of my friends or allies had sadistic tendencies, which was why they still lived. I would have to keep a remote eye on Millicent and her crew to make sure none of them became megalomaniacal tyrants or created anyone who might eventually become one.

"You're tired," Luc pointed out. "You should get some sleep."

Dawn had arrived and I didn't argue with him. Instead of retreating to the safe house for privacy, we opted to remain with our group. We searched for a room that wasn't occupied by soldiers and stripped down to our underwear. Dust also coated the furniture in the bedrooms, but I didn't have the energy to search for fresh linens. Neither did Luc and he merely turned the pillows over and stripped off the top coverlet. The bedding and mattress still smelled musty, but they would suffice.

Sensing that I wasn't in the mood for naked acrobatics, Luc gathered me in close and wrapped his arms around me. Still mourning for all that Kokoro had suffered, I slid into a deep sleep that was anything but peaceful.

# Chapter Twenty

When I opened my eyes, the ruins of an ancient building stared back at me. A low, full moon bathed the crumbling walls in a silvery light that made it seem slightly sinister. If I'd been human, I would have been terrified. Instead, I was merely curious. My dreams were usually messages of some kind and I was already intrigued by this one.

Only two walls still stood. They were made up of large brown-grey blocks and were covered in dead vines. A robed man stood unmoving directly in front of me. It took me a moment to realize it was just a statue. Skilfully made, it was very lifelike and was made of the same brown-grey stone as the rest of the ruins.

Moving closer to the statue, I examined it in detail. It stood in a carefully cut out section of the wall. Moonlight filtered through the archway, casting a deep shadow over the statue's face. Up close, I saw that a hood covered all but the mouth, which was grim and unsmiling. The figure held a large, shallow bowl that conjured up images of blood sacrifices. I went onto my tippy-toes to peek into the bowl. It was empty at the moment, but a dark residue remained. It might or might not have been blood and was too faint for me to tell.

Peering through the archway, I saw the edge of a cliff not far away. Behind the drop was a distant mountain range. Turning in a slow circle, I felt eyes watching me, but I saw and sensed nothing. Hearing stealthy movement behind me, I whirled around. A large, misshapen creature hulked on all fours in the shadows. Its head was higher than mine, but it was looking away from me so I couldn't see its face.

Turning to see what it was looking at, I heard a leathery flap of wings and something flew at my face. I ducked down and felt talons whoosh past my head. A few strands of my hair were yanked out. I considered myself lucky that I hadn't been scalped.

Standing up again, I turned and found myself teetering on the edge of a staircase. It was deep in the shadows and I hadn't even noticed the opening. Before I could regain my balance, the creature that I had yet to identify lunged forward and hit me with its shoulder. I tumbled head over heels down the stairs.

Thumping and bumping my way down two flights, I sprawled to a stop on my face. Metal grated on stone as something heavy was pushed over the opening. The moonlight disappeared, but faint light came from below. I climbed to my feet and descended another two flights of stairs to the bottom. A single light bulb weakly illuminated the hallway. A wide, long tunnel stretched out ahead of me with multiple doorways on each side. The doors were made of thick metal that even I might have had trouble breaking down.

Reaching the first door, I glanced through a barred window to see a pile of straw in one corner. My nose wrinkled at the smell of excrement that was smeared across the walls and floor. They weren't ordinary rooms at all, but were instead cells. Whatever had been kept in the cells hadn't been human. The jungle smell of wild animals permeated the entire hallway.

A different type of door waited at the end of the hallway. Also made of solid metal, it lacked a window or a handle and it didn't move when I pushed it. Abandoning my clothes, I reverted to tiny particles and filtered beneath the cracks to the other side.

Becoming whole again, utter darkness made me blink several times as my eyes adjusted to the lack of light. I went still as several large shapes moved when they sensed my presence. Red light flared to life and swung towards me. Staring up into the face of a creature that was both alien and strangely familiar, I felt huge claws close over my shoulders from behind as a face lowered towards mine.

Trapped between two monsters, I stared up at the thing towering over me in fascination. Twin horns curved upwards and were stained dark red, presumably from goring something, or someone, to death. A mouth opened to reveal fangs that were several inches long. Its head darted downward. I was thankfully woken up an instant before my face could be bitten off.

Grateful that I had avoided the imaginary pain of being de-faced, I opened my eyes to see Luc looking down at me in concern. "I take it you were having a bad dream?"

I nodded then grimaced. "I was having a nightmare about being locked in a dungeon with a bunch of creepy monsters."

"What did they look like?" Intrigued and knowing my penchant for dreaming about the dangers that we might face, he propped his head on his hand.

"They were like nothing I've ever seen before, yet they were somehow familiar," I replied. "I'm not sure what they were, but they were huge."

"Were they as large as a human that had been turned into a Viltaran clone?"

"Way larger. They were several feet taller and far bulkier. Their skin wasn't grey, either. It was a greenish-brown, I think." I'd only caught a brief glimpse of their bodies, not enough to give him much of a description. I could describe their horns and teeth with far greater accuracy.

"Hmm." Mulling over my dream, Luc's eyes dropped down to my chest and he lost his train of thought. An image of him burying himself inside me rose to the surface of his thoughts.

Sending out my senses, I found Geordie pacing the floor of the room he'd chosen across the hall from ours. "Let's go somewhere more private," I suggested and whisked us both to the safe house. The others might be used to having no privacy in the bedroom, but I wasn't and I doubted that I ever would be.

Away from the prying ears of the others, I was free to make as much noise as I wanted as Luc feasted on my body. His teeth grazed my neck as he joined us together and set a fast pace that quickly brought me to my peak.

Other girls might like to take things slow and easy, but I preferred to get to the good part quickly.

My eyes sprang open when Luc's fangs pierced my skin. I wasn't sure which of us was more surprised when he bit down and began to feed. I was instantly catapulted into another orgasm as he sucked hard at my throat. Then he was shuddering above me as he found his own release.

As my one true love collapsed beside me, I felt my neck. The skin was already unbroken. I felt shame emanating from Luc and took his hand. "I'm glad you bit me," I confessed. "Now I don't think I'll feel quite so bad when my minions' flesh hunger rises."

Rolling onto his side, Luc studied my face. "Why is that?"

"Because it felt pretty freaking awesome having you sink your fangs into me," I said with a grin.

Relieved that I wasn't angry or disgusted with him, he lifted my hand and kissed my knuckles. "I don't know what came over me. I've never bitten another vampire during sex before."

Doing so would have ended in his death, so I could understand why he'd resisted the urge. "You know my blood can't hurt you now." The army of soldiers that I'd created testified to that fact.

"Yes, but it was rude," he said almost primly.

"You have my permission to be rude anytime we're horizontal together," I said gravely.

"You truly enjoyed it?"

"Would I lie to you?"

Amusement glinted in the depths of his dark eyes. "Probably."

"If your blood didn't taste like arse, I'd bite you again,

too." The urge to bite down on the vulnerable flesh of his neck was almost overpowering at times. I'd succumbed to the impulse once and had been inundated with his memories, just as I'd been with Kokoro after our little experiment at prying into her thoughts.

"I distinctly remember the time you did," he said with a small smile. "I would not mind if you repeated the act, even if my blood tastes like arse to you." I smirked at him mocking my Aussie accent. "We'd best return to the others before they send out a search party for us," he suggested.

Luc searched the wardrobe and chest of drawers for a change of clothing and I did the same. A few of my belongings still remained from before I'd slunk back to Australia to sulk. "We should really try to find some new clothes for everyone," I said. Danton and his warriors still wore their sadly outdated robes and my soldiers desperately needed normal clothing.

"Gregor was going to hunt up something suitable for your men from the servants' quarters in the catacombs. There should be enough clothing for everyone."

Relieved that I had people on my team who were much better at planning than me, I realized that I'd have been lost without them. I couldn't even imagine a future without my close friends in my life.

Gregor had indeed been busy while we'd been sleeping and he'd scrounged up enough clothes for everyone. My soldiers would become far less conspicuous once they changed into their new clothing.

All of our friends were gathered in the living area when we appeared. Geordie gave me a reproachful look. "I know you like your privacy, but I wish you wouldn't disappear like that."

There was more behind his rebuke than mere worry, but I didn't pry. I'd promised him I wouldn't deliberately read his mind and I'd attempt to live up to it. "Sorry. I'll try not to let it happen again." While Geordie was mollified, Luc was dismayed. "Until this disaster is over," I added and Luc heaved a silent sigh of relief. I didn't mention that I'd dreamed yet another calamity might already be heading our way. We'd deal with one problem at a time and worry about what my latest dream might portend later.

Gregor thankfully changed the subject away from our sex life. "Have any of our enemies attacked land yet?"

Hidden in the catacombs, we had no access to the news, since the power had been cut when the mansion had burned down. Sending out my senses, I swept them outwards and hovered over an octosquid that was just retreating back into the ocean after destroying a town. My dismayed expression was enough to alert the others.

"Where did they strike?" Igor asked.

Reading the surface thoughts of the survivors, it was easy enough to figure out. "It wiped out a coastal village in China." The shocked images that I read from the few civilians who'd managed to escape were sickening.

"We need to see what kind of damage we can expect," Gregor murmured. "Do you think you can scrounge up a computer?"

I nodded. "I'll find one somewhere." Luc didn't protest at being left behind as I teleported to another location. Like me, he was feeling guilty. While we'd been feeding our flesh hungers, thousands of humans had been sucked into the maw of an octosquid. The creature had attacked during daylight, so I wasn't sure what we could have done to stop it, but it didn't lessen my guilt.

Materializing in the shadows of the nearby town, I honed in on a human that sold a range of electronic devices. He squeaked in surprise when I appeared right in front of him. The sun was still out and a shaft pierced the window and fell across my arm. The clerk looked down as smoke began to waft from my sleeve. Grabbing the man before he could scream, I darted into the shadows and captured him with my eyes.

"What do you need from me?" he asked as I put him under lightly.

"I need a computer that has a long battery life." It felt strange to be speaking fluent French, but I figured I'd get used to it eventually.

"I have a laptop with a battery that will last for eight hours."

A computer would be excellent, but I realized it probably wouldn't be much use to us without the necessary equipment. "We don't have internet access."

Waving the problem away, the clerk stepped over to a counter and unclipped a demonstration laptop. He spent a few minutes gathering items together, then went about setting up the laptop so that it would work for me.

"It is set up and ready to use," he said when he was done. "This is a mobile device that will allow you to use the internet anywhere in France." He dropped it into a bag, along with power cords for the laptop. We wouldn't be able to use the cords in the catacombs, but we could always use the safe house to recharge the batteries.

"Thanks. Forget you saw me and report the equipment as stolen."

Nodding, he turned away, already forgetting that I existed as I took the bag and transported myself back to the catacombs.

Ishida took the gear and set it up on a coffee table. His hands went to work and he called up a news article on the attack that had happened only a short time ago. Footage that had been taken by several survivors had already been sold to the media. The video was amateurish, grainy and had been taken from cell phones, yet the devastation was still clear to see.

What had once been a thriving fishing village was now a broken mass of rubble. The first short, shaky video showed hundreds of black tentacles emerging from the ocean in search of victims. The picture changed and zoomed in on an alien appendage. It wrapped itself around a five story building and plucked it from the ground like it was a flower. Peeling one side of the building off with a second limb, the octosquid held the building over its maw and shook it. Dozens of humans fell screaming into its gaping mouth, reminding me of raisins falling from a box.

The picture shifted to a tentacle that snaked across the road and grabbed a taxi. The passengers futilely tried to jump to safety. One fell ten feet and another tentacle appeared beneath him just before he hit the ground. He disappeared into one of the dozens of secondary mouths that ran up and down the limb. It was a blurry shot, but the ever gnashing teeth were still discernible. So was the spray of blood and chunks of flesh that erupted from the opening.

Ishida pulled up several news articles, then came across an urgent message directed at me. Commander Owens' face was shown in a clip beneath the title; World Leaders Call For Help From Natalie The Vampire.

"Catchy title," Geordie said mockingly as Ishida clicked

on the video to play it for us.

Clearly reading from a script, the commander made his plea. "Natalie, your presence has been requested at a meeting in London with concerned world leaders in relation to the attack that was recently made on China. Please meet me at the docks after sundown, so that I can escort you to the meeting."

His meeting place would be cryptic to all but a few. I appreciated his attempt at discretion even while shaking my head at their audacity. "After everything they've put us through, I can't believe they think I'm just going to waltz into a meeting with the same type of people who decided to kick us off our own planet."

Gregor watched the screen thoughtfully. "They were not this desperate ten years ago. After seeing the corpse of an octosquid and a live one destroying a small town, they are now aware of how much danger they face. Logically, our kind has the best chance of stopping them."

"Do you believe they will offer us aid?" Igor asked with a hint of derision.

Luc gestured towards the clip that Ishida had paused. "After seeing that, what choice do they have?"

"Yes," Gregor agreed. "I believe they will be far more amenable to working with us now that videos of the attack have spread around the world. Their people will lose confidence in them and the civilians will most likely begin to rebel if nothing is done to stop the aliens."

I could easily picture townsfolk rioting and chaos reigning if they became panicked. Humans could be highly irrational at times of stress and the octosquids were going to cause a lot of stress worldwide.

# Chapter Twenty-One

As requested, I met the commander at the docks, but I didn't go alone. I took my entire retinue of friends, allies and soldiers with me. Owens' eyes widened when we all suddenly appeared, but he didn't protest at our numbers. Nodding a greeting, he gestured towards a waiting truck. It was nowhere near large enough to hold all of us, but that wouldn't be a problem.

"Forget the truck," I told him. "Just think of where you want to go and I'll take us there."

He was disconcerted for a moment then nodded again. A picture of a multi-story redbrick building in the heart of London formed. Zeroing in on the location with my senses, I picked up on hundreds of humans. Scanning their minds, I found no hint of treachery, just an overwhelming sense of fright and desperation.

Changing my plan slightly, I turned to Higgins. "You

guys stay with the boat and make sure it's fuelled up and has some extra gas stored down below."

Wearing casual clothing, my soldiers looked far less sinister now that they'd ditched their orange prison uniforms. They were armed and their pockets bulged with spare ammunition and more of the explosives. Those without pockets still carried the satin bags. Charlie glanced down at his emerald bag and shook his head in embarrassment. "This bag doesn't go with my shoes at all." Geordie giggled and the redhead grinned back at him.

Gregor's and Danton's guards also stayed behind, but Danton stuck close to me, silently indicating that he wished to accompany us. Masterless for the first time in several thousand years, he lacked purpose now that the prophet was gone. Skimming his mind, I saw that he and Gregor had known each other long before the Court had been formed. Danton would fit in well with our group and his men were loyal to him, even if they weren't my minions. None harboured any thoughts of treachery, so I didn't mind them being part of our team.

Exclamations of alarm rang out when our party appeared in the room the commander had pictured. Soldiers from several nationalities raised their weapons. Owens and Danton were quickly shielded by my friends, since they were far more fragile than us. Danton might be a vampire, but a strategically place bullet could still end his life.

"Hold your fire!" a very British voice shouted. A tall, gangly man in his early fifties hurried over. Extending his hand, he smiled, but his eyes were worried. "Natalie, thank you for coming." His dark suit was probably expensive, but it was slightly short in the sleeves and hung on him awkwardly.

"Thank you for inviting us, Prime Minister Townsend." He had no way of knowing that I'd just plucked his name and title out of his head. He was a famous figure in the UK and he wasn't surprised that I knew of him.

Holding his hand out again, he offered it to Luc. "And you are?"

"I am Lucentio." Luc shook Townsend's hand, but he didn't offer a surname. One by one, my friends introduced themselves. Ishida didn't offer a surname either, or mention his former title.

"Welcome, all," Townsend said and gestured towards some chairs that had just been hastily brought in by his lackeys. A long, rectangular table sat in the centre of the room. It was large enough to accommodate the thirty representatives of several countries, but it would be squishy now that we'd arrived.

Not enough time had passed since the alien's attack on China for every world leader or their delegates to have arrived. Those that had come had brought along advisors as well as bodyguards. My personal retinue outnumbered theirs, but not by much. Only the highest on the political food chain would be able to sit down. Their minions, and my allies, would have to stand in the background.

After some hasty shuffling, we each took a seat at the table. Townsend, sitting at the far end of the table, kicked off the meeting since he was hosting it. "On behalf of everyone, I bid you a warm welcome and offer you our thanks for agreeing to meet with us."

Fairly ordinary in looks, Townsend gave off a pleasant vibe and didn't seem to harbour any malice towards us. In fact, he was a closet vampire fan and owned almost every known book and movie that was dedicated to our kind. I was both surprised and embarrassed to discover that a movie, several books and even a TV series had been created about myself and my friends. Geordie and Ishida would no doubt get a kick out of that. I'd rather stick a fork in my eye than watch or read about myself.

While it wouldn't be necessary to bamboozle Townsend into doing anything that needed to be done, the others were a different story. They were all petrified of us. More specifically, they were terrified of me. I'd cold-bloodedly murdered the President of the United States and was therefore unpredictable and untrustworthy.

"Commander Owens advised us that it was you and your people who killed the gigantic alien that is currently floating off the coast of Ireland," Townsend said.

"We did." I could tell they wanted more information, so I elaborated. "We borrowed a boat and used it as a lure." Shadow was supposed to be a secret, so I didn't mention it further. "It was an effective ploy and the octosquid swallowed us whole. Once we were inside its stomach, we cut our way up into its brain and blasted it apart with some weapons that we borrowed from your armed forces." Owens had already conveyed the details of our battle to them, but they wanted to hear it from us.

"I'd like to know how you not only knew that such highly classified weaponry existed, but how you managed to locate it," a British soldier said coldly. He wore an impressive swathe of medals on his chest.

"I knew about them the same way that I know your nickname was Prissy Pete as a child," I replied just as coolly. I could see how he'd earned the nickname. He was now sixty, but he was still uptight, rigid and prissy. His full name and title was Admiral Peter York. He was used to being shown respect, but he wasn't going to get it from me if he didn't have the courtesy of showing us some.

Flushing in embarrassment, he clenched his jaw. "Are you implying that you can read our minds?"

"No. I'm flat out saying it."

Excited rather than frightened by the prospect, Townsend moved forward until he was sitting on the edge of his seat. "Can you read the minds of the aliens as well?"

"Yes, but I can't read them as well as a human." No one was going to like what I was about to tell them. "They're pissed off that one of their friends is dead."

"Is that why they attacked my country?" the Chinese diplomat asked icily. His female advisor leaned over his shoulder and whispered caution for him to remain calm and not to anger me. She darted wary looks at me, but her gaze kept straying to Kokoro and Ishida. She was puzzled by their presence and wondered just how many Japanese vampires had survived the destruction of their island. I wasn't about to tell her that they were the only two left.

Gregor deflected the attention away from me. "It is one of the reasons why your country was targeted, but it could just as easily have been any coastal town or city anywhere in the world."

Townsend paled slightly. "Commander Owens told us that there are nine more of these creatures still out there. Is that true?"

Gregor nodded. Dressed in a fresh suit, he was the picture of elegant sophistication once more. "That is correct."

"Is there any way for us to negotiate peace with these aliens?" a Russian colonel asked.

"You cannot negotiate with creatures such as these," Igor replied. His accent was thick enough to make it difficult for some of the foreigners to understand him. Even with my gifts for languages, I still had trouble understanding him sometimes when he spoke in English. "They live to eat and their appetites are voracious."

"They are sea creatures," one of the European diplomats pointed out. "Surely they must remain in, or near water. If we simply evacuate the coastal towns, we can wait them out. Once their food runs out, they'll starve."

Despite the attack on China, and my earlier warning, none of the authorities had told their civilians about the impending doom and begun to move them inland yet.

Gregor shook his head regretfully. "I am afraid it will not be as easy as that. They are capable of leaving water and of moving around on land. Now that they've attacked humans without meeting any kind of resistance, I am afraid they will follow your citizens inland, gobbling them up as they go."

"What is the life span of these aliens?" an American asked. A quick trip into his mind told me he was from the US embassy based in London. He wasn't exactly high up on the hierarchy, but he was the best the Americans had in the country at the moment.

"They live for several hundred thousand years," Geordie said in answer to the question. One of the octosquids had revealed this to us during our trip to Viltar.

A shocked murmur ruffled around the table.

"Then we have no choice but to engage the aliens in battle and attempt to kill them," the Chinese diplomat said heavily.

"I am afraid so," Gregor confirmed.

"What can we do to help?" Townsend asked. He put on a grave face, but his eyes danced with excitement. Ever since we'd returned from outer space to save first Manhattan then Las Vegas, he'd been secretly hoping for a disaster to hit his nation so that he might one day be able to meet us. The near invasion of the UK was a dream come true for him, even if it was a nightmare for the rest of the world.

"You can keep us supplied with weapons and ammunition," Luc said. "We would also like to continue to use the boat that we've already borrowed once."

Townsend nodded his permission and his thanks for us keeping Shadow a secret. "Of course. Have you decided which of the aliens you're going to target next?"

All eyes swung to me. "I think we should track down the octosquid that attacked China. It has a taste for human flesh now and it will be more inclined to attack land again." The Chinese diplomat bent his head in a stiff bow of thanks.

"How are you going to get the boat all the way to the Pacific Ocean?" Townsend asked.

"I'll teleport it there," I replied and hid my grimace at how drained I would be once I did.

"We could use a few bags of blood for food," Kokoro said casually. It was a brilliant idea and I could have kissed her for thinking of it. She caught my gaze and gave me a tiny nod when she saw my gratitude.

"That can be arranged," the Prime Minister said and gestured for an aide. "Do you prefer any particular blood type?"

I vaguely knew the blood types were A, B and O, but

not much more than that. "Any kind will do." I didn't relish the thought of drinking cold blood, but Kokoro wouldn't have suggested it if it wasn't drinkable.

While we waited for the blood to be scrounged up from the closest hospital, Admiral York took a satellite phone out of his pocket and tossed it to me. "We'd appreciate it if you would keep us informed of your progress. Townsend's number has been input into the sat phone and you just need to hit the dial button. We'll let you know if there are any further attacks." His hard stare reminded me strongly of General Sanderson. While he didn't outright want us dead, he wasn't happy about becoming our allies. Neither was I, but we didn't really have a choice about it.

All too aware of just how treacherous humans tended to be, I made sure to capture everyone in the room. Without any of them being aware of it, I lay a light web of hypnotism over the entire group. Now they wouldn't be able to act against any vampire, unless I allowed them to, and that wasn't going to happen anytime soon.

My command over my body and mind had been honed far beyond the capabilities of any other vampire in our fifty thousand years of history. Fate had placed me in situations where I would gain the skills that I would need to battle each threat that arose. Seeing Luc blasted to pieces then thinking he had died had made me retreat deep inside my own mind.

During the months that I'd been a mausoleum-bound hermit, I'd mastered the art of mind control simply by mastering my own mind. No human, or vampire, was safe from my manipulation now. It was a frightening thought and it was a power that I had no desire to abuse. This was a secret that was probably best kept to myself. I wasn't sure how my friends would react if they knew just how formidable I'd become.

Still slightly sickened by the thought of having to become a puppet master, I was relieved when an aide eventually hustled in through the doors carrying a container full of blood bags. "This is all the hospital could spare, sir," he gasped to Townsend. "I had to promise that we'd donate more before they'd give it to us."

"Will that be enough?" the Prime Minister asked as Geordie and Ishida took a peek inside.

The teens nodded in tandem and I nodded at Townsend. "We'll let you know how we get on with the octosquid," I said as Ishida hefted the container.

"It was a pleasure to meet you all," Townsend replied. "Although I wish the circumstances weren't quite so grim."

Gathering in a circle with Commander Owens in the middle, I zapped us back to the docks. Higgins flashed a grin of relief when we reappeared. I smiled back and sensed his flesh hunger rise.

"Uh oh," Geordie murmured as the sensation quickly spread through the rest of my fledglings. "This can't be good."

"It appears that your babies are growing up, Ladybug," Luc said with a hint of a smile.

"And at the worst possible time," I murmured.

"Is this the flesh hunger that Gregor told us about?" Higgins asked uneasily. It had just been a momentary flicker and the urge was already dying down, but we'd have to do something about it soon.

"Yes. We'll deal with it after we take down the octosquid."

Charlie flicked me a miserable look. "We're not going to lose control and start raping women are we?"

So far, they'd proven to be very different from normal fledglings. They took after me and therefore had far better control over their hungers than normal. My blood and flesh cravings had only become close to being uncontrollable after I'd been fed the blood of four different imps. Even so, I'd mastered myself again fairly quickly.

"If rape wasn't in your nature before, then you won't be overcome with the urge now," I said to reassure my men. Relieved, the soldiers straightened up and waited for orders. "Is Shadow ready?" I asked Higgins.

"Yes, ma'am." American to the core, his automatic response almost made me snigger. We didn't use 'ma'am' and 'sir' very often in my country.

"Then let's go."

Owens and his men lined up on the dock to watch us as we boarded. I fired up the engine and Igor steered us through the gate and out into open water. Spreading out my senses, I located the octosquid that had attacked China and placed my hands on the console. In the space of a heartbeat, we shifted from one ocean to another.

# Chapter Twenty-Two

Braced for the toll that transporting the boat and its passengers would take on me, it was a pleasant surprise to find that it wasn't quite as bad this time. I only wobbled slightly before Luc's hand came around my waist.

Kokoro reached into the container at her feet and handed me a blood bag. The liquid was being kept on ice so it would stay fresh longer. I bit into the plastic like it was the neck of a human and made a face at the sensation of cold rather than warm blood as it went down. It tasted ok, so I drank the entire bag then held out my hand for another.

Refreshed and alert again after draining the second bag, I searched for our prey and found it skulking far beneath us. "I don't think this octosquid is going to be lured into swallowing us as easily as the first one," I told the others.

"Where is it?" Geordie asked, peering around the ocean.

There was no storm this time, but it was cloudy and the water was dark.

I pointed at our feet. "It's waaaay down there."

"Does it know that we're here?" Gregor asked.

Delving into the beast's mind, I shook my head. "I think it's asleep. It's dreaming about the meal that it had earlier." Its belly was far too vast to be full, despite the thousands of humans it had consumed, but it was feeling content for the first time in days. Apparently, humans tasted better than fish. *It must be all the fatty food they eat,* my inner voice said snidely. I'd once feasted on the same bad food, but I didn't remind my alter ego of that fact.

"Are you up to teleporting us directly inside the creature's stomach?" Luc asked in concern.

I was usually indestructible and he wasn't used to seeing me weakened like this. Neither was I and I didn't like it much. "It seems to be getting easier each time I use it, but you'd better have some blood ready just in case."

Closing my eyes, I pictured us inside the gut of the octosquid and opened my eyes to see that it had become a reality. I took the bag that Kokoro offered me and drained it dry. One was enough this time and I declined the second bag.

Staring out through a side window, Ishida's back went stiff. Standing beside him, Geordie made a small sound of grief. I didn't particularly want to see what had upset the boys, but I reluctantly joined them anyway.

Seemingly almost as vast as the ocean above, the highly acidic and stinky stomach juices stretched out as far as the eye could see. In the distance, I saw the remains of several vessels. One was far too large to be a boat and appeared to be a cargo ship. Objects floating nearby drew my attention.

Already decomposing from the gastric acid, the partially melted corpses of the victims from the Chinese coastal town bobbed in the water beside our boat.

"J-J-J." Higgins forced out a sigh at his inability to say 'Jesus'. "Let's kill this son of a bitch before it attacks any more innocent civilians."

It was a sentiment that I agreed with wholeheartedly and I turned to Gregor. "What's our best strategy? Should I just zap us all directly into the octosquid's brain?"

Weighing up our options, he shook his head. "We'd sink into it like pieces of fruit embedded in jelly. It might be quicker to transport yourself and Lucentio to the edge of the brain and begin carving a path. You can retrieve us in small groups and we can work our way deeper into its brain."

"We should find that darker purple section and destroy it first," Geordie suggested.

Gregor wasn't a fan of that plan. "I am not sure that that would be wise." He didn't offer us an explanation as to why he was against the idea. He was just guessing, but he briefly thought that doing so could result in disaster.

"It can't hurt to try," I decided. "It seemed to be the central thought processing area, so if we take it out first, it should become too stupid to think coherently."

"That is what I am afraid of," Gregor said almost too low for me to hear him.

Luc drew one of my swords and I drew the other. Concentrating on the brain, I shifted us both to the protective membrane that encased the organ. Working in tandem, we carved a path through the jelly-like substance whenever the twisted pathways meandered away from our goal. Leaving Luc to continue hacking out a path, I returned to the boat and brought my closest friends, Danton and his warriors back to the path first. After several more trips backwards and forwards, all of my warriors had joined us.

Far quicker than the last time, we located the cortex and blasted out a wide area around it to give us room to work. "Ready?" Igor called as several of us lined up in a semi-circle and levelled our guns. "Fire!"

A barrage of explosives blasted through to the darker purple mass that controlled the octosquid. Realizing that it was under attack, the alien was roused from its sleep and roared in fury. Its scream changed frequency and became higher pitched as the cortex began to break apart beneath our fire. Enraged, it surged up towards the surface, futilely searching for whatever was attacking it.

Linked to the monster's mind, I felt its ability to reason wink out as the plum coloured mass disintegrated. My shout of triumph died before I could even voice it when the creature's baser instincts kicked in. As usual, Gregor was right. He'd guessed that taking out the creature's ability to reason wasn't a good idea and he was about to be proven correct.

"Is it over?" Geordie asked hopefully then stumbled when the mammoth surged into motion.

Watching through the octosquid's form of radar, I saw thousands of bright red dots appear as it neared a small island off the coast of China. Instead of destroying its ability to think, we'd turned the creature into a frenzied killing machine. Knowing on some level that it was in danger, its instinct was to destroy.

"Keep shooting!" I shouted and wrenched myself away from the images of people being stuffed into our adversary's mouth.

Spreading out, we fired our guns and threw explosives until we'd destroyed a large enough area for Igor to begin firing his rockets. Half a dozen soldiers also began to use their rocket launchers, blasting chunks of brain everywhere. The rest of us did what we could to render the beast brain dead.

Efficient and methodical, our constant barrage eventually brought the monster to its figurative knees. Watching through its form of radar, it tried to brace itself with its tentacles, but didn't have enough control left. Few red dots remained in what had once been a prosperous city. I dreaded to see the havoc that the dying behemoth had caused to the island with my own eyes. It was bad enough seeing it through alien vision.

"You were right," I said to Gregor. I had to raise my voice above the shots that were still being fired so he could hear me.

Once again, he was covered in purple goo, as were we all. "What was I right about?"

"We shouldn't have attacked its cortex first."

"Why not?" Ishida asked. His gun looked too large in his hands, but he handled the weapon easily.

"Because we sent it into a frenzy and it attacked an island."

Concerned, Geordie touched my arm. "How many people were hurt, *chérie*?"

"Too many," I replied dully. "I doubt the Chinese government are going to be our friends after this all blows over."

Closing his eyes, Gregor mastered his regret quickly. "How many lives were lost?"

"Over eighty thousand." I knew the exact number down to the smallest child, but they didn't need to know that. It was enough that I would be burdened with the knowledge. As their leader, the guilt should and would fall on my shoulders.

Ever sensible, Igor waved at my soldiers to cease fire and spoke. "We have learned what not to do next time. There are still eight of these monsters left to destroy and I suggest we do not waste time wallowing in guilt. We should instead decide which alien we are going to target next."

"I think we might have something more urgent to take care of first," Higgins said. Hearing the strain in his voice, I turned to see my soldiers' eyes were blazing red. Their flesh hungers had risen again and all were shortly going to lose control.

Reading my panic, Gregor offered a solution. "I suggest you utilize another penitentiary, but choose a women's facility this time."

"We're not going to catch any diseases from the inmates, are we?" Sergeant Wesley asked uneasily.

"No," Gregor said, hiding his amusement. "We are immune to all human ailments."

Knowing we were out of time, I searched for the closest women's jail. "Just remember to put them under first so they won't feel any pain." Or terror. "Bite them as you become, er, intimate and they'll enjoy the experience as much as you will." I never thought I'd ever have to give sex tips to a vampire that I'd sired, let alone nearly two hundred of them. I never thought I'd ever sire a vampire at all, so this was all very strange for me.

Luc's lips twitched in a near smile at my discomfort as

he offered me his hand. "Shall we?"

Once everyone was touching, I transported us into a Chinese women's prison. My men didn't have time to be choosy and we didn't have time to search for a way to open the doors. As fast as I could, I shifted the men into the cells so they could perform their necessary business.

Luc and the others subdued the guards that came on the run. The uniformed men and women fell to our dark mojo and lined up quietly next to the wall. They wouldn't remember much of what was about to transpire and I envied them. I almost wished someone would hypnotize me so I wouldn't have to see my men getting it on with the inmates.

Screams of terror were replaced with sighs of lust as the women succumbed to my fledgling vampires' dark magnetism. I closed my eyes against the sight of naked flesh slapping together, but I couldn't shut out the sounds or the images that spilled into my mind. Through Higgins, I felt a petite prisoner grab him by the butt and watched her offer him her neck. His fangs sank into her vein and the sweet, salty taste of blood flooded into my mouth. Gritting my teeth, I rode out the wave of pleasure as my men satiated their flesh hungers for the first time.

"See?" Geordie teased, knowing how mortified I was. "That wasn't so bad, was it?"

Apparently, I was the only one who felt embarrassed by the near orgy that we'd just witnessed. I hadn't lived in the Court and I hadn't been subjected to the kind of environment that they were all used to. Even Danton and his warriors had spent time in the Court, so this wasn't a shock to them.

Kokoro took pity on my delicate sensibilities. She and

Ishida were no strangers to this kind of thing either. "We will see about freeing your men from the cells, Natalie. Perhaps you could retrieve the boat from the alien's stomach before it becomes corroded by its digestive juices."

I was grateful for an excuse to escape and it was a good idea as well. Luc took my hand and we left the prison and appeared in the cockpit of the boat. A moment later, Shadow floated in the ocean near the carcass of the dead octosquid.

Peering through the window at the ruins of the island, any thoughts of having a quickie with Luc fled. One sure way to curdle desire was to see the aftermath of a leviathan that had gone on a murderous rampage. The fact that we'd inadvertently caused the destruction weighed on me heavily.

Running his hand up and down my back, Luc offered me what little comfort he could. It was undeniable that we'd been responsible for the deaths of the humans that we were supposed to be protecting. I wondered uneasily if Fate would punish me for making the wrong decision about attacking the octosquid's cortex.

It was a mistake that we weren't going to make again, but the damage had already been done and it couldn't be reversed. While I had many strange and wonderful powers, resurrection wasn't one of them.

# Chapter Twenty-Three

Leaving Shadow floating near the carcass of the octosquid, we returned to the prison. The subdued atmosphere instantly alerted me that something was wrong. "What happened?" I asked my small circle of concerned friends.

"Please, let me feed," a female moaned in Chinese. "I'm so hungry!" *Well, that answers that question.*

"One of the inmates has turned," Ishida replied quietly and unnecessarily.

"Who sired her?" I asked. I kept my tone neutral rather than accusatory. I doubted she'd been turned on purpose, but this problem would have to be dealt with.

Shamefaced, one of my men stepped forward and could barely meet my eyes. "I'm responsible. I'm sorry, it wasn't intentional." Staring through the bars at the fledgling that he'd created, he sent me a pleading look. "Do I have to destroy her?" He'd only created her a short while ago and he'd already become attached to her. Unfortunately, I knew how he felt and I also knew how difficult it would be for him to watch her die.

Delving into the mind of the newly made vampire, I sorted through her whirling thoughts. At the moment, her craving for blood was overwhelming. Beneath that was a contempt and hatred for men. Her parents had wanted a boy and had never loved her. She'd been a burden to them and they'd neglected her terribly. They'd kicked her out of their home when she'd turned fifteen and she'd had nowhere to go and no one to turn to. She'd become a prostitute from sheer desperation and because she'd been starving.

During the next five years, she'd killed seven of her more violent clients. She'd been caught the last time, but had only been charged for one of the murders. If we allowed her to live, she would retain her homicidal urge and would kill again just for the sheer pleasure of it. She'd use men for their blood and would then take great enjoyment from mauling them to death.

Shaking my head, I shattered his hopes. "I'm sorry, she's too dangerous."

"If I'm her master, doesn't she have to obey me? I could just order her not to hurt people," he said in her defence.

"And if you died?" Ishida pointed out. "Who would control her then?"

Shoulders slumping, my minion conceded defeat. We stepped back out of the blast zone as he levelled his weapon and fired a single shot into his fledgling's chest. She exploded three seconds later and bright red blood coated the walls. It quickly changed to sludge and slid to the floor, blending into the stain that was the rest of her remains.

Geordie sidled up to me with sorrow in his black eyes. "We should have been keeping a better watch on your soldiers as they fed their flesh hungers."

"It wasn't anyone's fault. Accidents happen." I should know, they happened to me often enough. Gesturing for everyone to gather around, I made a short speech. "You probably think I'm cruel for not letting her live." Gazes were averted, telling me that I was right on the mark. "You have to remember that our purpose is to keep the humans from harm, not to inflict it on them. If any of our kind shows signs that they are dangerous to humankind, they have to be eradicated."

Grudging nods followed my words. "It won't happen again, Mortis." Higgins spoke for all of my men. The ancient title sounded strange coming from the young American. He used it to remind his fellow fledglings that I was more than their sire and their leader. I was a creature that had been fated for a specific task. I'd created them to assist me in that task. They needed to realize that we had a higher purpose than just to survive and to feed our hungers.

After our second battle with one of the monstrous octosquids, we were once again covered in purple brains and goo. Bunking down in the catacombs would keep us safe from being discovered, but they lacked certain amenities, such as showers and food. If the world leaders truly wanted to help us this time, then they could start by finding us decent accommodation. It was the least they could do, considering we were saving their butts yet again.

Remembering the satellite phone that I'd slipped into a pocket, I reached for it and hit the dial button. It barely had a chance to ring before it was answered. "This is Prime Minister Townsend." Townsend was aiming for brisk, but he sounded as excited as a kid at Christmas. He knew who was on the other end of the phone, but he was surrounded by people and he was trying to be professional.

"This is Natalie. We've taken down the second alien, but not without casualties. It went berserk and destroyed a small island near China before we could destroy it." I gave him a couple of seconds to process that information. "The eight remaining octosquids aren't going to be happy about this and they will probably retaliate again. Until we figure out which city is in danger next, my men need somewhere safe to rest."

Far less excited now, Townsend responded quickly and lowered his voice. "Thank you for informing me about the attack. I'll notify the Chinese delegate privately." His voice rose when he continued. "I have taken the liberty of readying accommodation for you and your soldiers. We'll be waiting for your return."

There was no point dillydallying, so I immediately teleported everyone back to the meeting room in London. Townsend whirled around and made a startled sound when we appeared behind him. He hadn't even had a chance to put his cell phone away yet. "I must say, I wasn't expecting you to arrive quite so quickly. This trick of yours is going to take some getting used to."

I glanced over Townsend's shoulder at the Chinese delegate, who was listening to his cell phone intently. His expression remained stoic as he learned the bad news that the small island had just been destroyed. "I understand," he murmured. "Do what you can for the survivors." Slipping the phone into his pocket, he hesitated, then approached us.

It was automatic for me to bow to the man. Ishida hid his smile at the manners his people had instilled in me during my four month stay on his island. "Please accept my condolences for the suffering of your people," I said in Chinese. I wasn't sure which dialect I was speaking, but it matched the one he'd used on the phone.

Bowing in return, the delegate graciously accepted my offer. "My government extends its thanks to you and your people for stopping the alien before it could cause any more damage to our cities." We exchanged bows again and Igor elbowed Geordie before he could unleash a giggle at our rigidly formal behaviour.

Gregor raised a brow at me. "It would appear that you have become somewhat of a diplomat," he said when the delegate retreated.

"You can thank Ishida and Kokoro for teaching me my manners," I said dryly. "But I'll leave the diplomacy up to you." I'd learned a thing or two about how to deal with officials, but I'd never be in Gregor's league when it came to dealing with people in power.

One of Townsend's aides approached us deferentially. "If you would follow me, we have transportation waiting to take you to your hotel." He was a small, fidgety man and darted looks at us rather than meeting our eyes. It was common knowledge that we could bedazzle humans with a single look. There was no way for him to know that I could take control of his mind without bothering to meet his eyes at all now. As far as I knew, I was the only vampire with that particular skill.

"Luc and I still have to return the boat to the dock for maintenance," I said to our friends. "We'll do that now and we'll catch up to you soon."

I didn't particularly want to be parted from our friends and allies, but it would be far less draining to shift two people rather than two hundred of them. None of the humans were planning on doublecrossing us. I figured my small army would be safe enough for the short time that we'd be gone.

Luc linked his arm through mine and I shifted us both back to the boat. It had drifted far enough away from the island that I could no longer see the town that had been decimated by the octosquid. Waves and the tide were pushing the alien out to sea. Seagulls circled overhead, not quite daring to land and taste the wealth of flesh that was large enough to be an island of its own.

I took a few moments to search for the surviving octosquids and found their minds roiling in fury. The last of their kind, their instinct was to fight back before they were all gone. They were enraged that such small and insignificant beings were cutting them down so easily. They were also beginning to suspect that something other than the fragile humans was behind the attacks. At the moment, they were too furious to plan a revenge attack. Once they'd calmed down, retaliation would be inevitable. If they couldn't find us and exact their revenge, they'd settle for destroying yet another city that was full of the small, but tasty civilians.

Zapping Shadow back to the docks, Owens and his men were waiting. Townsend had called to advise them that we were on our way. The commander winced at the state of the boat and sent a swarm of men forward to fix the damage.

"You'd better make the repairs as quickly as possible," I

informed my human puppet. "I have a feeling we're going to need Shadow again soon."

Nodding, Owens flicked a curious glance at the small container that Luc was carrying, then boarded the vessel to assess how extensive the damage was.

Luc opened the case and offered me a blood bag. I accepted it reluctantly. Fresh blood would have been far better, but I didn't want to waste the precious resources that had been grudgingly donated by the hospital. Biting into the plastic, I swallowed a single mouthful and grimaced. The liquid was lukewarm and tasted spoiled. "Gross," I complained. "I think it's gone off." Only a few bags remained, but I still felt guilty about wasting them.

"Then we'd best dispose of the rest," Luc decided and tossed the bag that I'd punctured back in with the rest. The ice had melted and a couple of inches of water sloshed around in the bottom of the container. It was already beginning to turn pink from the blood oozing out of the punctured bag when he put the lid back on.

I took Luc's arm and sent out my senses in search of our people. Locating my army, I transported us into the back of one of several trucks. One of my soldiers swore beneath his breath at our sudden and unexpected arrival. Thankfully, no one had been startled enough to fire their weapons. They were too well disciplined and too well trained for that.

"Is there any blood left?" Geordie asked when he saw the container in Luc's arms.

"There is, but I am afraid that it has expired," my beloved told the disappointed teen as he placed the container at his feet.

"I didn't know blood could expire," Geordie said.

"Anything can turn bad if it isn't stored correctly," Kokoro told the teen.

Her words rang in my head like a death knell and I had no idea why. All I knew was that she'd touched on something that was somehow related to my dream of the strange, yet familiar monsters beneath the ruins. I kept the sudden sense of doom to myself. It was too vague to pass on to them anyway and we already had one problem to deal with. Why worry them further with yet another disaster that was yet to happen?

The truck slowed down then came to a stop as we reached our destination. One of my men opened the door and we leaped to the ground. I tilted my head back to take in our accommodation. In the midst of being refurbished, the small hotel was empty of humans. A lack of twenty-four hour room service wasn't a deterrent for those of us who drank blood to survive. As long as I had access to a shower and a comfortable bed, I'd be happy.

Scuttling towards the door, the aide did a double take when he spotted me in the crowd. He waited for me to catch up before pushing the door open. "Fresh clothing is in those bags," he said and pointed to a large bundle of packages that'd been stacked off to one side. "The upper floors are being remodelled, so your men will have to pair up two to a room on the first three floors."

I put his nervous fears to rest. "That's fine. Pass on my thanks to your Prime Minister for the rooms and clothing. Tell him to call me on the satellite phone if he needs us."

Wringing his hands together, the aide nodded and backed away. Unlike his boss, he wasn't a fan of vampires at all and was afraid to turn his back on us. My men began sorting through the packages, trying to find clothing to fit them. Another small bundle sat by itself. Wesley took a peek inside and handed it over to Kokoro. The former seer delved into the bag and took out a black leather jacket. It was far too small to fit any of the men, with the exception of Ishida and possibly Geordie. While his torso was longer than mine, his shoulders were about the same width.

Kokoro raised her brows at me in enquiry.

"Try it on," I urged her, reading her surface thoughts that she wouldn't mind taking the jacket for herself. She'd once worn a traditional kimono, but had grown used to wearing more modern clothing.

Ishida whistled in appreciation when his maker donned the jacket. Gregor's grin grew decidedly lecherous when she withdrew a pair of tight leather pants from the package next. I wondered if the outfit had been intended for me, but I didn't begrudge Kokoro's interest in the leathers. We were a similar size and she'd easily fit into it.

"I think this one is meant for you," she said with a wink and handed me the shopping bag.

Glancing inside, I was stunned to see a familiar sight. "Holy crap! I never thought I'd see this again."

"What is it?" Geordie demanded and pushed between Luc and me to peer inside the bag. "Is that what I think it is?" His hands reached in and pulled out a red leather outfit. It was nearly identical to the one that Ishida's talented tailors had made for me to wear during my battle with the First.

Ishida's sorrow welled up before he could force it away. "Who is responsible for this?" Neither he nor Kokoro possessed the skill to work leather or to tailor outfits this well. That skill had died along with their people.

Sending my consciousness across London, I zeroed in on a target and skimmed his thoughts. "It was Townsend." Astonishment met my pronouncement. "He's a closet vamp fan," I explained. "He has a copy of the footage that was taken when Sanderson's men and I attacked the First. One of the videos was taken before my suit was torn apart." The Brit had fantasized about seeing me in the red suit for over a decade. Not in a sexual way, but more in the way that a sci-fi fan wanted to see a comic book character come to life. He'd personally paid a team of seamstresses to create the outfits in record time.

"Is Townsend going to ask you to turn him into one of us?" Luc asked curiously. I sensed a hint of jealousy from him at the thought. He didn't have a problem with me turning soldiers into my servants, but he didn't like the idea of someone who might be obsessed with me becoming my minion.

"I don't think so," I reassured him. "He's happy just to interact with our kind and to do his bit to help his fellow humans."

Igor's expression was doubtful at my assessment of the Prime Minister's feelings towards us. "It is rare to meet a human who doesn't want to kill us on sight. I find it difficult to believe that one would voluntarily want to be on our side."

"Not all humans believe that we are evil," Gregor said. "Some remember that we have saved them on more than one occasion and are willing to give us the benefit of the doubt." I wasn't sure if he actually believed his own words, or if he was just playing the Devil's advocate.

"We will see how they feel once we have saved them for a fourth time," the Russian responded dourly. "Based on their track record so far, we can expect them to try to find a way to eradicate us once we have finished killing the giant jellyfish."

"That isn't going to happen," I said grimly. "At least not by the people who were at the conference," I added slyly.

Danton realized what I meant at the same time that Gregor did. "You may have befuddled their wits, but their compulsion to obey you will eventually wear off," the monk warned me. Gregor nodded his agreement.

My smile was both smug and nasty at the same time. "Their orders won't wear off if I will them to be permanent."

Kokoro looked at me in astonishment. "How did you learn this skill?"

I flicked a pained glance at Luc and drew my friends off to the side to talk in private. "I learned how to read minds while I was pining away for Luc in the mausoleum," I explained as my men paired up and took the key cards that were neatly lined up on the counter. "I spent a lot of time in particle form, where I'm ninety-nine percent thought and only one percent substance. Without the distraction of a body, my subconscious took over and it started to wander."

"I take it your consciousness wandered to our meetings," Gregor said dryly as the last pair of soldiers headed for the stairs. The aide dithered for a few moments, making sure he wasn't needed, then darted for the door. He cast a final look over his shoulder, then disappeared in an almost palpable wave of relief that he'd escaped with his life and with his wits still intact.

"It didn't take me long to realize that it was you guys that I was being drawn to," I replied. "It was frustrating not being able to hear what you were saying, so I had the idea to possess one of you."

Geordie made a face. "Was it on purpose or by accident that you possessed me?"

I'd told them this much so I might as well remain honest. "I chose you on purpose."

"I am not sure if I should be flattered or annoyed," the teen said.

Thanks to her former talents, Kokoro was better equipped to understand the process that I'd gone through than the others were. "Being inside Geordie's body helped you to learn how to read his thoughts," she surmised.

I nodded, grateful that someone understood. "Once I figured out how to do it, it was easy to read everyone else. I just wish I'd known that I was reading Luc's mind and that I wasn't just hallucinating our conversations. As for my hypnotism being so much stronger now, I'm guessing it became powered up when I was infused with the nanobots on Viltar."

I'd been shot with around fifty syringes that had been filled with a mixture of Viltaran blood and microscopic computers designed to turn their targets into alien clones. My veins had already carried an ancient infusion of nanobots. They had probably saved me from being turned into a grey-skinned, hulking monster. It was strangely ironic that the Viltaran micro robots that had created our kind had made me what I was today; the weirdest and most powerful vampire that had ever existed.

"Fate is responsible for the time that we've spent apart," my one true love said. "She ensured that you learned everything you needed to know to face the battles ahead."

His thoughts echoed mine completely. I was still

concerned that the powers that I'd gained might not be enough. "I might've learned how to read minds and to control humans permanently, but I don't see how that is going to help us to kill the octosquids."

Kokoro and Gregor shared a disturbed look. "Perhaps these skills are designed to tackle a threat beyond the one that we currently face," the former prophetess said.

A resigned dread filled the silence. I wasn't the only one wondering if our task of saving the humans would ever be over.

# Chapter Twenty-Four

I knew it would be a bad idea to share the shower with Luc, yet I didn't complain when he stepped inside the bathroom shortly after me. At first, I could only see him as an indistinct blur through the glass before I wiped the steam away and created a small window. I enjoyed the show as he gracefully stripped off before pulling the door open and stepping beneath the spray. There was just enough room for both of us.

Taking the soap out of my hands, he lathered his palms and turned me around so my back was to him. His talented fingers started at my lower back and worked their way up, massaging my tension away. "You carry the weight of the world on your shoulders," he said as his fingers slid upwards and dug into my knotted muscles.

"Being Mortis can really suck sometimes," I agreed. "But someone has to do it."

His hands moved lower again and I sensed that he was contemplating something far deeper than mere sex. Respecting his privacy, I didn't attempt to probe his thoughts. His hands stopped just above my butt rather than dipping down and initiating what would probably turn into scorching hot shower sex.

"Why me?" Luc asked cryptically.

Turning around to face him, I could barely see his solemn expression through the heavy steam. I hadn't bothered putting the cold water on, since the heat no longer affected either of us. I did so now and the steam dissipated enough for me to see him clearly. "What do you mean?" Long, lean and with his dark hair slicked back, he looked like a model for an expensive cologne ad. If anyone should be asking 'why me', it was me, not him.

"Why did you choose to love me?"

For a short while, I'd mistakenly believed that Fate had forced him to care for me. I'd also momentarily doubted whether my feelings for him were true. I knew better now. My love for him was very real and so were his feelings for me. "I didn't choose to love you, Luc, I couldn't *help*, but love you."

Instead of smiling, he frowned. "I was the first vampire that you met after your master died. You did not really have much of an opportunity to get to know any others of our kind."

Silvius hadn't had a chance to enjoy having a new servant after he'd turned me. As soon as I'd realized that he was an actual flesh and blood vampire, I'd staked him to death. Luckily for me, I hadn't expired after killing my maker. If I'd been a normal fledgling, I would have perished along with him.

All thoughts of having mind blowing shower sex fled as I realized my beloved was feeling insecure. Putting my hands on his chest, I stared up into his dark eyes. "We haven't always been together during this long and strange journey," I reminded him. "I've met lots of other vampires along the way." A disturbing number of them had tried to kill me and had ended up dead for their troubles. "You're the only one that I've ever wanted to get naked with."

Instead of reassuring him, I'd made it worse. "Sex is simply a hunger that we must feed, it means little to creatures such as us."

It meant a lot to me, but he was a lot older than me and he was far more jaded. "Do you remember the first night we met?" He nodded and a tiny smile came and went. I'd been hopelessly unsophisticated and completely different from the courtiers that he was used to. "Do you know what I saw when I looked at you?" This time he shook his head. "I didn't see an attractive vampire that I instantly wanted to hump. I saw an intelligent man who I thought I could trust. My instincts were right and you protected me even after you knew that I was going to bring death to our kind. You cared about me, which is more than I can say any man has ever done before. You've been there for me through some really shitty times and I know you'll be there for me through eternity."

I twined my fingers through his as he processed that. "Do you know what I see when I look at you now?" He shook his head wordlessly. "I see the man that I'd go to hell and back for. I see the man that I'm going to spend the rest of my life with. I wish you could see inside my head," I said in frustration. "There are a million reasons why I love you and not a single reason why I shouldn't."

In the room across from ours, Geordie let out a sob. "That is the most beautiful thing I've ever heard," the teen blurted and dissolved into tearless weeping. Igor murmured something comforting to his apprentice.

"I will never again give you a reason to doubt my love," Luc promised and disentangled our hands. I caught a fleeting glimpse of the guilt he still felt about giving me the cold shoulder on Viltar. Then his hands were in my hair and his mouth descended on mine. I had enough presence of mind to whisk us both up to the top floor of the hotel. Hopefully, our flesh hunger wouldn't spread to my men on the lower floors. In a few more seconds, I'd be beyond the ability to feel concern for my soldiers.

A sheet of plastic covered one wall that had been removed during the renovations. Wind whistled in through the gaps as a storm hit the city. Lightning flashed as I pushed Luc down onto his back and rode him hard. Unlike the courtiers that he'd entertained during the first four centuries of his life in the Court, I didn't need him to perform for me. Our lives had been frantic and fraught with danger from the first moment that we'd met. Maybe one day I'd feel the need to explore my softer sexual side. Right now it seemed that every moment might be our last and that speed was of the essence.

Sensitive to my mood as always, Luc didn't protest at the fast pace that I'd set. Lying back, he put his hands on my hips and let me do the work. His eyes began to glow red and I knew he was close to the edge. Leaning down, our chests touched and I fastened my mouth to his neck. Remembering the pleasure I'd felt when he'd pierced my vein, I bit into his neck and he tightened his grip on my hips. Swapping our positions so I was on the bottom, his fangs pierced my flesh in turn and we fed from each other as he pounded us both into ecstasy.

Basking in the aftermath for a few seconds, I became aware of the horrible taste in my mouth and grimaced. "Your blood still tastes like butt," I told my beloved. "Why couldn't it turn yellow and tasty like mine?"

Not offended in the least by my criticism, he lifted my hand and kissed my knuckles. "Because it was you and not me who was destined to be Mortis." It was a fair point and I couldn't argue with him.

Still wet from our shower, we were covered in fine dust from our romp on the floor. In the blink of an eye, we were back in the still running shower. This time, we managed to finish washing without feeling the sudden need for privacy. Fortunately, our flesh hunger had been contained on the top floor and my soldiers hadn't been affected by our quick tryst.

We'd just finished donning our new clothing when the satellite phone rang. Luc finished tying the laces in the back of my new red leather suit as I answered it. "This is Natalie." Wearing the tight scarlet outfit, I had a sudden sense of déjà vu and flashed back to the battles we'd faced with General Sanderson. Unlike that traitorous bastard, none of the humans we'd had contact with so far would be able to plot against us.

"Natalie," Townsend said in a panic, dispensing with a greeting, "turn on your TV!"

Overhearing the request, Luc picked up the remote control and pressed a button. The television came to life, set on a low volume. The program had been interrupted by an emergency broadcast. A female presenter spoke in a grave tone as a camera depicted dozens of black tentacles emerging from the ocean. A gigantic, lumbering black body followed. "This video was filmed a short time ago by a brave survivor of an alien attack against Los Angeles."

We watched in horror as buildings collapsed under the octosquid as it heaved itself up onto dry land. Tentacles snatched humans from the streets and peeled them from their vehicles and dwellings. Entire blocks were buried beneath its appendages as it stuffed shrieking food into its mouth. Whoever was filming the devastation shook in terror, making the picture tremble as well.

"This isn't the only alien attack that is currently underway," the news presenter continued. "We have footage of two other colossal entities that are also attacking land as I speak."

I winced as the screen split into three separate pictures. Each one showed an enraged alien in the process of demolishing their chosen city. "As you can see," the reporter continued, "a Brazilian and Russian city are also being decimated. It is unknown what action the authorities could possibly take against creatures as large as these."

Luc muted the TV as Townsend barked a laugh through the phone. "What *can* the authorities do against the aliens? We can't nuke them." He hesitated for a second then asked, "Can we?"

"I wouldn't recommend it while they're still attacking land," I told him. "You could try it when they return to the water." I suspected it wouldn't do much good if they did.

"Do you think it would do any good?" he asked, eerily echoing my thought.

At a knock on the door, Luc opened it to let Gregor and Kokoro in. Our hearing was exceptional and Gregor had an answer ready for Townsend. "Tell the Prime Minister that it would most likely take several nuclear warheads to even make a dent in the aliens' flesh."

I relayed the information and Townsend sighed despondently. "Is there anything at all that we can do to stop them?"

Taking the satellite phone, Gregor spoke to the politician directly. "You could try to blast them with missiles, but I doubt the damage would be very extensive. You might just anger them further. We believe that they'll eventually heal any damage that is done to them. I am afraid that targeting the brain is the only effective way to kill them." It was doubtful that the humans would be able to penetrate the bodies of the octosquids deeply enough to be able to cause them any harm.

Gregor held the phone out so everyone could hear the Prime Minister's next words as the rest of our friends filed into the room. "The Americans and Russians are about to launch a counterattack against the aliens. They're sending fighter jets after them right now."

"They can probably kiss their jets goodbye," Geordie said in a tone that was too quiet for the Brit to hear. Ishida gave a single nod of agreement.

"How long will it be before they make contact?" Igor asked. Then said, "Never mind," as the jets appeared on one of the screens.

Circling the monster that was savaging Russia, the fighter pilots chose an angle to attack and unleashed their missiles. Just as Gregor had predicted, the leviathan barely felt the tiny gouges that appeared in its flesh. Half a dozen tentacles snaked out and smacked the jets from the sky like irritating mosquitos.

"Well, that was a waste of time and resources,"

Townsend mourned softly as he watched the debacle unfold on his own screen.

Word of the Russians' failure didn't spread to the Americans in time. Rockets were fired and more jets were slapped out of the air after causing very little damage to their target. We watched in silence as the trio of black aliens continued to rampage through the cities. Over a million humans in total had already been tossed into their gullets and they still weren't satisfied. This was just the start of what would turn into daily life as the monsters moved further inland to feed.

All trace of Townsend's boyish enthusiasm had disappeared after seeing the behemoths in action. "I know we've treated your people badly and we probably don't deserve to be saved again, but you have to stop them before they eat the entire population of the planet. Please."

His heartfelt pleas were unnecessary, but I hastened to reassure him. "We will," I promised. We had to. Not just because it was our job to rescue humanity, but because no one else could stop the aliens.

# Chapter Twenty-Five

"What is our best strategy?" Luc asked Gregor.

Gregor watched the TV intently. He shifted his attention from one octosquid to the next, studying them closely and searching for weaknesses that we could exploit. Far less agile on land, the leviathans lumbered deeper into the cities that they were feasting upon. They demolished anything that stood in their path, no matter how large or small. People looked tinier than ants beside the octosquids as they attempted to flee. Even LA looked like a model rather than a real city.

I was far from a master strategist, but even I knew that two hundred vampire soldiers weren't going to be enough to stop all eight of the aquatic creatures. Many more cities would be destroyed before we could kill them all.

Gregor agreed with my unspoken thought. "We need to recruit more soldiers if we want to stop our adversaries from decimating every coastal town on the planet." Once the coastal towns were gone, they'd have to delve deeper inland to search for more food. I doubted anywhere would be safe. *Except maybe the largest deserts.* They wouldn't offer much sanctuary to any humans that might survive, since they contained little food and even less water.

Igor was slightly sceptical of Gregor's idea. "Are we going to scour every prison cell in Europe in the hope of finding worthy fighters?"

Shaking his head, Gregor gestured at the satellite phone in my hand. "That will take too long. I propose that we ask for volunteers instead. Another fourteen hundred men and women should help to turn the tide in our favour."

"How can Nat possibly turn that many people?" Geordie protested. "She only has a limited amount of blood in her body!"

Already grimacing at the thought of slicing myself open over and over again, I touched the teen on the shoulder to calm him down. "As long as I feed every now and then, my blood seems to replenish itself quickly enough."

Geordie still wasn't happy with the idea and his shoulders slumped. "There has to be a better way than cutting yourself open to feed them your blood."

"There is a way," Ishida said as an idea occurred to him. "You could copy what the American scientists did to me and set up an intravenous system."

The experiment to replace Ishida's diseased vampire blood with human blood had nearly killed him. I'd be in no danger, since we would only be draining my blood. "Great idea, Ishida." He inclined his head modestly at my praise.

"Now we just have to convince more soldiers to join

us," Igor said. "If Townsend is truly our greatest fan, he should be happy to offer us his assistance."

There was only one way to test that theory so I dialled the Prime Minister. He answered almost immediately. "Townsend here."

"We've come to the conclusion that there aren't enough of us to tackle all eight of the remaining octosquids," I said bluntly. "We need soldiers to volunteer to be converted into vampires and we have to do it soon. The rest of the aliens won't be content with feeding on fish once they see how tasty humans are. Once they head for land," I cast a glance at the footage that was being shown in full colour on the TV, "well, you've seen for yourself what will happen."

He didn't need any further convincing. "I take it you are only interested in candidates trained in both combat and weaponry?" I caught his brief flare of regret that he was a politician instead of a soldier and therefore wasn't suitable to join our ranks.

"They'd be our first choice. Trained soldiers would be our best chance of beating these things. We'll need at least two hundred more soldiers per alien."

Doing the maths, Townsend exhaled in shock. "You want to turn another fourteen hundred people into vampires?" His voice lowered so no one would overhear him. A low hum of background noise told me that he wasn't alone.

"Yes." I didn't give him time to process the information. "We'll need someone to set up an intravenous system and a few people for me to munch on through the process. We'll also need more volunteers to feed the fledglings when they rise." All this would take time to set up and dawn was on its way.

"I'll make the arrangements," Townsend replied. "I'll contact you once everything is in place."

Several minutes later, and far sooner than I'd expected, the satellite phone rang again. Gregor frowned at the device as I answered it and held it out for everyone to listen in on the conversation. Danton, his warriors and most of my soldiers had crowded into the hallway and rooms nearby to listen in. A sinking feeling in the pit of my stomach hinted that our plan wasn't going to go the way we'd hoped.

"This is Natalie," I said.

Townsend's voice was heavy with regret and frustration when he responded. "Natalie, I'm terribly sorry to have to inform you that I am unable to assist you with your request for volunteers."

Incredulous exclamations swept through my troops. "Why not?" I could have gleaned the information straight from him, but everyone needed to hear this so I'd let him stammer his excuses.

We heard footsteps as he crossed the room, then he closed a door and the background voices became muffled. He obviously wanted to have this conversation in private. "I put your proposal to the delegates of the world leaders, mistakenly thinking they were of the same opinion as me, that you are here to help us. Unfortunately, they are of the opinion that this may well set you and your people up to take control once the threat of the aliens has been squashed."

"Are they crazy?" Geordie burst out. "Do they realize how many lives will be lost if they just leave it up to us few to kill the octosquids?"

Townsend's voice became small as he hit us with the rest of his message. Geordie had spoken loudly enough for him to have overheard. "That's another thing that I have to advise you of. They don't want your help anymore."

I blinked at that and almost laughed, thinking it had to be a joke. Giving into temptation, I sent out part of my consciousness and delved into his mind. What I saw there wiped away all traces of my momentary amusement. "They think we're behind the alien attacks," I told the others softly. "They believe we deliberately gave the Viltarans the Earth's location so they'd feel obligated to us when we returned and saved the day. It's apparently our fault that the octosquids hitched a ride and are now eating everything they come across." That last part *was* our fault, but the rest of their theory was completely bogus.

"I'm so sorry, Natalie," Townsend said. "I've tried to tell them that you're the good guys rather than the villains, but they don't trust you."

Igor gave the satellite phone a glare that would have stripped the hide off Townsend if he'd been there in person. "How do your 'world leaders' propose to fight these monsters?" he sneered. "Their missiles have no effect on them and they have no way of penetrating deep inside their bodies to destroy their brains."

Before the Prime Minister could respond, the door opened and feet stomped towards him. A moment later, the phone went dead. Still inside Townsend's mind, I looked through his eyes as Prissy Pete snatched the phone out of Townsend's hand. The glint in his eye was icy and disdainful as he placed his Prime Minister under guard. Two soldiers stepped forward to escort Townsend from the room.

Throwing the phone onto the bed, I bit back the urge to let out a string of foul curses. Luc's hand on my lower back had the calming effect that he was aiming for. "Townsend has just been put under guard, so we can't count on his help anymore," I told my small army.

Kokoro accurately summed up our dilemma. "So, it appears that Fate has once again taken control of our destinies. It is restricting our numbers and has taken away our hope of assistance from the armed forces."

"Now that we know the humans do not trust us, I suggest we leave this hotel immediately," Gregor said.

Sudden alarm thrummed through me and I sent out my senses. Just as Gregor had surmised, soldiers were already on their way to surround the building. While my six closest friends and I were indestructible, none of the others were.

"They've sent soldiers to attempt to eradicate us, haven't they?" Ishida asked.

I nodded unhappily. None of the delegates that I'd bamboozled had made the decision, it had come from higher up on the political ladder. "They'll arrive in a few minutes, so grab your gear and head for the lobby."

Everyone scattered to gather their few possessions that Townsend had thoughtfully provided for us. The approaching soldiers were only half a block away when I whisked my army back to the safety of the catacombs in France.

While my soldiers retreated to the rooms that they'd claimed earlier, Igor called the rest of us together. "Since it has been decided by the authorities that we can no longer be trusted, we should retrieve as many weapons and ammunition as possible from the underground warehouse before they shift them to another location."

Thankful once again for his practicality, I barely waited for the others to agree before moving into action. Danton and his five warriors accompanied us to the secret weapons cache on the outskirts of London. Stacking containers in neat rows, they continued to work as I transported the gear to the prison cells on the lower levels of the catacombs.

By dawn, we'd stolen everything that would be useful to us from the storeroom and returned to our hideout. We now had more than enough weapons and ammo to deal with the octosquids, yet the humans didn't want our help. Once again, they'd turned on us, but this time they hadn't waited for us to save the day first. They'd been on their way to stab us in the back, but this time I'd managed to avoid any losses on our side. I was frankly amazed that they'd even tried to plot against us after I'd bamboozled the American troops and had reduced the US president to chunks of meat. They were either very brave, or very stupid, I couldn't quite decide which.

Gathering in the plush living area of the courtier's former quarters, we dragged several sofas into a square. Geordie was pressed up against my left side and Luc was on my right. Once upon a time, I would have felt smothered by the contact. Now, I couldn't imagine not having them near me.

"What the hell are we going to do now?" I asked without preamble. "Do we just let the humans screw up and die?" I was under no illusions that they would be able to take on the gargantuan aliens and actually win.

"Now that Danton's master is deceased and I no longer have the gift of prophecy," Kokoro said, "we are unable to foresee the future."

Sitting on the other side of Geordie, Ishida leaned forward to see my face. "Natalie often has dreams of what is to come. Have you had any strange dreams lately?"

"The last dream I had was about a creepy old ruin that I think was an abandoned monastery. I haven't dreamed about the octosquids since we started fighting them."

Momentarily crestfallen at the reminder that he was masterless, Danton made a suggestion. "If Mortis is our only oracle, perhaps she should try to sleep and see what message her dreams bring us."

*I love it when people talk about me in the third person,* I thought wryly. Everyone acted as if Mortis was a separate entity. Latin for death, it was more than just a title. I *was* death and it now seemed that I always would be.

Luc made the decision for me and drew me to my feet. "Someone should stay alert and monitor the news. Wake us if any developments arise."

"I will keep watch," Igor volunteered.

"Do you even know how to operate a laptop?" Geordie asked his mentor with a hint of a grin.

Turning his shaggy head, Igor glowered at his apprentice. "I know how to operate a computer, you impudent whelp." He lunged at the teen and Geordie fled with a screech that was half laughter and half fright.

Smiling at their antics, I followed Luc to the bedroom that we'd claimed as our own.

# Chapter Twenty-Six

My mind was racing, making it almost impossible for me to fall asleep. Fate had created me to save the human race, but she'd just hobbled my ability to pull off another rescue attempt. She wouldn't allow me to create more of our kind, so I was at a loss as to what to do next.

Pulling me into his arms, Luc ran a hand up and down my back, lulling me towards the oblivion that my team was counting on. Eventually, my eyes closed and I succumbed to sleep.

Standing in the middle of a crowded street in London, I stared up at a gigantic TV screen. Motorists had stopped their cars and had climbed out to watch the scene that was playing out. Half a world away, four fighter jets menaced the octosquid that had just finished destroying LA. Finally satisfied with the destruction that it had caused, the gargantuan lumbered towards the ocean. It ignored the jets as they zoomed past.

The pilots waited for the creature to reach the water before firing their weapons. Instead of shooting useless missiles that did little damage, this time they unleashed a different barrage of projectiles. Shocked awe sighed through the crowd as they winced at the bright light that flared on the screen. Horror shivered down my spine when four distinctive and deadly mushroom clouds formed. The gigantic black alien disappeared from sight and I crossed my fingers that the nuclear missiles had managed to kill the thing.

A cheer rang out when the cloud dissipated and the creature appeared to be much smaller than it had been. The cheers died as they realized the pilots had just doomed any survivors of a once great city to death by radiation poisoning.

Cries and moans of disappointment swept through the crowd as the behemoth rose out of the water.

"Can't anything kill these monsters?" an agonized Brit shouted.

Only a small portion of its body had been damaged by the nuclear warheads and only I knew why. Back on Viltar, I'd witnessed them flattening themselves down to speak to their Kveet allies. Even now that they were gigantic, it seemed that they could still flatten themselves down low enough to be able to duck beneath the missiles.

Delving into the mind of the alien, I drew back from the enraged mental bellows as it called on its brethren to attack. This time, there wouldn't be three assaults on coastal cities, but eight. The humans had utilized their most fearsome weapons that were in their possession and they'd only succeeded in annoying their target.

Before I could wake and advise my friends and allies of impending disaster, I was sucked into another dream.

Once again, I stood in the ruins of a monastery. Before me, the robed statue held a bowl as an offering to an unknown deity. Nothing rushed forward to push me down the stairs this time, so I descended them voluntarily. I sensed no eyes watching me and the area felt deserted.

Darkness waited at the bottom of the stairs this time and I traversed the hallway with my senses on full alert. The heavy metal door at the end of the corridor was standing open a couple of inches. I pushed it open all the way and stepped inside.

The last time I'd been in this room, I hadn't really taken in much of my surroundings. The strange creatures had distracted me from the fact that I was in a laboratory. This time, the room was empty of life and I had the opportunity to examine it in greater detail.

A series of cages lined the far side of the room. Their doors had burst open and either hung askew, or had come off their hinges completely. The metal was marred by dents and claw marks that had been made by fists or feet. Each cage was large enough to hold even the tallest Viltaran that I'd ever seen, and Uldar had been eleven feet tall.

Whatever had been caged inside had broken free and had slaughtered their captors. Dried blood smeared the ceiling, walls and floor. Drag marks where the bodies had been carried away led to a different door and disappeared into another dark hallway.

The structure was ancient, but some effort had been made to modernise it. Repairs had been made to the rough stone, which was a direct contrast to the modern computers and other equipment. Gurneys had been tipped over and what appeared to be medical equipment had been smashed to pieces. Righting one of the gurneys, I took in the sheer size of it. Far larger and stronger than usual, it had been designed to carry something a lot bigger and heavier than a human.

I'd only caught a fleeting look at the creatures in my previous dream. The clues I was seeing now didn't help me much to determine what they were. The prophet had warned Danton that I had to be vigilant and my dream was telling me the same thing. I wasn't sure what was coming next, but it gave me hope that we would at least be able to vanquish the octosquids. Why else would Fate send me a preview of the next disaster before we'd finished dealing with the current one?

Snapping awake, I found Luc soundly asleep beside me. It would be safer to travel alone while I attempted to avert what would be an utter disaster, so I let him sleep. Dissolving my flesh down to dust motes and leaving my clothes behind, I teleported to LA. Through the eyes of one of the few survivors, I saw the fighter jets arrive. They circled the retreating octosquid, preparing to fire their deadly but ultimately useless weapons. Before they could unleash death on their own people, I split my consciousness.

Working simultaneously, I delved into the thoughts of all four fighter pilots. I'd never tried anything like this before, but it was surprisingly easy to issue the same order to all of them. I commanded them all to return to their home base without firing a single shot. *Tell your commanding officer that firing nuclear weapons at these aliens won't kill them. It will instead force all eight of them to attack.* I whispered the message into their minds and sent them home.

Returning to the catacombs, I re-formed my body and dressed. Luc heard me moving around and woke, instantly alert. He'd only been asleep for a couple of hours, but we didn't require much rest anymore. The Viltaran blood was still strong in our veins and I was pretty sure the changes were permanent.

Igor was watching the laptop intently when we entered the living room. Luc and I sat beside him as another reporter tried to describe the scene that was playing out. "I'm not sure what is happening," the attractive brunette said in confusion. "Instead of launching their planned attack against the aliens, it appears the jets are returning to their home base."

The Russian turned to me with an eyebrow raised. "I take it you are responsible for the aborted attack?"

Before I could respond in the affirmative, the satellite phone rang. Gregor had prudently brought it along with us and had placed it on the coffee table beside the computer. Luc handed it to me and I answered it, knowing who was on the other end even before he spoke.

"This is Admiral Peter York," Prissy Pete said stonily.

"What can I do for you, Admiral?" I asked. I suspected this wasn't a friendly call and I wasn't wrong.

"What right do you have to meddle in our affairs?" he demanded.

"Like it or not, I'm the custodian of the human race. Personally, I couldn't care less if you all became extinct," I told him honestly, "but something else seems to have other plans."

Fighting down his fury, the admiral paced the floor of what had probably once been Prime Minister Townsend's office. "We do not want nor need your help," he spat. "I personally absolve you of any perceived responsibility that you feel you have towards humankind. Stop hypnotizing our armed forces and let us do our jobs!"

Waiting for him to finish his rant, I found myself surrounded by my friends. Danton and two of his warriors were also listening in. Newly made, my soldiers had reverted to the death-like state that came with sunrise. They wouldn't wake until the sun had disappeared again.

"Are you finished?" I asked the admiral calmly and continued before he could reply. "You may not know this, but I can see the future. I just had a dream of the Americans bombing the octosquid and I saw the result of their attack."

"Really?" Prissy Pete said with heavy sarcasm. "What exactly happened in your dream?"

"The alien avoided the attack and was only slightly wounded by the nuclear warheads. The bombs only made it mad enough to call the rest of its friends to the attack."

Silence followed my statement. "How did you know they were going to fire nuclear warheads?" the admiral asked quietly.

"I told you, I can see the future."

"If you could see the future, you would have known that the Americans were going to send you into space ten years ago," he scoffed.

"I knew they were going to do something horrible to us, but my dreams aren't always easy to interpret," I responded. "This one was crystal clear. If you continue to bomb the aliens, it will result in the destruction of your world. You're probably doomed anyway, but it will happen much faster if you don't listen to my advice."

Stubborn to the last, he dismissed my warning. "Stay away from our soldiers," he repeated. "We'll face down this invasion without your help."

"Why are humans so stupid?" Geordie asked crankily as I tossed the phone back onto the coffee table. Landing with more force than I'd intended it to, it bounced off and fell to the carpet.

"They are afraid," Igor said as we watched the octosquid disappear beneath the waves on the screen. "They do not trust us and they believe their weaponry is sufficient to destroy anything."

Tucking his fist beneath his chin, Gregor sank down onto a sofa and watched Igor surf the internet for more information on the alien attacks. His stare became more intent as the Russian stopped on a map that had been marked with worldwide sightings of the creatures. "Are those markings accurate?" he asked me.

Sending out my senses, I picked up on the current locations of all eight octosquids. "More or less," I replied.

Ishida studied the markings as well and his lips quirked in a smile that disappeared just as quickly as it had appeared. "The aliens near Brazil and South Africa are quite close to each other," he pointed out.

Geordie shrugged his thin shoulders. "So?"

"So," the former child king said with a glance at Gregor, "perhaps we could perform a test to see just how territorial these creatures are."

Still clueless, Geordie's brows lowered in confusion. "How are we going to do that?"

"We'll need bait," Igor mused. "Humans this time, since

the jellyfish know we are a danger to them."

Gregor began to smile. "Bait can be arranged, but it will require skill and finesse to bring the two monsters together." He was smiling at me as he said that and it was my turn to be confused. I'd been accused of many things since becoming one of the undead, but I'd never been accused of having finesse before. "Exactly how many humans do you think you'd be able to transport on a large boat?" Gregor enquired.

Skimming his mind, I had to give it to the crafty old vampire, his plan was sneaky and it just might work. "There's only one way to find out," I replied. "Wish me luck."

It would be full daylight where I was about to go, so none of my friends could come with me. Geordie patted Luc on the shoulder consolingly before I disappeared. "Do not fear for Nat. She will be safe, Luc." My beloved sent the teen a sardonic glance when he used my nickname for him.

Arriving in South Africa, I dissolved my hands and head so they wouldn't melt beneath the unrelenting glare of the sun. The rest of my body would be safe for a few minutes. The red leather suit would protect me well enough.

Only my eyes remained solid as I searched the docks for a suitable vessel. With the threat of alien invasion imminent, no one was stupid enough to brave the ocean and the docks were empty of life. A short search rewarded me with a boat that was around the same size as Shadow. This one was far shabbier and was made of a much lighter metal. I hoped that meant it wouldn't take as much out of me when I was ready to teleport it. With the transportation sorted, now I just needed to round up the bait.

# Chapter Twenty-Seven

Sending out my senses, I located a large number of humans and whisked myself into their midst. Crowded into a stadium, they were watching a football match. Intent on the game, no one noticed the headless and handless vampire that was dressed in a vivid red leather suit.

A goal was scored and the spectators surged to their feet, screaming in either agony or ecstasy. Seizing the opportunity, I reached out and touched the closest meat sacks. I gathered as many humans into my net as I could and transported them all to the docks.

"What just happened?" a frightened man asked as he looked around wildly.

"Where are we?" someone else called.

Before panic could overwhelm the group, I drew them all beneath my spell. I no longer had to bamboozle humans individually and captured the entire group instantly. As long as I had contact with their minds, I could bend them to my will.

I'd gotten lucky and had snared nearly three hundred people to use as bait for my trap. At my command, they began to file onto the boat. When it was full, I escorted the extra sixty spectators back to their game. The match had been halted and security guards were attempting to clear the stands. Exclamations of fright sounded when some of the members of the crowd who had so mysteriously disappeared returned just as unexpectedly. Their hypnotism would wear off quickly, but none would remember where they'd gone or what had happened to them.

Returning to the boat, I was hidden from the sun in the cockpit and re-formed my flesh. As docile as sheep, my minions made no sounds of protest as the docks disappeared and they were suddenly surrounded by open water.

Apart from a faint gnawing hunger, I hadn't been affected by shifting the large weight of a fully loaded boat. Just as I'd hoped, it seemed that my teleportation was growing stronger with practice.

Deep in the water beneath us, the hungry octosquid was slumbering. Unlike it's comrade who'd fed on the coastal town in Brazil, this one had yet to go in search of human treats. Sensing that some had come within its grasp, it stirred and woke. Sending out its radar, it identified the humans as food and sped towards the surface.

Timing would be crucial to pull this off. I waited for the last possible moment before zapping the boat out of the alien's reach. From a safe distance, I watched the octosquid explode out of the water with its mouth wide open so that it could swallow us whole. Its body followed, rising up and up out of the water and throwing us into its shadow. Closing its mouth, it swallowed. Even from several hundred yards away, I heard the rushing sound of tons of water disappearing into its gullet.

Tentacles fanned out to break its fall as it descended back into the water, sending a ripple of waves towards us. Settling back down until just the top of it was showing, it became aware of us at the same time as it realized it had just swallowed nothing but sea water.

Covered in endlessly gnashing mouths, dozens of gigantic black tentacles boiled towards us. I skipped the boat out of reach as the leviathan lumbered after us. I'd only ever seen one of the creatures move quickly in a dream and I was astounded by its speed when it raced through the water towards us. Concentrating fiercely, I skipped us backwards, keeping most of my attention on the pursuing alien. It was hungry, confused and enraged that we were able to stay beyond its reach. Surrounded by humans, it didn't detect me on its radar and I hoped it didn't realize that I was leading it into a trap.

Far to the northwest, the second octosquid sensed a rival closing in on its territory as we rapidly shifted closer. Still sated from its large meal of Brazilian civilians, it wasn't particularly hungry, but its territorial instincts were roused as it realized its comrade wasn't going to stop at the invisible border of its realm. It sent out a telepathic warning to the approaching alien, but it was ignored as the rival octosquid doggedly chased its prey.

Just as Gregor had predicted, it took all of my skills and even greater finesse to remain just ahead of the Goliath that pursued us. I split my concentration between the two hulking beasts as we moved across the invisible boundary line between their territories. The instant the rival jellyfish crossed the line, a confrontation became unavoidable.

Defending its watery domain, the octosquid at our back roared a challenge and charged. We were caught between the two beasts, but I wasn't about to teleport to safety until I knew that my trap had worked. The extra-terrestrials raced towards us as I skimmed the boat rapidly along the surface of the water. Each of the beasts had a different intent. One wanted to feed on us and the other wanted to destroy its rival.

I sensed the change as the hungry alien finally realized that it had encroached on another's territory. Caught in a figurative land that didn't belong to it, it was now obligated to defend itself. It instantly forgot about us and turned its attention to its former ally.

My bait would no longer be necessary, so I teleported the boat back to the docks. I could have kept track of the monumental battle remotely, but I felt compelled to watch the two leviathans duke it out with my own eyes. Leaving my clothing and the humans behind, I became floating particles and returned to witness the encounter.

Reaching the pair, I formed eyes just in time to see them clash. Tentacles shot out, landing blows that tore hunks of tough flesh away. Their numerous mouths bit and chewed anything they came into contact with. Roaring in rage, their mouths gaped wide open and several rows of scissor sharp teeth descended.

Grabbing hold of the interloper, the defending octosquid lurched forward to bite deeply into the body of its rival. The second alien inserted a dozen tentacles into the gnashing mouth, stopping it from taking out a chunk of flesh. Purple blood gushed as the tentacles were severed, but more appendages lashed out, boring through the thick black hide.

Grappling, biting and causing mini-tsunamis to form with each lurch, they fought for supremacy. Turning a portion of my attention away from the battle, I sent out my consciousness and found the other six aliens awaiting the outcome of the clash with interest. Earth was a small planet and the fewer rivals they had, the more food there would be for the rest. They might have been allies on Viltar, but now that they were fully grown, there wasn't enough life to sustain them all. Since this was a battle to the death over territorial rights, there would be no retribution towards the humans. None of them knew that this encounter had been engineered. At least I hoped they didn't know. I didn't sense any suspicion amongst them.

Twisting out of the rival's grasp, the defending monster reared up out of the ocean. Like something out of a nightmare, it rose high into the sky before crashing back down on top of its enemy.

Shrieking in pain, the interloper's tentacles went limp as it came close to losing consciousness. The defending octosquid latched onto the semi-conscious body of its adversary and shoved half a dozen tentacles into a deep wound in its hide. Rooting around inside, it ignored the weak struggles of its enemy and held on tightly as it strove to reach the brain.

Knowing that it was about to die, the rival went into a frenzy. Its tentacles clutched at the air and water as it felt the membrane that protected its thought centre break apart. Its bellows rose in pitch then suddenly ceased as the arms of its enemy lashed around, destroying its brain utterly.

Casting aside the body of its foe, the winner lifted its

gory tentacles into the air and let out a roar of triumph. It had just secured more territory, which gave it a greater chance of survival. The remaining six rivals mentally saluted the victor, while secretly coveting more water for themselves.

My bamboozled human minions were waiting for me when I returned to the dock. Pouring my particles into my clothes, I transported them back to the mostly deserted stadium. Several police officers shouted and ran towards the crowd as I released them from my mental bondage. They wouldn't be able to tell the authorities what had happened to them while they'd been gone. My friends, allies and I were the only ones who would know that they'd been used as a lure for a ravenous alien.

# Chapter Twenty-Eight

Luc was sitting on the edge of the couch when I reappeared in the catacombs that had become our temporary home. Sending me a relieved smile, he patted the empty seat beside him in invitation.

Geordie plopped down beside me as I settled next to Luc. "You were gone for hours," the teen complained. "Did your plan work?"

Gregor took a seat opposite from me and waited expectantly. Kokoro and Ishida sat on either side of him and Igor and Danton shared another couch. Danton's warriors stood guard behind him. They weren't expecting treachery from us, it was just habit for them to stand guard duty.

"It worked perfectly," I said, much to their relief. They were silent as I gave them a brief rundown of the operation.

"The remaining seven octosquids have no idea that you orchestrated the battle?" Gregor asked me shrewdly.

"Nope," I said with more than a hint of smugness. "Each of them is hiding it from the others, but they're planning on being the only one of their species left on our planet."

Gregor wasn't at all surprised by that revelation. "The Earth cannot sustain even one of their kind forever, let alone seven of them."

Lounging beside him, Ishida cocked his head to the side in query. "Do you think we will be able to use this ploy again?"

Nodding, the crafty old vampire smiled. "I do not see why it wouldn't work a second or even a third time, as long as we are careful."

Without needing to be urged to, Igor performed another search on the internet and pulled up the world map again. Eight red dots still appeared, but we knew one of them could now be discounted. None of the other aliens were in danger of trespassing on each other's domains, but I'd just proven that it was possible to force two of them together. I just needed the appropriate bait to dangle in front of them.

"Which aliens should Natalie target next?" Kokoro asked her beloved.

Studying the screen that Igor had angled towards him, Gregor narrowed his eyes as he went deep into thought. "I believe we should turn our attention to these two." He pointed out the octosquid that had devastated the coastal town in Russia and the one that had attacked LA. "They have both tasted human flesh now and seemed to have found it to their liking. They are much more likely to continue to search for their food on land."

I was doubtful of his plan for one reason. "I'm not sure one small boatload of people will be enough of a lure to get them to follow me. Not if they know there are millions of meals on nearby land."

As always, he was one step ahead of me. "How many humans do you think you're capable of transporting?"

I'd picked up three hundred easily enough and I had a feeling I could have snatched up many more. "Several hundred, I guess. I doubt I'd be able to teleport that many if I have to transport them on a boat." The larger the group was, the bigger the boat would have to be. Moving inanimate objects seemed to be more difficult than teleporting living or undead beings.

"What if you didn't bother with a boat?" Ishida asked.

He was turning out to be almost as crafty as Gregor. A brief trip into their minds showed an almost identical plan. "Just to be clear," I said, "you want me to kidnap hundreds of humans, dump them in the ocean without a boat and use them to lure one of the octosquids into their rival's territory?"

Exchanging glances, the vamps nodded. "Precisely," Gregor confirmed.

Showing his sentimental side, Geordie made a protest. "Won't the meat sacks, I mean humans, panic and drown?" He frowned at me when I sniggered at his usage of my pet name for the humans.

"They won't panic," I reassured them. "They'll be totally unaware of what is happening to them." He still wasn't appeased, so I heaved a mental sigh. "I'm aware that we're supposed to be saving them, not drowning them. I'll make sure they have life jackets."

Still suspicious, Geordie gave me a grudging nod. "Where will you get life jackets from?"

"From a boat, I guess." I was a bit vague on that point, but we'd figure it out.

"It will be dark soon," Danton observed. Even when we were deep beneath the surface, we could still sense the sun. "Once your men awaken, perhaps we could all assist you with obtaining enough life jackets for the meat sacks."

Geordie's lips quivered at the deadpan expression on the monk's face. Ishida sniggered, I sniggered then all three of us were laughing. Luc raised his eyes heavenward and I caught a fleeting thought that I was just as much of an adolescent as the teens. Strangely, he seemed to think my childishness was part of my charm.

When my warriors woke, their hungers woke with them. Still fledglings, they had yet to master their desire for blood and sex. At least being sired by me, they had far more control than any other newly made vampire. It helped that each of them had years of training and discipline from being in the military or a member of a police force.

Since it had worked so well last time, I teleported our group back into the women's prison in China. We subdued the guards and the inmates once again fell beneath the spell of my soldiers as they satisfied their hungers.

This time, I forced myself to remain rather than scurrying away to protect my delicate sensibilities. If my blood had been normal, red would have stained my cheeks from the embarrassment of listening to my men make the female prisoners cry out in pleasure. The bones of Luc's hand groaned in protest when my grip became too tight. A faint red light glowed from my eyes as I fought down my own need for sex. I was supposed to be a leader and it was about time I acted like one.

Grinning from ear to ear, Higgins exited the cell of his chosen morsel and saluted me. "Corporal Higgins reporting for duty, ma'am."

"You've got blood on your chin, Corporal," I said dryly.

Charlie elbowed Higgins as the abashed soldier wiped his chin with his sleeve. "That'll teach you not to be a smartass," the redhead whispered.

Spying Ishida leaving one of the cells, my mouth almost dropped open in surprise. Luc tightened his grip on my hand when Geordie emerged from another cell. His glance warned me not to make an issue of the teens feeding their hungers. The inner prude in me shrieked in hysterical laughter as the adolescents sent me a shamed glance. Geordie guarded his thoughts so strongly that I caught only a bare whiff of his loneliness. Ishida's needs were different, he'd just missed having regular sex with multiple humans. He'd had to settle for only one this time, but one had been better than none, apparently.

Keeping my expression carefully neutral, I waited for everyone to gather into a tight circle before transporting us to Commander Owens. We might not need Shadow right now, but we could definitely use some of the other equipment that was stockpiled in the buildings. I figured asking him for the life jackets would be quicker than searching a bunch of boats for them.

The commander was advised of our arrival and rushed to meet us. "I am afraid Shadow has suffered some structural damage," he told me when he reached us. "It will take us at least another day to fix it."

I waved away his concern. "We just want to borrow some life jackets. How many do you have on hand?"

Confused, he didn't bother to question me as to why I needed them. "Around a thousand, I believe. How many do you need?"

I had no idea how many humans I could shift, but it wouldn't hurt to err on the side of caution. "We'll take the lot."

Owens sent dozens of his men to gather the life jackets. When deflated, they were fairly easy to carry. Each of my soldiers took a bundle until we'd depleted Owens' stocks. "I'll try to return them to you soon," I promised the commander before shifting my troops to eastern Russia.

It took time to round up and hypnotise a large number of humans. The town I'd chosen housed several hundred thousand souls. Most were huddled in their homes, worriedly watching the news for further attacks on their homeland.

Working in pairs, we spread out to recruit people to use as bait. "This should be enough," Gregor decided when we'd gathered nearly a full thousand. We quickly handed out the life jackets. Beneath our spell, the humans docilely donned the bright orange vests then inflated them and awaited their fate.

"I want to come with you this time, Nat," Geordie said. Expecting a refusal, he wrung his hands together. Luc stepped up beside the teen, also intent on joining me on my hunt.

Surrendering to the inevitable, I mentally threw my hands in the air, but kept my tone calm. In their position, I'd probably want to come along and witness the battle as well. "Who else wants to come with me?"

Gregor, Ishida, Danton, Higgins and half a dozen others put up their hands. I cocked an eyebrow at Igor. "I will remain with your soldiers and keep them out of trouble," the Russian declared. The truth bubbled to the surface of his mind. He hated being in open water out of sight of land. It was a fear he'd harboured as a child and the phobia had never left him in all of his fifteen thousand years.

Kokoro's reasons for remaining behind were more practical. She didn't want to ruin her new leather suit. Neither did I, so I reduced all but my head and hands down to the consistency of fine ash and left my clothes behind. My body was a vague outline of constantly shifting particles.

"Is everyone ready?" I asked and received nods from all who hadn't been bamboozled into an almost catatonic state. According to my built in radar, our quarry was a couple of miles out at sea. I also picked up on several thousand humans heading towards it.

"What is wrong?" Luc asked as I hesitated.

"The Russian warships have arrived and they're moving in to surround the octosquid."

I wasn't the only one to turn to Gregor to gauge his reaction. It only took him a few moments to assimilate the information and to tweak my rather simple plan. "We should allow the warships to attack the alien," he decided.

"I thought their missiles weren't strong enough to hurt the jellyfish," Geordie protested.

"They aren't," I replied. "But they'll help to work the octosquid up into a rage."

"Is your intention not to intervene and to let the humans die?" Danton asked. His question was curious rather than judgemental.

My nod was resigned. "Our job is to save the majority of the human population, but not even we can rescue

253

everybody."

Ishida was more practical. "They have refused our help and thus have hindered our ability to dispose of the aliens quickly and efficiently. We must use the tools that are at our disposal. If a few thousand souls are sacrificed for the greater good, then so be it."

Geordie sent me a miserable glance and stepped back from the crowd. "I have changed my mind. I have no wish to witness this slaughter."

Cut to the quick by the teen's accusing gaze, I hardened my resolve. I was Mortis, not a miracle worker. "Everyone who is going with me, hold hands," I ordered. My minions, friends and allies obeyed. A second later, we were treading water.

# Chapter Twenty-Nine

Keeping our distance from the fray, we watched as the four warships circled their target. Painted light grey, they looked like bath toys beside the immense black even with most of the creature still hidden below the water. The first shot was fired and exploded against a tentacle. The octosquid flicked the appendage in annoyance and a large wave sloshed over the ship, causing it to rock alarmingly.

More shots were fired and they lit up the night sky in orange bursts of light. Still nowhere near full after devouring an entire city, the octosquid sank lower beneath the water and ignored the barrage. The top of what would be a head on any other creature dwarfed the attacking vessels.

All firing ceased as the captains of the warships presumably conferred. Changing their tactics, they all aimed at the same spot in the centre of the black mass and fired together. Ripples spread out as the alien flinched from the impact and a small crater appeared in its hide. It was proof that the weapons could at least inflict some damage, even if it was minimal.

Roused to anger, the beast surged upwards until it towered over the warships. Slow and cumbersome, the vessels didn't stand a chance of fleeing. We watched helplessly as a tentacle whipped out and sent one of the warships into a dizzying spin.

Sending my consciousness out, I found the sailors of the crippled vessel in a panic. To abandon ship and try to escape on lifeboats would be suicide. Staying on the ship would also result in their deaths. None of the other ships could come to their aid, since they were currently being buffeted by the enraged alien.

With Geordie's accusing gaze still haunting me, I made a snap decision. "I'm going to try to help them," I told my friends and teleported onto the sinking ship.

Still mostly in particle form, I appeared in the cockpit. Grief stricken that he was about to lose both his ship and his men, the captain was frozen in indecision. He focussed on me and superstitious dread washed through him. "Have you come to take my soul to the afterlife?"

"No. I've come to take you and your men to safety," I replied in his native tongue. "Tell your men to gather on the deck."

Succumbing to my unholy allure, the captain woodenly gave the order through his radio. The milling mass of doomed sailors changed direction and gathered at the back of the ship. I was sure it had a more technical name than that; stern, aft, bilge or whatever, but I frankly didn't care.

The sailors made way for their leader when he appeared

on the deck. I followed him in an almost invisible cloud of molecules. Only when the men had crammed together did I re-form my head and hands. Whisking the men to the nearest Russian shore, I left them in a state of utter confusion and returned to my friends and the bait that we'd gathered.

"Did I miss anything?" I asked when I appeared amongst the bobbing humans and vampires.

"Not much," Ishida responded. "The ships have given up their attack and are on the run. The jellyfish appears to be toying with them."

Sure enough, the gigantic black tentacles were teasing the three warships as they attempted to outmanoeuvre the alien. All three had been rounded up and two were in danger of ramming into each other. The other had a gaping hole in its side and was listing dangerously. Far more decisive, the captain of the damaged ship had ordered his men into the lifeboats. Some were in the water and were frantically rowing for safety. Tiny with distance, their screams floated over to us as a tentacle reared up and came slashing downward.

I was on the move before I'd fully formed the intention of going to the rescue again. I reached the flimsy rubber lifeboat a bare instant before the tentacle could crush them. The sailor's cries of terror were piercing as they covered their heads and cowered in the bottom of the boat. I teleported them to safety and left them, boat and all, beside the still confused group of sailors from the first warship.

It took me several trips to scoop up the sailors in the lifeboats, then a few more to rescue the rest of the crew from the doomed vessels. Still too enraged to realize the tasty treats had been evacuated, the octosquid gave up its game and opened its maw. All four warships were sucked inside and were swallowed, disappearing into the stomach of the leviathan. They'd soon be eroded by its digestive juices alongside the hundreds of thousands of civilians that it had already consumed.

The activity had done more than just stir the creature's anger, it had also roused its hunger. My catch of bait might be small, but I hoped it would be tempting enough to lure our prey towards a confrontation with its closest rival.

Sensing the gargantuan turning back towards land, I shifted my bait to its far side then prodded its mind. As I'd hoped, I drew its attention. Seeing a free and easy meal, it surged towards us. I teleported the group a safe distance away, but remained close enough to entice the target to follow.

Frustration warred with anger as the octosquid pursued its prey. The rage the warships had stirred within it escalated. Propelling itself to its fullest speed, it surged through the waves, intent on devouring the appetizers that continued to elude it.

Splitting my senses, I kept one remote eye on the creature that had eaten LA and steered the rival towards it. We were moving far quicker than any seaborn vessel could hope to match as we remained just out of reach of the black tentacles that strove to grasp us. As we crossed the invisible line between one octosquid's territory and the other, the second monster was roused from its sleep deep beneath the waves. The close proximity of an intruder alerted it that its domain was under threat.

Once allies, if not friends, the two aliens became instant enemies. Speeding towards the surface, the defending leviathan roared a challenge at the interloper when it surfaced. Immediately losing interest in us, the creature that we'd lured across thousands of nautical miles went on the attack. Using the speed that it had built up in pursuit of us, it rammed the defender. Purple blood flew as their tentacles grappled. Ever biting, the multiple mouths chewed through flesh and severed appendages flopped into the water.

My friends watched in awe as the two Goliaths battled for supremacy. Like the two biggest hippos in the universe, they tore at each other's flesh. They gouged deep holes as they struggled to reach the nerve centre hidden in the depths of their enemy's body.

Both aliens were strong from their feasts of humans and neither were about to concede defeat. To do so meant death. Their struggles became slower and more calculated as they began to tire. The water around us turned lilac from the amount of blood that had been shed. Severed tentacles drifted around us. They were whale sized or even larger in some instances.

Making a last ditch effort, the defender reared up and slammed down on top of the interloper. Flattening itself down to absorb the blow, the trespasser wrapped its tentacles around the body of its enemy and drilled deep inside, searching for a weak point. Thrashing and bellowing in agony, the defender reciprocated. The ocean turned a darker shade of purple as fresh blood sheeted from their wounds.

Probing deep inside the body of its adversary, the interloper's tentacles located the brain and tore it to shreds. Weak from loss of blood, it wearily pushed the corpse of the fallen away and sank down out of sight, too tired and in too much pain to celebrate its victory.

"Is the octosquid as grievously wounded as it appears to be?" Gregor asked. Even drenched in sea water with his hair slicked back, he was the picture of elegance.

Still mostly in particle form, my head nodded. "Yes, but it'll start to heal pretty quickly."

"Perhaps we should strike while we have the chance," the most crafty of our kind suggested.

"Good idea." I liked the way he thought and went into action.

I whisked everyone back to the Russian town where we'd snatched the humans from and found Kokoro dressed in a different outfit of jeans and a t-shirt. Her leather suit lay neatly folded on the ground beside mine. She held out a bundle of clothing to me. "In hindsight, the suits aren't very practical for wearing into battle with sea creatures," she said.

My smile was grateful as I took the bundle. I'd had practice at pouring my molecules inside my clothing and became solid in seconds. I was dressed nearly identically to Kokoro. Ishida took Geordie aside for a private chat as my men prepared for the fight ahead. Sidling over to me when Ishida had filled him in on the action he'd missed out on, Geordie shamefacedly held out my twin swords that I'd left with the red suit. "I hope you can forgive me for doubting you, *chérie*."

I donned the sheaths so they were crisscrossed on my back then took Geordie's hand. "You know, I've been thinking about why the six of you survived our trip to Viltar and the reason why you were turned into immortals."

Watching my face cautiously, still expecting anger, the

teen grew hopeful that I wasn't going to berate him. "What conclusion have you come to?"

"It's obvious to anyone who knows me that I'd fail if I tried to figure all this out on my own." Gathering around, none of my closest friends argued with me. "I think you were all picked for a reason."

Gregor looked at me thoughtfully. "You believe that we all have certain skills or attributes that will assist you to perform the tasks that Fate has set for you?"

Ishida flashed a grin of amusement. "What skill did I lend you, Mortis?"

"You have helped me in two ways," I told him seriously. "Your greatest warrior taught me how to fight, but you taught me how to be a ruler."

Ducking his head almost shyly, he offered me a bow. "I am honoured."

Bowing in return, I shifted my gaze to Kokoro. "I'd be lost without your kindness, wisdom and insight."

She also bowed and Ishida allowed her to pull him to her side. "It is we who are grateful," Kokoro said on their behalf. "Without you, our entire nation would have been destroyed. While there are only the two of us now, our history will not be forgotten and we will always remember our people."

Wearing an ironic grin, Igor raised one eyebrow in challenge. "What possible use could you have for me?"

"That's easy," I grinned back. "You're the practical one of our little family. You keep us on track and you don't let us lose sight of the current objective."

The Russian gave me a salute of acknowledgement of his skills. "That is true. You are easily distracted."

It wasn't necessary to spell out why Gregor was so

invaluable, but I did so anyway. It was time I let everyone know just how much I needed them. "Gregor, you've orchestrated most of the battles that I've fought. If I didn't have you on my side, I'd stumble around without a clue of what to do." Every time I'd gone out on my own, I'd ended up embarrassing myself horribly. Thankfully, nearly everyone who'd ever witnessed my bumbling antics had died at my hands.

"In all honesty, I haven't had this much fun in all of my three thousand years," he replied. "At one time, I was an advisor to a king and helped him to conquer several neighbouring countries. That pales in comparison to aiding Mortis." His dark eyes twinkled in merriment, but I sensed he was deadly serious.

I turned to Luc and his lips twisted briefly in a wry smile. I caught a flash of why I was important to him. Sliding my hands around his waist, I tilted my head back and forced him to look me in the eye. "You have been my protector from the beginning. You found me in the mausoleum in Brisbane and took me under your wing, knowing who and what I was. You're the bravest, most loyal and honourable man that I've ever known. You're my strength, Lord Lucentio. Without you, I wouldn't be Mortis, I'd just be Natalie, the clumsy and inept vampire."

Geordie tried to giggle, but it transformed into a sob when I turned to him. "You do not need to invent a reason why you keep me around," the teen said. "Everyone knows that I am not important."

After more than two hundred years of being ridiculed by the courtiers he'd once served, his self-esteem was understandably low. Even after all we'd been through together, he still didn't realize how much he meant to me.

"You might be the most important friend I have, Geordie."

Astounded, he lifted his eyes to mine. "Why?"

"Because you are my conscience." Confused, he turned to the others and received nods of confirmation. "You're the only one who can stop me from turning into a heartless monster," I told the teen. "I need you, Geordie." A lump tried to form in my throat and I swallowed it down. "I need all of you. I can't do this job without you. I *won't* do this job without you. You're my family now."

Bottom lip quivering, the teen wrapped his skinny arms around me and sobbed on my shoulder. "I love you, *chérie*," he whispered. Luc's arms came around us, wordlessly telling Geordie that he was cherished by us both.

I wasn't used to professing my feelings out loud, but the kid was French and it seemed to come naturally to him. "I love you, too, kiddo." He was nearly two centuries older than me, but he'd always be an adolescent and he would always need someone to look out for him.

Igor blinked hard a few times and tried to pretend he wasn't close to breaking down. He was more than Geordie's mentor, he'd been his pseudo father for all of the teen's existence. He sent me a grateful nod that I returned with a smile that trembled a little.

Once Geordie had regained control, I held him at arm's length. "Are you ready to kick some alien butt?"

Nodding, he deftly caught the gun that Ishida tossed to him. "Let's do it!" His voice only wavered slightly as he replied. He might be a teenager on the outside, but on the inside he'd become a warrior. A small part of me mourned the mischievous soul that he'd once been. I wondered if he'd ever be as carefree again. *Will any of us ever be the same again,* my inner voice whispered. Somehow, I doubted it.

# Chapter Thirty

With Shadow currently out of commission, we were without transportation. Well aware of the contents that were now floating around in the octosquid's stomach, I transported my army inside. We appeared on the wreck of one of the warships that had so recently been swallowed. Once again, the bodies of townsfolk bobbed in the noisome stomach juices nearby. They were mostly skeletons. Even the bones were dissolving in the stomach juices.

Whole buildings were crammed inside the alien's gullet. A quick search of my senses found no survivors. The air inside the beast's belly wasn't breathable. Anyone that might have survived the trauma of being swallowed wouldn't have remained alive for long.

Luc accompanied me when I teleported to the membrane that protected the octosquid's brain. The rival alien had dealt out some damage of its own and the protective sack had been ruptured in several places. Huge tunnels had been bored through the light purple jelly. The damage was already starting to be repaired, but the gargantuan had subsided into a semi-coma while it healed.

It wouldn't be necessary for us to carve our way to the centre of the brain. Enough damage had been done that we really just needed to finish off our target. I left Luc behind and was back with the rest of our troops before he could even begin to miss me.

Shouldering our weapons, we fired at the already mangled purple jelly-like substance as we worked our way to the cortex. There was too much damage to the rest of the brain for the creature to become frenzied once we destroyed its central thought processing area. I fired the first volley into the darker purple mass.

The octosquid expired without a fuss and much more quickly than the previous deaths that we'd meted out. Splitting my consciousness, I checked on the reaction of the remaining extra-terrestrials and found no trace of suspicion towards the humans this time. While pretending to mourn their fallen brethren, their secret wish to reign supreme swelled even further.

Whisking my army back to dry land, we retrieved the life jackets that our bait had deflated and had then stacked into neat piles. I released my hold over the humans and silently ordered them to return to their homes. Unaware of the events that they'd been a part of, they drifted away in a daze, shivering from being immersed in cold seawater.

We returned to Owens to drop off the life jackets. His hypnotism had worn off enough that he was able to follow current events and ask questions. Enough bamboozlement remained that he couldn't even contemplate the idea of trying to turn on us. "How many aliens still remain?" he asked.

"Five," I said wearily. I'd used a lot of energy to lure the two beasts together and needed either sleep, a snack, or both.

"I've heard rumours that the world leaders no longer want you to destroy the creatures," the commander said with a hint of anger. "I've seen their attempts to stop them and it's obvious they're going to fail. We might not like it, but it's up to you and your men to save us. If there is anything my sailors or I can do to help, let me know."

Skimming his thoughts, I saw that his offer came honestly and not from the spell that I'd put on him. "Thank you, Commander. For now, my men could use a meal."

He nodded briskly and came close to saluting me. "I'll see to it."

"Only half of the jellyfish are left now," Geordie said in wonder as Owens used his radio to round up his men. "Do you think we will be able to use this same tactic again?"

"I'm not sure," I replied honestly.

"If we attack them directly, more cities will be destroyed in retribution," Igor pointed out. "We must decide whether it is worth the risk, considering that the beasts will eventually head for land no matter what choices we make."

I turned to Geordie. "What do you think we should do?"

His eyes went round in surprise. "You're asking *my* opinion?"

"You're my conscience, remember?"

Disturbed at being singled out, he sought assistance from the others, but didn't find it. "I don't want to be responsible for anyone's death," he said in a small voice.

"I'm not trying to lump responsibility on you," I said and hugged him to my side. "I just want to hear your opinion. No deaths are going to be on any of you." They would be on me. I was Mortis, after all.

Struggling with the idea of sacrificing a few to save many, the teen's shoulders slumped as he reached his decision. "I suppose I would target each one as quickly as possible and hope to kill them all before they could destroy too many more cities."

"That's what I was thinking, too," I told him and he gave me a quick smile of relief.

We all turned to Gregor next. "We should return to the catacombs and rest while I ponder on this," he said after a thoughtful pause.

Rather than being disturbed that he didn't have a plan ready, I was glad that I'd get the chance to rest. Blood would restore my strength, but sleep would still be welcome. I had a feeling that Fate had a message for me that I'd need to hear, or to dream about in this instance.

After feeding from the sailors that Owens rounded up, we took the time to use their facilities to get cleaned up before returning to our hidden base. My soldiers headed for their bedrooms with the knowledge that they would be safe from discovery in the catacombs. No one knew where our hideout was. The French and American governments knew that the vampire Court had once resided in the mansion, but they didn't know about the catacombs, or so I hoped. They were probably responsible for razing the buildings to the ground. They'd done their best to eradicate us, so why not destroy the house where a large number of our kind had once lived?

I changed into the spare t-shirt Prime Minister Townsend had provided and left my leather suit hanging up in the closet. The night might come when I would need it but, as Kokoro had said, it wasn't practical for fighting aquatic monsters.

Wearing only a pair of black boxer shorts, Luc slid into the bed beside me. He'd been quiet and contemplative since I'd divulged the reasons why I needed my close friends around me. He waited until my head was resting on his chest before speaking. "I feel as though I should apologize to you."

"For what?" I didn't try to skim his thoughts. He'd closed a mental door against me and it would be rude to try to pry it open.

"I thought you valued me more for the pleasure that I could give you rather than for my moral support."

"To be honest, it's fifty-fifty," I confessed. "I love your body as much as I love your personality."

"Since we are being honest," he replied. "I feel the same way." His hand moved to cup my butt, but I slid into sleep before my flesh hunger could rise.

Expecting to see the ruins of a monastery, I instead found myself standing next to a chair on a small stage. Upholstered in a plush maroon fabric, the delicate chair was made from a dark wood that had been inset with gold. A backdrop had been erected behind it. The backdrop was of a library scene, with shelves that reached high enough that a ladder would be required to reach them if they'd been real. A small round table made of the same dark wood sat beside the chair. It was stained with several rings from glasses that had spilled their contents.

Turning, I saw three cameras on tripods aimed at the chair. Each one would capture a different angle of whoever sat in the seat. Overhead spotlights would shine brightly on the stage when the filming commenced.

"Ok," I said out loud. "This is weird." I had no idea why I'd been sent to this particular dream. Whatever message Fate was sending me, it was beyond my comprehension.

There were two doors in the room. Picking the one to my right, I opened it and stepped out into a city.

Turning in a circle, I took in the empty streets and buildings. Sweeping my senses out, I detected no signs of life anywhere. A door to a nearby house banged shut as a gust of wind rose. Half torn off its hinges, it listed badly. I knew the house was empty, but my feet carried me towards it anyway. Wherever I was, it was a city that was foreign to me. The buildings were of varying heights, colours and sizes and were all crammed in tightly together. I had a feeling I was in the poorer part of the city.

The living room furniture had been tossed around as the unknown intruders had searched for victims. The smell of death permeated the air and drew me towards a hallway. Three doors stood open, one was smeared with blood. A bare foot caught my eye as I approached the first door. Pushing it open, my eyes travelled up the foot and stopped at mid-thigh. The rest of the leg, not to mention the body that it belonged to, was missing. Blood coated the bed where the grisly remains of another human rested. Thick liquid had dried to a dark brown stain on the floor, walls and ceiling. The smell of more death carried me back into the hallway to the last door on the right.

Filled with trepidation, I entered the room of an infant. A crib stood in the corner, but I had to step over the carcass of a large black dog to reach it. The animal had died while defending the occupant of the room and its owners would never know of their pet's bravery. A gigantic hole in its chest was the cause of death. Its heart had been torn out and lay on the blood soaked floor beside the animal.

My hands were trembling as I leaned over the crib. At first, I thought I was looking at a discarded doll's head. Then I saw the dark stain of blood from where the baby's head had been torn from its shoulders. Newly born, the baby must have been a delicious snack for whatever had bitten its head off and then spat it back into the crib.

Fighting down sudden rage, I teleported into the centre of the city. Death surrounded me as I sent out my senses to find whatever had slaughtered the inhabitants of this town. Widening the search, I found only emptiness in each city or town that I touched. There were no humans left on whatever island or continent that I'd dreamed myself into. There was also no sign of whatever had killed them. On that thought, thousands of red eyes appeared in the shadows. I didn't have time to brace myself before dark, misshapen creatures came thundering towards me.

Luc started awake when I flailed my hands to ward off a blow that never came. Capturing my hands, he folded me into his arms. If I'd been human, my heart would have been racing. Instead, it lay inside me, inert and lifeless.

"I take it you had an unpleasant dream," my one true love said quietly. Gregor was the only one still awake, but he was too far away to overhear us, as long as we whispered.

"It was a doozy," I replied and tried to push the image of the decapitated baby from my mind. The suffering of small children affected me far more than I cared to admit. I was pretty sure Fate had used that particular image on purpose. She knew me better than I knew myself. She was aware of which buttons to press to get me to do what she wanted.

"Tell me about it," Luc said. I related the dream to him and waited for his verdict. "Do you have any idea what any of it means?" he asked.

Glad that I wasn't the only one who was clueless, I shook my head. "Nope. Maybe Gregor will have an insight."

Rising, we dressed and quietly made our way to the living area. Now wearing black jeans, a dark blue t-shirt and black leather jacket, I sank onto the couch beside my beloved. Wearing clothing that was similar to mine, Luc was dressed far more casually than I was used to, but the outfit suited him. Gregor seemed uncomfortable in his less than expensive outfit. He'd no doubt prefer to don one of his custom made tweed suits. They'd be ruined each time we entered the brain of our adversaries, so he had little choice but to put up with the casual clothing for now.

Quirking an eyebrow, Gregor looked as grave as I felt. "Has something happened?"

"Not yet, but it probably will," I replied cryptically and related my dream again.

Baffled, Gregor also had no explanation for the images that had been sent to me. "I am sure it will become clear in time."

That was what Danton had said after relating the vision his master had received. I hoped both messages would become clear soon. "It'll become clear when the shit has already hit the fan and it's too late to stop it," I grumbled. "Why can't Fate, or whoever it is that sends me these dreams, just be clear for once?"

"Perhaps Fate thinks that would be too easy," Luc said dryly. "I sometimes feel as though we are facing a test and the ultimate outcome depends on how we deal with each threat that arises."

Gregor nodded slowly in agreement. "I have often had that same feeling."

Now that they'd pointed it out, I also had the sensation that it would be crucial for us to make the right decisions, or else we'd fail and the Earth itself would be damned. *No pressure,* I whined, but I kept the thought to myself.

# Chapter Thirty-One

Gregor had been keeping track of octosquid activity while the rest of us had been sleeping. The laptop battery had almost run out. We'd have to charge it again if we wanted to keep up to date. Since he'd had time to kill, he'd drawn a detailed map of the world and had found five pins to mark where each alien had last been sighted.

"How accurate is the map?" he asked.

A quick search found all five octosquids. Two had been marked correctly, but the other three had moved closer to land. They'd depleted the oceans and seas of life in their immediate vicinities. These three had yet to feed on coastal towns and hunger was driving them in search of two-legged food. Interestingly, two were drifting towards South America from opposite directions.

"We might be in luck. It looks like these two are heading towards Chile and Argentina." I shifted two of the pins to indicate where the aliens were now. "They're moving slowly, but they should encroach on each other's territory sometime in the next couple of hours." Once that happened, an inevitable battle would ensue and we could then move in to take down the victor.

One by one, our friends woke and joined us. Danton was the next to rouse once the sun departed from the sky. His five warriors broke free from their death-like states shortly after. My newly made vampires were slower to rise, but became alert within seconds of each other.

The seven of us who could wake at will had been keeping watch over the aliens' activities via the pins that I kept moving on the map. I frowned when one of the octosquids changed direction. "One of them is moving away," I warned the others as my soldiers filed into the room. Dressed and armed, they were ready for action, which was handy since we'd have to act fast.

"Should we round up some more human bait?" Ishida asked. He had cleared the furniture from a small area so he could practice his sword technique. He'd borrowed one of my swords since he didn't have one of his own. He was only slightly shorter than me, so the weapon suited him well enough.

He handed my sword back and I slid it into its sheath as I answered him. "We don't have time for that." I stood and urged everyone to gather around. Once we were all touching, I whisked us to the dock and on board Shadow.

Several sailors were still tinkering with the vessel. Used to seeing us popping up unexpectedly, they merely filed out onto the dock instead of screaming and fleeing in alarm.

"Has Shadow been fully repaired?" Igor asked one of

the men.

"Yes, sir," the sailor responded and saluted. One of Igor's eyebrows rose in amusement as he returned the salute.

Locating the alien that was straying off course, I made sure we were within shooting distance when I zapped us to it.

"Fire!" Igor ordered and the soldiers out on the small deck obeyed. Their weapons were far too puny to inflict much damage on the monster's hide. It had the effect we were hoping for and caught the beast's attention.

Faster than I'd anticipated, it whirled around and sent a dozen tentacles shooting towards us. I skipped the boat backwards, staying just out of range and the chase began. Firing the occasional shot to work the alien up into a rage, my soldiers made sure they kept its attention on us.

The second octosquid became aware of the interloper approaching its territory and charged in our direction. Teleporting Shadow for a final time, the boat landed directly between the former allies that had turned into enemies simply by their close proximity.

Tentacles lashed out, but not towards each other. They instead wrapped around our boat before I could shift us to safety. We were lifted into the air and my attempt to teleport the boat to safety failed. With two immense aliens holding onto us, there was far too much weight for me to shift. They'd turned our trap against us and not even Gregor had foreseen this outcome.

Caught between the two mammoths, we were in a titanic tug of war that made the hull squeal in protest. The windows buckled, then disintegrated as Shadow was twisted in opposite directions. Losing his balance, Igor fell through one of the windows. Geordie's hand reached out and caught his mentor's foot. He was left holding his shoe as Igor dropped. A tentacle swept up towards him. Its hungry mouth opened and closed as its teeth gnashed the air in anticipation of a meal.

"Save him!" Geordie screamed at me, but I was already on the move.

Appearing beneath Igor, I caught him an instant before the teeth could tear him to pieces. I zapped us both back onto the boat just in time for it to be torn in two. In horror, I watched as my army fell and it was suddenly raining vampires.

Time seemed to slow down as I realized I couldn't save everyone. Kokoro and Gregor fell together. Hand in hand, they were resigned to their fate. Ishida coolly fired his gun into the mouth that would shortly turn him into chowder. Geordie screamed shrilly, reaching for Igor as his mentor dove out of my arms after him.

Danton, his warriors, Higgins and the rest of my men would die and my friends would become a mangled ruin. Luc and I were the only ones who were safe. We were suspended in mid-air as my body had automatically turned into whirling particles. He'd grabbed onto my semi-solid shoulders before he could fall.

"No." I shook my head in denial, refusing to allow my people, the remnants of our entire species to be destroyed. Reaching out with my mind, I snared them all in a mental net. Without physically touching any of them, I willed us all directly into the brain of the interloping alien.

Still screaming and holding onto Igor's shoe, Geordie plopped into the gooey, purple brain beside me and instantly became mired. Thrashing around, his screams petered out as he realized he wasn't going to be cut to pieces by the ever gnashing teeth embedded in a tentacle. Astonishment replaced his terror. He spotted me and stared with something like awe. "How did you manage to save us all, *chérie?*"

A bit dazed myself, I checked and found everyone to be safe and sound. "I'm not sure," I confessed. "I think I somehow linked my telepathy with my teleporting skill and willed us all here."

Swimming through the thick substance, the teen wrapped his arms around me and smacked a kiss on my cheek. "Ugh," he said with an instant grimace. "You don't taste very good."

"I'm kind of covered in brains," I reminded him.

"How are we going to get out of this glop?" Ishida complained.

I still had my swords on my back and Luc pulled one free. "Natalie and I will cut a path to freedom." Even covered in goo, he was gorgeous. Giddy with relief that I'd saved my people from certain death and dismemberment, I pulled him in close and kissed him hard.

We both grimaced at the same time as the hideous taste of alien brains invaded our mouths. "Geordie's right, that tastes pretty nasty," I complained.

Mired a few yards away, Gregor's expression of distaste had nothing to do with Luc and I showing our affection in public. "Can you please hurry?" he requested. "I have brains in my sinus cavities."

Ishida, Geordie and I burst into laughter, instantly incurring Igor's annoyance. The Russian doggedly swam his way through the purple mass to deliver a slap to the back of Geordie's head. Stopping long enough to grab his shoe out of the teen's hand, he turned his sights on Ishida. Much smaller and slimmer than Igor, Ishida giggled as he propelled himself towards me. With his hand clamped around my waist, I had little choice but to take him along. I transported Luc, the teen and myself into one of the narrow tunnels that ran haphazardly through the giant organ.

Regaining his dignity, Ishida offered me a bow. "Thank you. You saved me from much embarrassment at being chastised by Igor."

"He'll get you sooner or later," I warned him. He'd probably get me, too, for that matter.

"I know," the teen replied. "But it is fun to make him chase me." He had a mental flashback to when he'd wanted to chop Igor's head off for daring to smack him that first time and felt ashamed.

"Igor doesn't hold that against you," I told him softly.

Well used to having his mind read, the former child king looked at me hopefully. "Are you certain?"

"Yes," I replied as Luc began to carve a path through the gooey brain. "Igor had an extremely cruel and sadistic master and was forced to serve him for many thousands of years." He'd managed to murder his master by spooking his horse over a cliff. Since he hadn't directly killed his creator, he'd survived the experience. "Nothing much could faze him after that."

"I would like to make it up to Igor, but I am unsure how." Ishida had changed substantially since I'd first met him. He'd lost some of the imperial reserve he'd had to wear in front of his subjects. He was attempting to just be a normal vampire rather than a beloved ruler.

"You've already made it up to him by being friends with

Geordie."

Ishida's expression was troubled. "Geordie has not had a pleasant life as a vampire."

Being turned by a thirteen year old girl in the hopes that he would kill her master, Geordie had been ridiculed by most of the courtiers and their servants for all of his two hundred years. It showed how much he trusted his new friend if he'd told Ishida about his torment. "We'll have to make sure his life is better now," I responded. I knew Geordie felt alone even when surrounded by his friends, but I wasn't sure how to fix his problem. *Worry about that later,* my inner voice recommended. *You've got aliens to kill, remember?*

Stepping up beside Luc, I helped him to carve a path towards the centre of the octosquid's brain. Testing my new ability, I searched for Gregor and willed him to me. Landing on his feet, Gregor wiped purple jelly from his face and nodded his thanks. "I hope our weapons are still operational after being immersed in brains."

"Let's find out," Ishida said and fired a shot back down our path. The bullet lodged in the membrane wall and exploded three seconds later. "They appear to be fully functional."

"I thought our guns would have a better chance of working if I transported us here rather than dunking them in stomach juice," I said to Gregor over my shoulder.

"Forgive me if I seemed to be critical of your plan, Natalie," he said. "You acted quickly and it was a remarkable feat to have rescued us all as you did." I could see the wheels turning as he factored my new ability into his plans.

Igor joined us next. Reaching past Gregor, he delivered

a slap to Ishida that sent him stumbling into my back. "Told you he'd get you," I told the teen over my shoulder as he rubbed his head ruefully. Igor contented himself with a warning glare at me rather than assaulting me for being childish.

Now that we had more room to move in, I retrieved Geordie, Kokoro and Danton at the same time. "Finally!" Geordie complained. "I thought you were going to leave me in that purple slop forever!"

"You're welcome," I said dryly. No matter what mysterious powers or abilities I developed, I could always count on my friends to bring me back to reality before my ego had a chance to become too large.

"Why didn't the aliens attack each other?" Danton asked from his position in the rear. The rest of my soldiers appeared behind him. Most were still shell shocked at their close brush with death.

"I believe the octosquids set a trap for us," Gregor replied. "They are aware of our tactics now and they're intelligent enough to use them against us."

"What are they doing now?" Kokoro asked.

"They're trying to figure out where we went," I replied. Being inside the brain of one of our enemies, it was almost impossible to ignore its thoughts. Confused, they searched the ocean for us while tromping down hard on their instincts to battle for their territory. "Once we start shooting, they'll figure out where we are soon enough."

"I believe we should attack the cerebral cortex immediately in this instance," Gregor said.

"I like the way you think," Igor complimented the strategist of our group.

"Won't that make the jellyfish go crazy?" Geordie asked.

He was following right behind me, staying close enough to almost tread on my heels.

"That is exactly what we want to happen," Igor told his apprentice.

Realization dawned and Geordie grinned. "Oh. I get it now."

Altering out path slightly, we headed for the darker purple tissue that ruled the thought process of the alien. Clearing the area around the cortex, we formed a half circle and fired a barrage of explosives at it.

Roaring in alarm, the alien's bellow changed to rage as we blasted the cortex apart and its ability to reason fled. It turned to attack its tentative ally and we were thrown off our feet as the two monsters clashed. I watched through the strange radar vision of the leviathan that we'd invaded as they landed blows on each other. Unable to think beyond the need to destroy, the interloper drilled deep inside its enemy's hide in search of its only vulnerable area.

Someone let out a shout as the tip of a tentacle swept through the already damaged tissue just above our heads. We all ducked reflexively and stayed down. Thrashing, writhing and clutching each other in a death grip, the monsters sank beneath the waves as they gored each other. The defending monster's appendages stiffened, then went lax as its own cortex was destroyed, along with most of its brain.

Bellowing in triumph, the interloper surged back towards the surface, heading for land to feed on the unaware citizens of South America. Climbing to his feet, Igor fired a rocket into the ruined depths of the octosquid's brain. We kept up a sustained barrage of fire until the creature first slowed then stopped. I was relieved to discover that it had come to a halt just short of land. It became yet another casualty in our war and floated listlessly on the currents.

"Why are you smiling like that?" Higgins asked me suspiciously.

"Because there are only three octosquids left now and they're running scared." I couldn't see it, but I suspected that my smile was rather malicious.

"They picked the wrong planet to try to eat," Geordie stated as he rested his gun over his shoulder. "They should have known we wouldn't just let them take over our world."

Kokoro tried to see it from our enemy's point of view. "They are simply doing what we would have done if we were in their situation."

"What do you mean?" Ishida asked.

"They are the last of their kind," his maker told him gently. "They do not wish to die any more than we would." My feeling of triumph dissipated and I wasn't the only one who felt a tug of remorse for our plan to stamp the aliens out. "It is our duty to keep our planet safe, but that does not mean that I will relish the task of eradicating an entire species," Kokoro said. Gregor put his arm around his lady love's shoulder and she leaned against him gratefully.

"I don't like it either," Geordie agreed. "But it is our job and we have to finish them off."

I hadn't been wrong when I'd named the teen my conscience. He'd just articulated exactly what I was feeling.

"Can you sense what the three remaining aliens are thinking?" Gregor asked.

Splitting my consciousness three ways, I found a trio of

identical thoughts and the news wasn't good. "They know that they're doomed and they're going to cause as much damage as they can before we kill them all off." Just like us, it wasn't in the aliens' makeup to go down without a fight.

"Then I suggest we find another boat, restock our ammunition and start hunting them down one by one," Igor said.

"I sincerely hope we can shower and change before we embark on our next hunt," Gregor murmured.

"Don't worry, we all look like we're covered in purple afterbirth," Geordie told Gregor helpfully.

"Thank you for that stunning visual picture, Geordie," our master planner said dryly. He cocked a goo caked eyebrow at Ishida when he made a sound of amusement.

On the edge of breaking into hysterical laughter, I zapped us all out of the carcass of the monster and back to dry land.

# Chapter Thirty-Two

Once again, we returned to the catacombs to restock. Gregor was the only one who felt the need to change. The rest of us didn't bother, since we were heading straight back out into another battle. I briefly wondered where I was going to house my soldiers once this was all over, but quickly abandoned that line of thought. First, we had to survive our clashes against the three remaining aliens. Each one would be only too happy to rend my army to pieces.

My troops scattered to the cells below to retrieve more ammo. The rest of us gathered in the living room and huddled around Gregor's map. We were too filthy to sit, so we stood around the coffee table. I bent and removed all but three of the pins, then shifted them around to display the new locations of the behemoths.

"They each appear to be heading towards small islands," Gregor observed. "They will be able to wreak utter destruction in a short amount of time."

One octosquid was arrowing towards an island to the north of Norway, another was aiming for New Zealand and the third towards Japan. Since Japan was by far the most heavily populated area, it made sense to go to their aid first. "Does everyone agree that we should head to Japan first?" I might be their leader, but I valued the opinions of my friends.

Geordie raised worried eyes to mine. "Are we just going to abandon the other islands to their fate?"

"I don't like it either," I admitted. "But we can't be in three places at once."

"Perhaps we should advise the humans of the impending attacks," Igor suggested. "They might be able to use their ships and jets to at least slow the aliens down."

Gregor nodded in instant agreement. "They will most likely prove to be ineffective, but we should at least give them the opportunity to try to hold off the attacks."

"I'll update Owens," I said. "He can spread the word while we head for Japan." No one objected, so I linked my arm through Luc's and transported us to the commander's office.

Owens was on the phone and trailed off in mid-sentence when he saw us appear. "Hang on for a moment," he said then covered the mouthpiece. "What do you need?"

"There are only three aliens left now, but all of them are heading for land with the intention of causing as much destruction as possible," I told him bluntly.

Already pale from fatigue and worry, his face went a shade whiter. "Can anything be done to stop them?"

"That is up to you humans," Luc said. "I would suggest

you alert the authorities in Norway and New Zealand and tell them to do what they can to slow the attacks."

"What about the third alien? Where is it heading?"

"Japan," I replied. "We're going to target that one first. Unfortunately, my men aren't able to function during the day, so I highly doubt we'll be able to save all three islands from destruction."

The commander nodded in understanding, silently thankful that he didn't have to make the decision that would affect millions of human lives. "I'll do what I can to alert the authorities," he promised and hung up on whoever he'd been speaking to.

"I'm afraid I have some more bad news," I told him before he could spring into action.

His shoulders tensed and he guessed what I was about to say. "Shadow?" At my nod, he sank back in his chair. "How bad is the damage?"

"It was torn in half by a pair of octosquids," I explained. "It isn't salvageable." We left him to grieve the loss of his prized boat. His job had been to look after the vessel and it was now gone. He couldn't be held accountable, since he'd been under my hypnotism, but he would probably be punished anyway. That was how the armed forces seemed to work. If they couldn't castigate the guilty party, they'd discipline whoever was at the top of the chain of command instead.

My men were ready when we returned to the catacombs. The night was waning and we'd have to move quickly if we wanted to intercept and destroy the octosquid that was heading towards Japan before daybreak came.

No one wanted a repeat performance of being mired in brain jelly. I took the group to a dock in Japan and searched for a boat first. Igor led the search and shouted to alert us when he located a suitable vessel. Examining the tourist boat, it was a far cry from the sleek ride we were used to. There was enough room for everyone and no one had to cram down below. That was a good thing, because there was no below decks this time.

Larger in size, but lighter than Shadow, I zapped us all into the stomach of the rapidly approaching Goliath. Instead of landing in stomach juices, we thudded down on a large object and immediately began to slide backwards. I threw a frantic look out the window, spotted open water and teleported the boat to safety.

Still clutching the railing, Geordie tilted his head back to examine what we'd accidentally landed on. "Is that what I think it is?"

Peering out through the window, Ishida was the one to respond. "If you're thinking it's a whale, then yes, it is what you think it is."

Blubber oozed through tears in the dark hide that had been made by the alien's several rows of sharp teeth as it had swallowed the whale. Still relatively fresh, its flesh was slowly being eaten away by the digestive juices.

Something bumped against our hull and Higgins leaned out the window to investigate. "It's another whale," he reported. "A baby, I think."

Other whale carcasses were spotted and were pointed out by my men.

"It must have eaten an entire pod," Kokoro realized out loud.

Whales were the largest living creatures on our entire planet and a single octosquid had chewed up a bunch of them and had swallowed them down like popcorn.

Leaving the others behind, I transported Luc into the brain. None of the organs were exactly the same. We followed the natural tunnels where we could and continued to cut a path that would take us roughly towards the centre. Now that I didn't have to physically touch someone to transport them, I reached out with my mind and began bringing my troops to us in small groups. It was an even quicker method than returning to pick them up in person.

Startled to find himself suddenly standing beside me, Geordie grinned. "You have become very proficient at moving us around like chess pieces, *chérie*."

"It is a pretty handy skill," I agreed then turned to help Luc chop through another barrier.

Finally in the general centre of our target, we began firing into the soft tissue. Practiced at destroying the jelly-like substance by now, we reduced the brain to mush as quickly as we could without touching the cortex.

Watching through the leviathan's version of radar, I saw we were too late to save Japan completely. Reaching the coast, tentacles hauled the gigantic black alien onto land and it began stuffing terrified humans into its maw. Buildings were torn apart in its mission to eat and destroy. Still, we didn't attack the dark purple casing that protected its motor functions. We had to wait until we'd wrought as much damage to its brain as possible before targeting the cortex. If we didn't, we'd just make it worse for the civilians.

Ishida worked in stolid silence, ignoring the sympathetic glances Kokoro sent him. Their small island had been destroyed over a decade ago and now Japan was under attack again. Proving that he was far more mature than his façade suggested, he remained calm and shot with precision rather than firing wildly in revenge.

When the beast began to falter, I turned towards the protected cortex and fired the first shot. Igor's rocket blasted it apart and the octosquid collapsed. Seeing through its eyes, I watched as it thrashed, destroying more buildings in its death throes. It finally went still, but I felt little satisfaction as I drew my senses back in. Too many humans had died and many more were now homeless.

*There are still two more to take down,* my inner voice reminded me. *There's no way you'll be able to stop them before they attack. Dawn is almost here.* So it was, in Japan anyway. The island to the north of Norway was at least several hours to the west and the sun wasn't scheduled to rise there yet. It was already too late to attempt to save New Zealand. We would have to abandon them to their fate.

Seemingly reading my mind, Gregor caught my eye. "If we remain here, your men will shortly fall asleep and will become useless to us."

Anguished that I couldn't be everywhere at once, I hoped aid was being sent to the Kiwis. Australia would undoubtedly send help in the form of both ships and jets. It was small consolation, since they'd had very little effect against the invading aliens so far.

Geordie put his arm around my waist in commiseration of the difficult choice I'd had to make. "You can't save them all, Nat. You are only one person," he reminded me.

*But I'm not a person,* I wailed inside my head. *I'm Mortis and I'm supposed to save the human race, not sit back and watch them being eaten by giant alien squids!* "I know," I said instead and shifted my army back to the tourist boat.

I waited for everyone to reload from the containers of

ammo that Igor had brought along. When everyone was ready, I shifted the boat westward. Sensing a group of humans, I stopped short of teleporting us directly into the stomach of the leviathan. I deposited the boat into the ocean instead.

Warships surrounded the alien. They stayed at what they believed was a safe distance from it as they fired their guns and missiles. The octosquid proved their estimations to be wrong by reaching out and snaring one of the vessels in two of its tentacles. With a rending crunch, the ship was torn in two. Bodies began to fall and I automatically went into action.

Blinking out of the air, the humans reappeared on the decks of neighbouring ships. I missed a couple that fell into the secondary mouths on the tentacles, but the bulk of them survived. They wouldn't survive for much longer. Even now, the monster reached towards another ship for some tasty treats.

"Wait here," I told my army unnecessarily. "I'm going to try to evacuate them all to land." Appearing on the boat that was about to be attacked, I sent out my senses and snared all of the humans in my mental net. Delving into the mind of the captain, I identified where their base was and transported them back to it.

Several trips later, the sailors were back on land and the octosquid was smashing two of their ships together in a fit of pique that it had been denied a meal.

I returned to the tourist boat just in time to see darkness enfold it as the mammoth swallowed it whole.

# Chapter Thirty-Three

Teleporting the boat before the approaching teeth could tear it apart, I relocated it and my army into the beast's stomach.

"That was a close one," Ishida said with a small grin of relief.

"Only two left to go now," Geordie said with pretend brightness. We all knew we might be able to stop this alien from causing too much damage, but the final one was out of our hands. God only knew how many people would die when my army fell into a sun-induced coma. It didn't seem right somehow, that Fate expected us to rescue everyone, but had prevented us from creating more soldiers. Then again, we'd done well so far. Even if we'd had the extra soldiers, they wouldn't have been able to save the Kiwis.

Following the same plan as last time, Luc and I cut our way through the octosquid's brain as I brought the others up to join us in small groups. A nagging feeling of impending catastrophe wouldn't leave me as my beloved took the lead. He fired into the gooey walls of the organ to begin taking the creature down.

With only half of my attention on what I was doing, the rest was watching through the other alien's radar as it approached New Zealand. Several warships were on their way, but they'd never make it in time to avert the coming disaster.

At the last second, the alien swerved away and detoured around the north island. A disturbingly familiar feeling of doom settled into my stomach as the octosquid changed course and started for my home country. Some sixth sense had told it that it would find a far larger meal if it kept heading westward.

I continued to fire, breaking down the brain of our enemy as its comrade closed in on Australia. I watched helplessly as it eventually spied land and increased its speed. In dismay, I recognized the unique roof of the Sydney Opera House when it appeared on the murky picture that was the alien's radar. It was still distant, but it was closing in on the harbour fast.

Just like in one of my dreams, one of the greatest, most recognizable icons that Australia possessed was about to be destroyed and my army could do nothing to stop it. My soldiers would instantly fall into comas and the rest of us wouldn't be enough to take the beast down alone if I teleported them to my home country.

*Think outside the box,* my subconscious urged me. *If you can't use your army to destroy it, think of something else that you can use.*

As Igor fired the first shot into the dark purple cortex of

one monster, I teleported myself to Sydney to confront the other one. My clothing and weapons fell to the ground and I reduced myself down to molecules before the sun could fry me. Screams of panic and terror were a barrage of noise that I read in the minds of thousands of humans as thc alien was spotted. It was just a dark dot on the horizon, but it was rapidly growing larger and would soon be within touching distance. Once that happened, the Sydney Opera House and Sydney Harbour Bridge would be smashed to pieces and the inhabitants of the city would be eaten.

Re-forming my eyes, I searched the harbour in desperation as the very sky seemed to darken from the approaching leviathan. Docked for some kind of ceremony, a warship caught my eye. Most of the staff was on land, attending the festivities and only a few were left on board. *It's too heavy,* I told myself even as I blinked myself inside. *I'll never be able to move something this big.*

Safe from the sun inside the ship, I became whole and sent out my senses to zap all of the humans onto land. Now empty but for me, the ship was far more immense than anything else I'd ever tried to shift before. Through the cockpit window, I saw hundreds of tentacles swarming over the buildings that lined the outer edge of the harbour and I knew that I was out of time. *Here goes nothing.*

With only one shot at stopping the octosquid, I allowed my instincts to take over. Putting my hands on the console, I willed the ship into motion. For three agonizing seconds, nothing happened. Then darkness enveloped the ship as it was shifted directly inside the alien. Purple blood and gore splattered the windows as the warship ploughed through the octosquid's brain. It turned the organ into mush much faster and far more effectively than any number of explosives or rockets could have.

The warship tore directly through the cortex, laying ruin to around eighty percent of the organ during its journey. The momentum of the ship was great enough to tear through its hide and emerge into sunlight on the other side. I left the vessel to drift and willed myself back to land. Still alive, but heavily crippled, the monster dragged itself through the water and across land. Mortally wounded, it was still intent on causing pain and destruction before it expired.

I stood in the shade of the Sydney Opera House as a dozen tentacles emerged from the water and crept towards the iconic building. More appendages knocked down the expensive houses and buildings that ringed the harbour, but there was little I could do to save them. I was determined to keep the building behind me intact. My weapons lay on the ground with my clothing, but my swords came to my hands when I called for them. Black chunks of flesh flew as I sliced the tentacles apart.

Close to death and running out of energy, the creature grabbed me with one tentacle and reached out towards the building that I was trying to protect with another. I screamed as the ever gnashing teeth chewed into my flesh and sheared my legs off. Humping along the ground, the other arm stretched out, then reared back to strike at the Sydney Opera House. I had only one weapon left in my arsenal and I called on the power of my holy marks. I didn't have time to let it build and blindly lashed out with it instead. An invisible wave cut through the air and hit the tentacle as it began to fall. To my astonishment, the limb instantly withered and turned to ash. It left a charred stain against the side of the building when it fell, but it caused no structural damage.

The tentacle that was holding me went lax as the final remaining octosquid gave up its hold on life. Naked, legless and badly wounded, I reduced myself down into molecular form and was whole and uninjured once more when I re-formed. It was an even faster method of healing than letting myself heal naturally.

Transporting my filthy clothing to me from where it had fallen, I poured myself into them and shifted back to the deceased alien near Norway.

Geordie gave a glad cry and enveloped me in a hug when I appeared. "What happened? Where did you go?" They'd finished off the alien while I'd been gone and had been waiting for my return.

"The last octosquid changed course and headed for Australia. I had a dream a while ago about Sydney being destroyed and I couldn't let that happen," I explained.

"Are you feeling well?" Kokoro asked me, concerned by my appearance.

I wasn't sure what I looked like, but I was more exhausted than I'd ever felt before. "Now that you mention it, I'm feeling kind of crappy."

Luc caught me as my legs buckled. "You need blood," he said as he swung me into his arms.

"We're not going to find any here," Igor pointed out.

"Do you think you can teleport us to safety?" Gregor asked.

"She is already beyond exhausted," my beloved said tightly.

Too tired to argue, I concentrated and zapped my small army directly back to the catacombs. We might not have a supply of blood handy, but at least we'd be safe here.

Luc strode into the bedroom we'd chosen and lay me on the bed. "Sleep," he said as he stretched out beside me. "I will watch over you."

It was taking all of my concentration to remain awake. Now that we were safe, I allowed myself to spiral into darkness.

Images awaited in the gloom. Three plain wooden doors appeared and I opened the one on the left first. Inside, the Earth was an empty wasteland, devoid of all life, but not because of alien invasion. Only the undead survived in this scenario, but not any undead that I'd ever seen before. They lurked in the shadows, giving me only glimpses of misshapen flesh and scarlet eyes.

Behind door number two, I saw another post-apocalyptic world where the humans had gone into hiding. Like the Kveet that had been enslaved on Viltar, they lived in caves deep beneath the ground. They were afraid to ascend for fear of dying from the toxic air that had been left behind after a nuclear war had decimated almost all life.

The third door drew me and I hesitated in dread before opening it. Instead of ruin and destruction, I saw worldwide peace and general happiness. It wasn't a perfect world and never would be, but it was as close to it as it could possibly get.

Puzzled by door number three, I turned and saw a chair floating in the darkness. It was the same maroon chair that I'd seen in my last dream. There were no cameras or backdrop in sight this time, but I sensed the chair would be pivotal to whichever future that the Earth would face.

"It's just a chair," I said out loud and Geordie gave a glad screech.

Opening my eyes, I was lifted up and plopped on the teen's lap. He hugged me so hard that I wouldn't have been able to breathe if I'd been human. "Oh, *chérie*, we were so worried about you." He buried his face in my shoulder and began to sob.

Luc burst into the room, dressed only in a towel and dripping wet from a shower. He closed his eyes in relief and sagged against the doorframe when he saw that I was awake.

Patting Geordie on the back, I became aware that I was clean and naked beneath the blanket that was barely covering me after being dragged onto the teen's lap. My close friends all piled into the bedroom, thankful that I'd returned to them. I caught glimpses of their memories of me remaining asleep for far too long.

My men required regular food, so Gregor had decided to move us back to his mansion. Luc had bundled me into a blanket after I'd fallen unconscious while Igor had located the closest exit from the catacombs. I'd forgotten that several emergency exits had been created in the cave system beneath the destroyed Court mansion.

Gregor, Kokoro and Ishida had escorted my soldiers out to feed each night. They'd managed to keep our presence a secret, but feeding nearly two hundred men in the same town each night would be noticed eventually.

"How long was I asleep?" I asked. Still slightly groggy, I felt much better than I had before I'd fallen into my coma.

Pulling back, Geordie answered me. "You were unconscious for seven nights." His shoulders were still heaving, but he regained enough control to give me a wobbly smile. "We weren't sure if you were ever going to wake up."

Sensing my discomfort about being practically unclothed in front of our friends, Luc removed his towel and held it out to me. I kept my eyes above his waist, not wanting my flesh hunger to flare up. As soon as it did, it would alert everyone in the house that I wanted to have some private time with my one true love.

Pulling the towel around my body, I climbed out of Geordie's lap and slid to the floor. "Thanks," I said to Luc and went up on my tippy-toes to give him a kiss.

"Did I hear you say something about a chair?" Gregor interjected before the kiss could turn into far more.

Utterly comfortable with his nakedness, Luc leaned against the wall beside me as I remembered my dream.

"Yeah," I said. "It's fading now, but there was something about a chair and three possible outcomes for the human race."

"What were the outcomes?" Igor asked.

I counted them off on my fingers. "Total destruction by yet another undead attack, almost total destruction from nuclear war, or worldwide peace and general happiness."

"Can we go with option number three?" Ishida asked dryly.

"What does the chair have to do with anything?" Geordie asked.

I shrugged, then grabbed the towel before it could fall. "I have no idea, but I sense that it is somehow pivotal to whatever happens next."

Kokoro made a noise that sounded suspiciously like a weary sigh. "So, our task is not yet over?"

"Nope," I confirmed, much to everyone's unhappiness. "But I do have some good news."

"What's that?" Geordie asked with a profound lack of hope.

"I'm pretty sure that this will be the last threat that we'll ever have to face."

Astonishment followed that statement.

"What makes you so sure?" Gregor asked.

"Fate told me."

Ishida's eyes widened slightly. "Fate itself spoke to you?"

"Not with actual words." Not this time anyway. "I just had the sense that this would be it. If we can somehow save the earth one last time, there won't be any other threats to deal with."

"What is this last threat?" Igor asked.

I was forced to shrug again. "I don't know." I was positive that we'd all find out what it was soon enough.

"Now that you are back with us and there are no immediate threats on the horizon," Gregor said, "there is a loose thread that needs to be addressed."

I could have delved into his mind to learn what he was talking about, but it seemed rude.

"What loose thread?" Geordie asked.

"Now that Natalie has the ability to teleport inanimate objects, I think it would be a good idea to retrieve the Viltaran Seeker ship from the river in Manhattan," Gregor replied.

Igor nodded in immediate agreement. "We do not want the humans to discover it."

I'd almost forgotten about the alien spacecraft that we'd stolen and had returned to Earth in. "What do you want me to do with it?"

"I believe merely shifting it from the Hudson River into a far deeper ocean would suffice," Gregor said.

I saw a picture in his mind that was the deepest spot he knew of. "Ok. I'll take care of it."

Luc didn't want me to go alone, but this was a task that would be easier if I went solo. "Return soon," he told me softly. I felt his flesh hunger stir and I teleported away before I could become ensnared by it. I left him the towel, just in case he felt the need to hide his all too obvious and highly visible need from our friends.

# Chapter Thirty-Four

I materialized in a dark alley in the heart of Manhattan. Dawn was only a short hop away and there were few people out and about. Hunger cramped my insides. I'd used up all of my energy killing the final octosquid and I hadn't eaten for a full week, thanks to being in a coma. I'd have to find food before I went in search of the alien spaceship.

Searching the minds of the nearby slumbering humans, I found a female who was roughly my size and shifted into her bedroom. She slept deeply and didn't sense me as I pilfered some of her clothes. Call me a prude, but I wasn't about to feast on a sleeping human while I was buck naked.

Dressed in jeans and a t-shirt, I left my feet bare and willed myself up to the next floor. My chosen meal lay on his side, dreaming about his fiancé. She was away visiting her family and he felt lonely without her. He barely even felt it when I sank my fangs into his neck. I drank a few mouthfuls and left him smiling happily in his sleep.

I visited two more male occupants of the apartment building and built my strength back up to its usual levels. While my senses couldn't exactly detect inanimate objects, I pictured the small black alien ship and an instant later I was floating in its belly. The Americans hadn't discovered it yet and it still lay on the bottom of the Hudson River.

Even full of water, it was far lighter than the warship that I'd used to demolish the final octosquid's brain. Using the image Gregor had given me of a deep part of an ocean, I transported the ship to it, then whisked myself away before I could be crushed by the pressure. The Seeker was most likely crumpled into an unrecognizable mass of alien metal. It might be discovered one day, but it could never be reconstructed now.

Fully dressed, Luc was waiting for me when I returned to the bedroom. Taking in my dripping state, he ruefully handed me the towel that I'd left behind. "I take it you were successful?"

"Yep," I said as I rubbed my hair dry the old fashioned way with the towel. I could have reduced myself down to particle form then become whole again, but that seemed almost too lazy.

"There is a spare change of clothing in the wardrobe," Luc told me.

The glint in his eye made me suspicious, so I crossed the room and opened the door of the antique piece of furniture. My red leather suit hung on the coat hanger. "Isn't there something less...conspicuous that I can wear?" I asked. The suit was awesome, but it did tend to stand out.

"Humour me," Luc requested. He rummaged around inside a chest of drawers and handed over some underwear. Naturally, they were my exact size. "Kokoro did some shopping while you were recovering," he said with a smile.

I was glad Geordie hadn't been the one to do the shopping, he'd probably have bought me some kinky crotch-less panties. Luc watched as I stripped down, towelled myself dry then squeezed into the red suit. "How do I look?" I asked and turned in a quick circle after he finished tying the laces.

"Good enough to eat," he replied. The glint in his eye had increased and a hint of red glowed in their dark depths.

"Cut it out, you two!" Geordie complained from down below. "In case you've forgotten, we apparently have another crisis to face."

"We can get naked together later," I promised my one true love and linked my arm with his. We walked down the stairs and into the library. A fire blazed and our friends had gathered on the chocolate coloured leather sofas. More chairs had been brought in to accommodate everyone. Danton sat at a small table, furiously typing away on a laptop. I cocked an eyebrow at Gregor and cut my eyes to the monk.

"Danton has decided to chronicle everything that has occurred since you rose as Mortis," Gregor advised.

"*Every*thing?" I asked in alarm. Many of the events that had transpired had been pretty embarrassing, for me anyway.

"Do not fear, Natalie," Danton said without raising his

head. "Only we vampires will have access to the chronicles."

"Gee, that makes me feel so much better," was my sarcastic reply. "Why do you want to write all this down?"

Finishing his sentence, he swivelled around to face me. "Now that my master is gone, I lack purpose. You and your friends all have their parts to play, but I have no tasks to perform." It was said without rancour and more as an observation. "I am long used to recording the Prophet's words and I wish to keep a record of your history. I feel it is the only way that I can contribute to our species."

"Wow, Natalie," Ishida said with mock awe, "you have your own personal scribe."

"I *am* supposed to be the Queen of the Vampires," I said self-mockingly. "I don't have a problem with you writing down our story," I told Danton, "but at least let me read it so I can tell you if any of the details don't match up."

"Of course, my Queen," Danton said with a small bow and a smile.

"I think her official title should be Queen Natalie Ladybug Mortis the First," Geordie said, then giggled at my instant grimace.

"How about you all just keep calling me Nat or Natalie?" I suggested.

"As you order, my Natalie," Ishida said with a bow, mocking the long dead Nicholas.

*I'll always be able to count on my friends to keep me grounded,* I thought as I took a seat on the couch beside Luc. They wouldn't let me turn into an unfeeling tyrant.

"Now, about your dreams," Gregor said and the mood immediately shifted back to being sombre. "I confess that

I have no idea what any of them mean. You were warned several times of another undead infestation, so we should probably concentrate on that first. Can you sense anything anywhere that might be considered a threat?"

Closing my eyes, I sent my senses out far and wide. Apart from the two hundred vampires on Gregor's property, I sensed only a few scattered vampires across Europe, and Millicent's dozen that were still in China. I picked up no signs at all of any other vampires, imps, aliens or clones of any kind. I opened my eyes again and relayed my findings. "As far as I can tell, there's no undead out there at all, apart from us."

"Could you sense the rats that you sired?" Igor asked.

"I didn't sense them as the undead," I admitted. "But I felt a connection to them."

"You felt a connection because you sired them," Gregor said. "You may not have directly created the second rat, but it still originated from your line."

"Can you imagine an infestation of vampire rats?" Kokoro asked and shuddered. "They'd swarm the cities, killing every living being and leaving only corpses behind. It would not take long for them to reduce the entire planet into a lifeless wasteland."

Geordie's eyes were wide with alarm. "Do you think that is the next threat? Hordes of vampire rats?"

"No," I said and he slumped in relief. "But they definitely won't be human. What I saw of them in my dream told me they were a lot bigger than us, but they weren't quite identical, like the clones were."

"Could you not tell what creatures they originated from?" Luc asked.

I shook my head in frustration. "They were like nothing

I've ever seen before. Until they turn up and we see them in the flesh, we're going to be in the dark."

Gregor wasn't happy about that. He liked to plan ahead whenever possible. This time, he wouldn't be able to think of a way to take down this new threat until after it had appeared. "We will have to keep our eyes out for news about any strange sightings."

"Why do your dreams have to be so vague, *chérie*?" Geordie complained. "It's like Fate wants us to flounder around like idiots."

Sadly, I agreed with his assessment. Fate did like to make us jump through hoops and the next hoop seemed to be almost out of our reach. After the ordeal that we'd just faced, I despaired at the next task that was lined up for us. I only hoped I'd attained all of the abilities that I would need to finally be able to put an end to our constant struggle to save the humans.

This next task would be the last one, but the outcome was uncertain. My dreams seemed to hint that the decisions we would make would result in one of three outcomes. The humans would be utterly wiped out, they'd be all but destroyed, or they'd be saved. As Ishida had said, I hoped we would be able to choose option number three.

Printed in Great Britain
by Amazon